Marian was being stalked.

It started with a long shot of the two of them at the outdoor café near Lincoln Center. Then the camera zoomed in on Marian talking on her phone. The lens moved over to Holland, showing him slowly savoring his food as he watched Marian.

The last pictures were of Marian coming out of the Galloway Building and telling the reporters gathered at the entrance that there would be no statement until the next of kin had been notified.

Then, after a break, the camera lingered on what looked like a large poster board with a message stenciled on it: *If you want to see her alive again, you're going to have to do something for me. Something big.*

★

"...classic, no-nonsense, police-procedural style."
—Santa Rosa, CA *The Press Democrat*

"...a compelling thriller."
—*Mystery News*

Full Frontal MURDER

Barbara Paul

WORLDWIDE®

TORONTO • NEW YORK • LONDON
AMSTERDAM • PARIS • SYDNEY • HAMBURG
STOCKHOLM • ATHENS • TOKYO • MILAN
MADRID • WARSAW • BUDAPEST • AUCKLAND

FULL FRONTAL MURDER

A Worldwide Mystery/September 1998

This edition is reprinted by arrangement with Scribner, an imprint of Simon & Schuster, Inc.

ISBN 0-373-26284-1

This book is for
the Avon-Without-Guilt gang.
Have fun. :)

ONE

MARIAN LARCH looked at the brightly wrapped box that had just been placed in her lap. "But you're the one going away," she protested. "Shouldn't I be giving you a present?"

"Open it," Kelly commanded.

The bow was lopsided; Kelly had wrapped it herself. Marian pulled off the ribbon and opened the box to find a fanny pack wrapped in silver tissue. Lovely brushed gray leather, reeking of money, so soft to the touch as to be sensuous. Three zippered pockets, not one of them deep enough to hold a gun.

"It's beautiful, Kelly," Marian said, awed. "Where did you get it?"

"Siena." Kelly Ingram had flown there to make a quickie TV movie before heading to California to make a real movie. They were sitting in TWA's VIP lounge at Kennedy, waiting for the Los Angeles flight to be announced. "Leather shops all over the place there," Kelly said, meaning Siena. "I wanted to get one of those fanny packs for myself, but they cost too much," she added straight-faced.

Marian laughed; Kelly probably had three. She was going to miss her friend. Kelly had left Hollywood seven years earlier as a former starlet going nowhere. A television series shot in New York had made her a name, and a successful Broadway play had made her an actor. Now she was headed back to La La Land in triumph to make the movie version of *The Apostrophe Thief,* the play that had given her stature.

"I'll probably have an entourage by the time I get

back," Kelly said glumly. "It's a capital offense in Hollywood to go anywhere alone."

That was a joke Kelly was making. "What would you do with an entourage?" Marian asked, amused.

"Oh, I don't know. Pay 'em to stand around and look impressive, I guess. Isn't that what entourages are for?"

"You're asking me? I thought they were to provide moral support."

"Oh, that." Kelly dismissed the notion with a wave of her hand. Other passengers in the VIP lounge kept glancing at Kelly out of the corners of their eyes, trying not to appear impressed by the presence of this particular celebrity among them. Kelly was dressed for traveling in faded jeans, a white T-shirt, and what appeared to be a fisherman's vest. She looked like a million bucks.

"Ms Ingram?" An airline official had appeared by Kelly's armchair. "Would you like to board now?"

"Yes, thanks." Kelly and Marian both stood up. "Time for me to go, Toots."

"Don't stay any longer than you have to," Marian said.

"Don't worry about *that*." They followed the airlines official through a door leading to the boarding ramp. Kelly paused and said, "And I hope you catch your bad guy."

Marian sighed. "Which one?"

Kelly winked. "Whichever one you're thinking about right now." She turned and headed up the ramp.

Good exit, Marian thought. She raised her hand in response to Kelly's wave just before her friend disappeared into the connecting tunnel.

Dammit. Marian missed her already.

Kelly knew her pretty well, Marian mused as she made the drive back into Manhattan. Never completely out of her mind was whatever crime-of-the-moment was taking up most of her working hours, spending the taxpayers' money, plaguing her sleep. But at the moment she was more concerned with the gap Kelly's absence would leave in her life.

Cops rarely had friends who were not also cops. Street cops especially had trouble talking to outsiders; only other cops understood what it was like. Marian Larch had put in her time as a street cop, living with the constant tension, never knowing whether the next door she pounded on would be opened by a frightened citizen or a crazy with a shotgun. Afraid that her fear might paralyze her at the very moment she needed to act fast to save her own life. Just wearing the uniform had made her a target in some of the neighborhoods she'd had to go into. How did you explain living that kind of life without sounding like a lunatic with a death wish?

After Marian had earned her gold shield, those moments of intense fear had not disappeared—but they had become spaced further apart. As a detective, she had breathing room she'd not had as a street cop. But then a new kind of intensity had appeared, an incessant pressure to *get it right*. Again, it was something only other police detectives understood.

That was one reason Kelly Ingram's friendship was so precious to Marian. Kelly and her extravagant, funny, somewhat nutty world of show business had given Marian's life a perspective it had never had before. It was an odd pairing, the grimly real world of crime and the world that made make-believe enchanting and necessary. Kelly had opened a door for Marian; she'd become friendly with both Kelly's co-star and the woman who'd written the play they were filming. Now all three of them would be in California for months, and Marian's contacts with other people would all be in the field of law enforcement.

Even Holland.

She parked in one of the diagonal spaces in front of the Midtown South Precinct stationhouse. "Morning, Lieutenant," the desk sergeant greeted her when she walked in.

She went through the good-morning ritual with everyone she passed on the way to her office, knowing the respect shown her was only mouth-honor from those men who still resented taking orders from a woman. Their problem.

Dowd looked up from his desk right outside her office door. "Captain wants to see you. Toot sweet, he says."

She nodded. "And I'll want to see Buchanan and Campos when I get back." She locked her shoulder bag in the bottom drawer of her desk and headed toward Captain Murtaugh's office.

The captain was looking worried, but then he always looked worried. He'd put on a little weight over the winter that he hadn't gotten rid of yet, but he still appeared long and lanky even when sitting behind a desk. Marian knocked on the open door to get his attention.

"Ah, Marian—have a seat. Something I want you to do."

"Sure." She shut the door and sat down.

He took a swallow of coffee from the oversized mug he kept close at hand all day long. "The Galloway case. The attempted kidnapping."

Marian did a quick mental run-through of her detectives' case assignments. "Yeah, O'Toole caught that one. Little boy snatched away from his mother on the street. Mother convinced the father was behind it even though she didn't know the guy who grabbed the kid. Beat cop saw it happening and intervened. Kid safe, perp long gone."

"I want you take that one on yourself."

She was surprised. "Okay, but O'Toole can handle it."

"He could if it were an ordinary domestic squabble. But this one may have a little more involved. I just got a call from the kid's grandfather, Walter Galloway." He paused. "Galloway Industries. The Galloway Foundation. Galloway Charitable Trust."

Oh. *That* Galloway. "So there's more than just parental feeling involved."

"Walter Galloway thinks so. He thinks it was an attempted kidnapping for ransom. Did O'Toole turn up the connection to Galloway Industries?"

Marian frowned. "I don't know, I'll have to check. But he would in time—this just happened yesterday."

"That's the problem," the captain said. "If someone is trying to snatch the boy, we don't have a whole lot of time. Old man Galloway has hired a bodyguard for the kid, but the mother is screaming harassment and won't let the bodyguard into the house. She says the hired muscle is just a cover-up, that the boy's father is the one they have to be afraid of. It's a mess."

"And the poor little rich boy is caught square in the middle. How much money are we talking about here?"

"Enough to buy the Lower East Side out of pocket change. I want you to find out who's really behind that attempted kidnapping and forestall the next attempt, if you can. If the father checks out okay, talk Mrs. Galloway into accepting the bodyguard. But for now, put a police officer in that house."

"Right. Seventy-two hours max?" The standard period of police protection.

"Let's see what you turn up first."

Marian left in a hurry; if the grandfather was right and the child was still in danger, there was no time to waste. As she passed O'Toole's desk, she tapped the young detective on the shoulder and said, "Bring the Galloway case file into my office. Right now." He grabbed a folder and followed her.

Sergeants Campos and Buchanan were waiting for her. Buchanan, the seasoned veteran, seated facing her desk; and Campos, the angry young Latino, lounging against a file cabinet. She held a finger up. "One phone call." Marian called the Chief of Patrol's office and arranged for around-the-clock protection for the Galloway boy. She read the address out of the folder O'Toole handed her.

"What's up, Lieutenant?" Sergeant Campos asked. He'd assigned the Galloway case to O'Toole.

"A complication. O'Toole, did you know these Galloways are the Galloway Industries people?"

He cleared his throat. "I'm still running a background check."

Campos made the connection. "Ransom."

"It's a possibility," Marian said. "O'Toole, I'm going to be running the case but you're still on it."

O'Toole said, "Hey, Lieutenant, I woulda found it!"

She flapped a hand at him. "I know. But our time schedule has just been goosed up."

Sergeant Buchanan shifted his weight. "Somebody wanna fill me in?"

Campos gave him a quick run-down. "Looked like a straight domestic snatch when it came in. Husband and wife separated, both want the kid."

"Have we ruled out the husband?" Marian asked.

"Not yet," O'Toole answered. "Mrs. Galloway didn't know the perp, but the husband coulda hired himself some talent."

"Mug shots?"

He shook his head. "She couldn't ID anyone. I got an APB out."

"Where's the husband staying...oh, you've got it here. Sutton Place?"

"His father's place."

"Walter Galloway. O'Toole, I want to talk to all these Galloways. Set up appointments—the sooner the better."

"Right." He left to start phoning.

Marian turned to Buchanan. "Is Perlmutter working on anything you can't assign to someone else?"

He squinted his eyes, thinking. "Naw. You can have him."

"Good." Marian shifted mental gears and looked at the

two sergeants. "You know why I called you in. The Sergeants Exam." Buchanan grunted, Campos nodded.

The Midtown South Precinct had been working one sergeant short for over a year. As lieutenant, Marian was supposed to oversee three squads of seven or eight detectives each, each one headed by a sergeant. But Campos and Buchanan had been shouldering the load by themselves, with Marian picking up as much of the overflow as she could. To add to the difficulties, Buchanan was scheduled for retirement at the end of the year. They needed not one new sergeant but two.

So when a new Sergeants Exam was announced for October, Marian had called Buchanan and Campos in and *ordered* them to find volunteers to take the test. "Well? Got any names for me?"

"Perlmutter," said Buchanan. "And he'll ace it."

"Good." Marian was pleased. "Who else?"

Campos grinned. "O'Toole volunteered." Buchanan grunted while Marian shook her head. O'Toole was still too green.

Buchanan scratched the side of his nose. "Dowd says he'll take the test but he won't study for it."

"Then forget Dowd." No way anyone could pass that test without studying. "Any others?"

They had three others—all three of whom had taken the test before and failed. "Perlmutter's our best bet," Campos said.

"Which still leaves us one sergeant short."

"What about your buddy down in the Ninth, Lieutenant?" Buchanan asked. "Gloria Sanchez? Is she still dead set on *not* taking the test?"

Marian sighed. "Don't know—I haven't bugged her about it for a while. I'll give her a call. Okay, then. Keep trying." She shooed them out.

She was at a loss to understand the reluctance of so many detectives to take the Sergeants Exam. The exam wasn't given all that often, and it was a detective's only chance for advancement. Captain Murtaugh once suggested that police detectives didn't need another failure to carry around with them; and if they didn't take the test, they couldn't fail.

And it was true, the exam *did* have a high failure rate. But still. Marian herself had jumped at the chance, taking the test the first time it was offered after she made detective. And passing it. She was concerned that the seeming lack of ambition in the Midtown South detectives might be a sign of early burnout.

She pulled the Galloway case file toward her and started reading, grateful for all these distractions that kept her from brooding over the fact that her closest friend was on an airplane headed away from New York.

TWO

RITA FAIRCHILD GALLOWAY had taken her four-year-old son Bobby to a puppet show for preschoolers at the Little Church around the Corner on Twenty-ninth. They came out around three o'clock, planning to stop somewhere for ice cream and then take a cab home. Outside the church, Mrs. Galloway had let go of Bobby's hand long enough to bend down and tie one of her shoelaces that had come undone. At that moment a man appeared "out of nowhere," snatched Bobby up under one arm, and ran.

The combined screams of mother and son had attracted the attention of a patrol car cruising the street. The cops chased the kidnapper down to Madison Square Park, where one officer jumped out of the patrol car and tackled the perp. The two men were struggling for possession of the screaming boy when the second police officer came running up. The kidnapper relinquished his hold on Bobby and fled. The second officer took off in pursuit but lost him in the crowd. Young Bobby Galloway suffered nothing worse than a scraped elbow.

But his mother was in hysterics. Rita Galloway immediately accused her estranged husband of staging the kidnap attempt and demanded that he be arrested. She said he was a ruthless man who'd stop at nothing to get what he wanted, and what he wanted was Bobby.

Mother and son had been driven to the Midtown South stationhouse, where Bobby's scraped elbow was disinfected and adorned with a Mickey Mouse Band-Aid. Rita Galloway had looked through mug shots but recognized no one. Detective O'Toole called the number Mrs. Galloway had given him and spoke to her estranged husband.

Hugh Galloway had come to the stationhouse immediately, demanding to see for himself that Bobby was all right. His wife accused him to his face of engineering the kidnapping, and the two almost came to blows. A police officer drove Rita and Bobby home.

Even though he'd looked as if he wanted to punch someone out, Hugh Galloway had stayed to answer O'Toole's questions. He denied all knowledge of the kidnapping. O'Toole had added the comment that Mr. Galloway appeared sincerely outraged by what had happened.

And that's where it rested until Hugh's father, Walter Galloway, had called Captain Murtaugh that morning. If Hugh hadn't tried to kidnap Bobby, then someone else had.

Of course Walter Galloway would not think his son capable of kidnapping, Marian mused. And of course a bitter, estranged wife would. Poor Bobby, caught in such an ugly tug-of-war; all too common a picture, unfortunately. If Hugh Galloway was indeed innocent, and if O'Toole's APB didn't bring in the wannabe kidnapper—then this one was headed straight for the dead file. *Can't let that happen.*

Marian put O'Toole to work finding out as much about Hugh Galloway as he could and took Detective Perlmutter with her on her interviews. Rita Galloway and Bobby lived in a four-story town house on East Seventy-fifth, until recently also the home of Hugh Galloway. A lifelong apartment dweller, Marian always felt a twinge of envy when calling on people who had an entire house to themselves. But her nesting instinct had never been strong enough to make her do anything about it.

"Money," Perlmutter said as Marian parked by a fire hydrant, the only space left on the street. "I'm going to feel like a bum again."

"Hazard of the profession." They got out of the car and started toward the building. "What do you want to bet they have a place on Long Island as well?"

"Tuxedo Park. Snootier."

"Not that we prejudge people."

"Naw, we never do that."

"Well, well—look over there." Directly across the street from the Galloway house was a parked car with a man inside busily taking pictures of them. Marian and Perlmutter strolled over to him.

She held up her badge. "Lieutenant Larch. Will you identify yourself, please?"

"Oh, you're police." He fished out some ID. "Name's Jarvik. I'm with Heron Security."

His ID checked out. "Who hired you?"

"Mr. Galloway."

"Which Mr. Galloway?"

"Mr. Walter Galloway."

Marian returned his ID. "Okay, Jarvik. Anyone watching the back?"

"No rear access. They got a patio out back, with a high wall marking off their property limits. Another patio on the other side—the back of the property on the next street."

"Walls can be climbed."

"Yeah, I know, Lieutenant. But the lady, she won't let us inside. There's no way we can watch that wall from the street."

Marian nodded. "They had any callers since you've been here?"

"Just one. Cop answered the door, made the guy wait while he checked with the lady. Guy's inside now. I got him on film."

She frowned; the cop shouldn't have let *anyone* in. Marian and Perlmutter left the security man to his watch and crossed over to ring the doorbell.

The officer who opened the door was unknown to Marian, but he knew her. "Hello, Lieutenant." He stepped

back to let them in. When asked, he said his name was
Bartolomew.

"Bartolomew, weren't your orders not to let anyone
in?"

"You mean Mr. Fairchild? He's Mrs. Galloway's
brother, Lieutenant. I didn't think I was supposed to keep
family out."

No, he wasn't. "That's all right, then. Where are they?"

Officer Bartolomew led them through a sitting room so
full of light and color that it made Marian pause. A south
wall fronting on East Seventy-fifth contained a floor-to-
ceiling stained-glass window; the summer sun cast a pattern on the opposing wall—bold, vivid colors in the shape
of a dragon. Wonderful combination of color and form,
and an attention-catching one.

"Pretty, ain't it?" Bartolomew said with a grin. "It
changes as the sun moves."

"Ptolemy would love it," Perlmutter said.

"They're in the studio," the officer told them, heading
down a hallway and up a flight of stairs.

"What kind of studio?"

"Mrs. Galloway paints. Just watercolors, though."

"Way I hear it," Perlmutter said, "watercolor is one of
the most difficult mediums for an artist to work in."

"Yeah?" Bartolomew knocked and opened a door; they
stepped into another bright and cheerful room with a number of worktables and easels displaying sketches and unfinished watercolors. Under one window sat a little boy at
a child's table covered with crayons, construction paper,
blunt-end scissors, a jar of paste—busily working away on
a project of his own. The two adults in the room broke off
their conversation when Bartolomew said, "Here's Lieutenant Larch to see you."

O'Toole must have said *she* or *her* when he made the
appointment, because Mrs. Galloway and her brother did
not assume Perlmutter was the lieutenant, as often hap-

pened. "Lieutenant?" the woman said, approaching Marian. "Have you arrested Hugh?"

It was obvious these two were brother and sister just from looking at them. Both tall, with broad foreheads over wide-set, moist-looking eyes. Narrow shoulders, curly reddish brown hair, thin lips. Long thin fingers. Very intense looking people, but that could be a reflection of their concern over Bobby.

"Alex Fairchild," the man said, sticking out a hand.

Marian shook it, and then explained that they had no evidence linking Hugh to the kidnapping. "That's why we're here. To see if you can tell us something more."

"What more is there to tell?" Rita Galloway exclaimed. "Hugh knew we were going to that puppet show. How else did the kidnapper know where to find us?"

"He could have followed you there."

Mrs. Galloway glanced over at the boy at the little table. "Let's go outside." Then, to the child: "Bobby, we're going out on the balcony for a few minutes."

"I'll stay here," Officer Bartolomew said before anyone could ask him to.

The balcony was a long one, running along the back side of the house with another door opening on to it; her bedroom, Mrs. Galloway said when Perlmutter asked. They were overlooking the patio; the furniture below was wrought iron with padded cushions on the seats and backs. The stone wall marking the property boundary was about ten feet high. "Is that wall wired?" Perlmutter asked.

It was; alarms would go off both there and at the security firm's monitoring center. But Rita Galloway had already made arrangements for a new security system to be installed. "They're coming tomorrow," she said. "Hugh had the present system put in, and it's not beyond him to cancel the contract without telling me. He could slip in any time he wanted to."

"The locks have all been changed," Alex Fairchild

added. "But that wall could pose a danger. Anyone determined to get in could scale the wall and hurl one of those iron chairs through the glass patio doors. The alarms would all be going off, but the system was designed to deter burglars, not kidnappers. And the police officer can't watch the front door and that wall at the same time." He looked at his sister. "We're going to have to hire some protection."

She sighed. "I know."

Marian remarked, "There's a security-agency guard sitting outside your house right now."

Fairchild laughed shortly. "Hugh's man. Or his father's man. Same thing."

"He's from a reputable agency. Why won't you let him in?"

Brother and sister exchanged a look. She said, "He's not there to protect us, Lieutenant. He's there to spy on us, on Bobby and me. To look for evidence that I'm an unfit mother. And no, I'm not being paranoid. Hugh's done it before. He replaced one of the cleaning service's regular crew with someone he hired to snoop through my things."

Fairchild confirmed her story. "I caught her at Rita's desk, going through her checkbook. Credit card statements were out, so she'd probably gone through those as well." He looked Marian straight in the eye, his own moist eyes gleaming. "Do you know how Hugh was able to replace one of the cleaning crew? He bought the business. He bought the whole goddam cleaning service. Just to put a spy in this house."

No one spoke for a moment. Then Marian said, "Mr. Fairchild, could you take Detective Perlmutter around the house and show him the complete security system here?"

He looked amused. "The security system that's being replaced tomorrow? Certainly. And how long should it take me to show Detective Perlmutter everything?"

"At least twenty minutes, I'd say."

"I think that can be arranged. Detective?" The two men went back into the house.

Marian stepped closer to Rita Galloway. "Mrs. Galloway, did your husband ever strike you? Or threaten you?"

The other woman shook her head. "I've not been physically abused. Or threatened. Oh, no...Hugh is too civilized for that." The sarcasm made her voice ugly. "Hugh is a master of emotional torture—the put-down, the belittling, the sneer that's not quite a sneer, if you know what I mean. No, the abuse has all been psychological."

"That's a little harder to prove," Marian said reluctantly. "But not impossible. If you want to—"

"In all the time we've been married," Rita Galloway interrupted, caught up in her own thoughts, "I've been made to feel inadequate. I don't quite measure up to the high standards a Galloway is expected to meet. Hugh's just like his father-they're never satisfied. Not to mention the fact that Hugh's been cheating on me consistently from the day were married."

"From the *day* you were married?"

The other woman's mouth was grim. "That's right, Lieutenant. He got up from our wedding bed and went to a prostitute."

Marian was appalled and dubious at the same time. "How could you know that?"

"He told me. He took great pleasure in telling me. Laying down the ground rules, you see. He could do whatever he wanted, and I had to take it."

Whew. "Why did you stay with him?"

"I was pregnant. When Bobby was born, Hugh did settle down pretty well. But it didn't last. He's back to his old habits now."

"Are you legally separated? Did the court award custody of Bobby to you?"

"Legally separated, yes. The court, in its infinite wisdom," more sarcasm, "decided Bobby would spend six months with me and then six months with Hugh. Next year when Bobby's old enough to go to school the custody arrangement is to be reviewed. But this is *my* six months! Hugh has no right to him now!''

''How long have you been separated?''

''Only two months—no, it's been ten weeks. Oh, what does it matter!''

''Mrs. Galloway, if you can give us something more than your supposition that your husband tried to kidnap Bobby, we can arrest him. The man who took Bobby— you've never seen him before?''

''No. And his picture wasn't there either, in those I looked at at the police station.''

''Could you sketch him for us?''

She spread her hands. ''I'm sorry, Lieutenant, but I'm not much good at catching likenesses. Faces are my brother's talent.''

''Then the next step is for you to go in to the station and help one of our graphics technicians build a face on the computer. The sooner the better, Mrs. Galloway. Can you go in today?''

''Yes…yes, I'll go today.''

''Has your husband tried to steal Bobby before?''

''He's tried to pick Bobby up from preschool a couple of times—no, three times. I take Bobby in four mornings a week, so he'll have other kids to play with. Three times Hugh showed up right before noon when I pick Bobby up, but the school director wouldn't let him take Bobby. I'd informed her of the separation.''

Marian asked for the name and address of the preschool. ''That was a violation of the court's order. Did you do anything about it?''

''My lawyer advised me not to. He said Hugh would just claim it was a misunderstanding and I couldn't prove otherwise. Like now. I can't *prove* Hugh was behind the kidnap attempt.''

That struck Marian as odd legal advice, but she said nothing. "One thing. What if he succeeded in stealing Bobby away? How could he hope to get away with it? He'd be breaking the law."

Mrs. Galloway was at a loss. "I've wondered about that too. But I'm sure he has something worked out. Hugh's very deliberate about what he does. He never rushes into things. Like the time he tore up my watercolors. He didn't do that in the heat of anger—he did it in cold deliberation."

"He tore up your watercolors? All of them?"

"Not all of them. Just enough so that I would understand the extent of his displeasure. I don't even remember what he was displeased about, that time. But he destroyed some good work, and I'll never forgive him for that. Understand, Lieutenant, Hugh Galloway is a cold, calculating son of a bitch. Do you know what he's doing now? He's sending Bobby a present every day. *Every* day. Big, expensive presents, all with cards signed 'From your Daddy, who misses you.' He's trying to buy Bobby away from me."

"Are you letting Bobby keep them?"

"A few. Bobby's only four years old—how can he understand what his father is doing? Most of the presents are locked away upstairs." Her voice was bitter. "Now Hugh can go into court and claim I intercepted gifts he'd sent to his son. He wins either way."

No wonder Rita Galloway suspected her husband; Hugh Galloway sounded like a grade A bastard. But Marian hadn't heard his side of it yet. "Do you think your brother could stay with Bobby for a while? While you go to the police station?"

"Probably. I'll ask him."

They went back into her studio, where Marian asked if she could use the phone. Mrs. Galloway pointed to one on a worktable and went on out. Bobby had tired of whatever he'd been working on and was stretched out on his stomach on the floor turning the pages of a picture book. Officer Bartolomew was sitting on a high stool looking bored with his baby-sitting duty.

Marian called in and arranged for a graphics tech to be waiting when Rita Galloway got there. When she hung up, she turned her attention to Bobby. Such a quiet little boy.

And so small, to be the spoils of a war.

. . . . .
. . . .

THREE

BOBBY GALLOWAY looked up from his picture book when Marian hunkered down in front of him. Black eyes full of curiosity. Hair not his mother's reddish brown but coal black, thick and a bit long. Rather large ears. He looked like a little elf.

"Hello, Bobby," Marian said slowly. "I'm Lieutenant Larch."

He stared at her, unspeaking.

"Hmm, that's a mouthful, isn't it? Tell you what. You call me Marian. Mar-i-an."

A little smile. "Mary Ann."

"Yes, that's better. I heard about what happened to you yesterday. That was scary, huh?"

He nodded soberly.

"You did the right thing when that man grabbed you. You yelled. You yelled, and the police heard you."

Bobby lifted his right arm to display a now somewhat soiled Mickey Mouse Band-Aid on his elbow. "P'lice gimme."

"Mickey Mouse, huh? Bobby, I'm with the police."

The four-year-old scoffed. "You're not p'lice!" He pointed to Officer Bartolomew. "He's p'lice!"

"Well, I don't have a nice uniform like the officer's, but I am a cop. Bartolomew, tell him."

"That's right, kid," Bartolomew said. "She's police. In fact, she's my boss. One of 'em."

Bobby's mouth made an O.

Marian said, "Bobby, that man who grabbed you—did you ever see him before?"

He shook his head. "He smelled funny."

"You mean he smelled bad?"

"Not bad." Bobby tried to think of another word but couldn't. "Funny."

Marian thought a moment. "It was a new smell? Something you'd never smelled before?"

"Yeah," Bobby agreed. "New, funny smell!" He liked the sound of that and laughed. "New, funny smell!" he said again.

Thinking she needed to brush up on preschool humor, Marian got to her feet just as Perlmutter came in. "Mrs. Galloway's calling a car service to take her to the station," he said. "The brother's going to stay here."

"Did you get Fairchild's address and phone number?"

"Yes, and business address too. He's a photographer."

"In business for himself?"

"Uh-huh." Perlmutter grinned. "He seemed surprised I hadn't heard of him."

Marian sent Officer Bartolomew back to keeping an eye on the front entrance, informing him of the Heron Security man taking pictures from a parked car across the street. "He's legit, I saw his ID. But he may be here for reasons other than surveillance. Don't let him in under any circumstances."

"He won't get in," Bartolomew assured her.

Marian turned to Perlmutter. "Talk to Bobby. The kidnapper had a distinctive smell that was unfamiliar to the boy. See if you can get him to tell you more about it. Sweet, sour? Like mothballs, shaving lotion? He said it wasn't a bad smell."

"Okay." Perlmutter went over to Bobby while Marian made her way downstairs to the room with the stained-glass dragon.

Rita Galloway and Alex Fairchild were both there. He was peering through a piece of clear glass. "Car service is here."

His sister said, "I have no idea how long this will take."

He waved a hand. "Take as long as you need."

"It shouldn't be too long," Marian told them. "Computerizing the process has sped it up enormously. You'll be able to come up with the kidnapper's face in less than half an hour, I'll bet."

Mrs. Galloway's face brightened slightly at that. In the entryway off the dragon room, Officer Bartolomew opened the door for her and then stood in the doorway a minute after she'd left, a very visible cop-on-duty.

"I think I've persuaded her to hire a bodyguard," Alex Fairchild murmured, still gazing through the dragon window. "Nobody likes a stranger hanging around all the time, but it's going to be necessary until this business is settled."

"I'm surprised she needed persuading," Marian remarked.

"She's still in shock, Lieutenant. She'd have thought of it herself in a day or two."

Marian sat down on a white armchair and regarded him. An attractive man, in an offbeat sort of way, and deeply concerned about his sister and his nephew. "Do you think Hugh Galloway was behind the attempt to kidnap Bobby?"

He turned from the window. "Oh, there's no doubt of that. What Hugh wants, Hugh gets." Fairchild sat on a sofa, facing her. "What Rita has trouble accepting is the fact that Galloway married her because he needed a broodmare. She's his second wife, you know. He divorced his first when they learned she couldn't have children. Gotta keep that Galloway name alive, you know."

"Bobby's an heir to the Galloway money?"

"He's *the* heir. The Galloways used to be a big clan, but most of them died off. Now it's down to Walter Galloway and Hugh. Hugh's a younger son, but his brother died seven or eight years ago. No children. So it all comes down to Bobby to perpetuate the family name."

"Big responsibility for such small shoulders. Hugh could marry a third time and try again."

"And he undoubtedly will. But Bobby's his insurance policy. No, he's not going to give up on Bobby. And don't forget, Hugh did know where they were going to be yesterday."

"How did he know?"

"How? Well, he called Rita and asked if she'd let him take Bobby to a ball game yesterday afternoon. She told him she'd already promised Bobby he could see the puppet show."

"Were you on an extension phone when the call came?"

"Was I...no, of course not! I wasn't even here."

"Then you didn't hear the conversation."

Fairchild flared. "If you're saying my sister is lying—"

"I'm saying Hugh Galloway is going to paint quite a different picture from the one I'm seeing here, and I need all the details I can get. Was he in the habit of calling and asking if he could take Bobby out?"

He relaxed, a little. "I think Hugh had called a couple of times before, but Rita always said no. The court granted no visiting privileges, to either one of them. Bobby is Rita's alone for six months, and then he's Hugh's alone for six months."

Marian let a small silence develop and then deliberately changed the subject. "You're a photographer, Mr. Fairchild? What kind of pictures do you take?"

"Good ones." He wasn't joking. "I take the kind of pictures that magazine editors are currently calling Life Studies. I've been concentrating on New York's street people lately. Hustlers, rap-dancers, hot dog vendors, mimes, twelve-year-olds who walk along Fourteenth Street talking on pocket phones. Those nuts who wear billboards announcing the end of the world by next Tuesday." He smiled. "Cops."

"Hmm."

"It's the faces that fascinate me," Fairchild went on. "I don't do straight composition photography anymore. I have to have a compelling face in there to bring the picture alive." He gave her a searching look. "I'd like to photograph you."

Strange sort of compliment. "Well, thanks, but I do all my posing for *Cosmo*."

He had the grace to laugh. "Think about it? I'd like to come into your police station—Midtown South, isn't it? I could get a whole series of shots there. Would that be possible?"

"Not up to me. Call Captain James Murtaugh. But have a very good reason for wanting to go around taking pictures."

"Murtaugh," Fairchild repeated. He pulled out a pen and looked around for something to write on; Marian tore out a sheet of paper from her notebook and handed it to him. "Thanks." He wrote down the captain's name. "If you'd like to see the kind of work I do—let's see, I should have a couple of invitations with me." He felt through his pockets and came up with an unsealed envelope, which he held out to Marian. "I have an exhibition at the Albian Gallery on East Fifty-seventh. That'll admit you and a guest."

Doubtfully, she accepted the envelope. "Is this an opening?"

He laughed at her expression. "No, the opening was four nights ago. This is a private showing for people who hate the cocktail party atmosphere of openings as much as you do."

Marian smiled. "In that case, I'll certainly try to make it."

"I hope you will. Thursday night, any time after nine."

They heard Bobby's high little voice calling out "Giddyap!'' A stooped-over Perlmutter came into the room with Bobby riding on his shoulders.

Fairchild stood up and went to meet them. "So, you've found a new horse, have you?" He lifted Bobby off Perlmutter's shoulders and placed him on his own.

Perlmutter straightened up. "Thanks," he said in relief.

Bobby pointed a finger at Marian. "Uncle Alex, Mary Ann's a p'liceman!"

"Yes, she is, isn't she?" Fairchild jumped up and down in place, making the little boy squeal with laughter.

Time to go. Marian thanked Fairchild for his help, said good-bye to Bobby, and nodded to Officer Bartolomew holding the door for them.

"Don't forget Thursday night," Alex Fairchild called after them. The door closed.

"You got a date with Fairchild, Lieutenant?" Perlmutter asked, deadpan.

"Exhibition of his photographs. Some gallery on Fifty-seventh." Jarvik, the Heron Security man, was still at his post across the street. "Did you get anything from Bobby?"

"I'm not sure." Marian unlocked the car and they got in. "I tried to get him to tell me something the smell reminded him of," Perlmutter said, "and the closest he could get was the bathroom man."

"Who?"

"I think he meant the cleaning service guy who does their bathrooms."

Marian chewed her lower lip. "Cleaning solvent?"

"Or something like it. Not ammonia, because Bobby said it was kind of sweet."

"Pine? Floral scent? That doesn't really get us anywhere, though."

"Naw, the kidnapper could just have cleaned something before he went after the kid. Is that our only clue?"

"Looks like it. And how reliable is a four-year-old's memory of a new smell anyway?"

"Yeah. Dead end." He changed the subject. "Lieutenant, you getting hungry?"

She was. "Let's fuel up before we tackle the Galloways."

"But not in this neighborhood. They'd charge you ten bucks for a cup of coffee."

They found a place on Third Avenue more suited to a cop's salary and took stools at the counter. Over grease burgers and coffee Marian told Perlmutter the substance of her talks with Rita Galloway and Alex Fairchild. "They make a pretty good case for Hugh Galloway's being behind it. Number one, he's tried before. Number two, he planted a spy in the household. Number three, he knew they were going to the puppet show."

"One and three could be irrelevant," Perlmutter pointed out. "Maybe he just wanted to spend the afternoon with Bobby the times he tried to pick him up at the preschool. And his knowing they were going to the puppet show doesn't mean he did anything about it."

"And number two?"

"That's harder to explain away. The guy's out to get the goods on his wife, and he doesn't seem to care how he goes about it—so he plants a spy in her house? No wonder she feels threatened."

"I wonder how much of this Bobby understands." Marian thought of something else. "That studio. Rita Galloway has several easels in there. I thought watercolorists always worked on a flat surface."

Perlmutter swallowed a mouthful of cholesterol and said, "Not if they're using drybrush technique. Very little water, so it doesn't run down the paper. Some of those things she was working on were pretty big."

"So easels are not unusual?"

"Well, they're not exactly *usual*. My brother-in-law

teaches art at CUNY, and he uses an easel for large watercolors." He wiped his mouth with a paper napkin. "Did you take a close look at her work?"

"Not really. Why?"

"It's good. I mean, it's *good*. This is no rich man's wife looking for a hobby to fill up her hours, if that's what you're thinking. The lady is a real artist."

Marian nodded, accepting his evaluation. They ate in silence for a few more minutes, until Marian's watch told her they had twenty-five minutes to make their appointment at Sutton Place. "Finished?" she asked Perlmutter. "Then let's go meet the Galloway monsters."

FOUR

THE GALLOWAY HOME on Sutton Place had tighter security than the Midtown South stationhouse. Marian and Perlmutter had to show their ID to three different keepers of the gate before a manservant finally let them in to the hallowed sanctuary of the Galloway empire.

Both father and son were waiting in a room that was cavernous and quiet—and aggressively masculine: dark wood paneling, heavy leather furniture. The place reminded Marian of those London men's clubs she'd seen in the movies. The younger of the two men rose to greet them; he had the same coal black hair and oversized ears that Bobby had.

"Lieutenant Larch? Thank you for coming. I'm Hugh Galloway and this is my father, Walter Galloway." He did not offer to shake hands.

Marian introduced Perlmutter and they all sat down. But before Marian could say anything, Walter Galloway rasped out a question. "What have you done to find the *real* kidnapper?"

This one was not going to be easy. "We've put out an all-points bulletin based on Mrs. Galloway's description of the man. She's at the station right now helping a graphics technician reconstruct his face."

"That's all you have to go on? That woman's description?" He snorted. "Then you have nothing."

"That about sums it up," Marian replied crisply. "Only she and Bobby got a good look at the kidnapper. The police officer who struggled with him never did have a clear view of his face. The officer told us the man is about six feet, maybe a little more, and heavy—close to two hundred pounds. Could you identify someone from that description? Without a face, we have no chance of finding him."

"And with a face?" Hugh asked quietly.

"A slight chance. But there is this. Bobby is probably safe. Kidnappers depend on the element of surprise, of the unexpected. Now that you're on to them, they'll most likely move on to a different target."

Walter's clawlike hands gripped the arms of his chair. "Then you've ruled out this nonsense that Hugh arranged the kidnapping of his own son?"

"No, I'm sorry, but we haven't." Marian turned to Hugh. "Your wife says you've tried to get Bobby away from her before. She says you tried to take Bobby out of preschool three times without her permission."

Hugh made a sound of exasperation. "Once. I went there once. And that was…a misunderstanding."

"Like hell it was," Walter Galloway growled. "For god's sake, Hugh—tell them."

Hugh smiled wryly at his father and nodded. "I'd asked Rita if I could have Bobby for one afternoon. That's all—just a few hours. She said yes. Then later she claimed I'd misunderstood her."

"She changed her mind?"

"She set him up," Walter said tightly. "It was deliberate."

Hugh was nodding. "I'm afraid he's right. What you have to understand, Lieutenant, is that Rita is the biggest liar on the face of the earth. She lies instinctively, about everything, even about matters that don't *need* to be lied about, if you follow my drift. That's what started the trouble between us. The constant lying."

"Not your adulteries?" Marian asked calmly.

A silence fell on the room. Then Hugh said, "I had one affair. If you can call it an affair—it lasted two weeks. And I went into that one like any stupid teenager who's been hurt and wants to hit back. I'd just found out that

Rita would sleep with anything in pants. After she'd drop Bobby off at the preschool, she'd go *cruising,* for god's sake!''

"Oh. A liar *and* a nymphomaniac.''

He flared. "She's still in therapy for it! She didn't mention that little fact to you? No? What a surprise.''

Perlmutter pulled out his notebook. "Name of the therapist?''

Hugh gave him a name and address without having to look it up. "I've been writing checks to that quack for over two years. He hasn't done her a bit of good. But Rita won't change therapists. She says he understands her.''

Walter Galloway snorted. "He's shtupping her himself.''

"Dad.'' Mild reprimand from Hugh.

"Why not? Everybody else is. She's a tramp. Worthless. My son married a tramp.'' The old man sneered. Hugh's face darkened.

Well, well—a sore point? Marian took the opening. "Did you oppose your son's marriage, Mr. Galloway?''

"Of course I did!'' he snapped. "No man wants his son marrying a tart.''

"Then you knew she was a tart before they were married?''

A pause. "I sensed it. Women like that send out signals.''

And the signal *he* was sending out was that he wasn't going to budge on the matter. Back to Hugh. "There's one more thing. Your wife claims you hired someone to pose as a housecleaner and spy on her.''

"*What?!*'' roared Walter Galloway.

His son looked equally startled. "Oh, that's a new one! Very good, Rita...very good indeed. What's she claiming, that she found the cleaner reading her mail?''

"The cleaner was going through her checkbook and

credit card statements. And it was your brother-in-law who found her doing it, not your wife."

"Fairchild?" He mulled that over. "That casts a different light on things."

"How?" his father asked. "That brother of hers is no better than she is. They both spend their lives making pretty pictures. Reflections of life." He sniffed. "*Reflections,* not the real thing. They see things the way they want to see them."

Hugh made a dismissive gesture, as if he'd heard all that before. "Fairchild isn't the pathological liar that Rita is, but of course he'd lie to help her. But if he wasn't lying, I suppose the cleaner could just have been nosy about the people whose house she was cleaning. Still, couldn't she have been planted there by the kidnapper?"

Perlmutter spoke up. "That's not likely. Too complicated. And someone who wanted to grab Bobby for ransom wouldn't need to look at your wife's checkbook to see if the Galloways could pay the ransom."

Hugh wasn't ready to concede the point. "But it's an anomaly. It ought to be checked out."

"Don't worry," Marian assured him. "It will be. But Alex Fairchild said you bought the cleaning service. That would make it easy to slip a ringer into the house."

Hugh leaped angrily from his chair. "I bought *three* cleaning services! We're merging them into one. Good lord, Lieutenant, it was an ordinary business transaction!"

His father huffed. "Small potatoes."

"With a potential for growth that you simply *will* not see! Those three piddling little businesses are just the starting point." Back to Marian. "But that's neither here nor there. Now I am accused of hiring a spy in addition to everything else? I'm calling my lawyers. I'm sure that's grounds for a libel action. Rita's gone over the edge. I've been trying to handle this problem in a civil manner, but the woman is beyond reason. I will *not* allow my son to grow up under her influence. She's already poisoning him against me.''

Marian wondered if that was true; the little boy she'd talked to that morning seemed unaware of the war being waged by his parents. But then, she hadn't spent much time with him. She waited while Perlmutter got all the details of the proposed merger from the younger Galloway.

Hugh Galloway showed all the symptoms of any father caught in a tug-of-war over custody of a child; he was feeling harassed and worried. There was only a hint of the high-powered businessman, the wheeler-dealer determined to get what he wanted at all costs. Walter Galloway had once been a dynamo; now he was an old man in an armchair who liked to snipe at his son for not managing his affairs better. But there was no real tension between the two men; their relationship seemed one of accommodation, of acceptance of their changed roles. Hugh was alpha now, not his father.

When Perlmutter nodded that they were finished, Marian said, ''Mr. Galloway, why did you tear up your wife's watercolors?''

''What? I never tore up her watercolors!''

''She says you did.''

He heaved a big sigh. ''I told you what a liar she is. I never destroyed anything she—'' He broke off, remembering. ''Wait a minute. I did tear up a sketch. Just a sketch, and only the one. Is that what she's talking about?''

''She said 'watercolors,' plural.''

''No. I did no such thing.''

''Damned woman,'' Walter muttered from his armchair.

''All right, then,'' Marian went on, ''why did you tear up the sketch?''

Hugh closed his eyes, opened them again. ''It was a sketch she'd done of me.'' It was obvious he'd have preferred not to talk about it, but he went on. ''She'd drawn me wearing ballet slippers. And a tutu.''

Marian managed to keep her face straight.

A rumbling erupted from Walter's armchair. "You never told me about that!"

"No, I probably didn't," Hugh said tiredly. "It was just one of a thousand ugly little things that happened." He smiled wryly at Marian. "Rita has interesting ways of letting you know what she thinks of you."

"Are you sure the sketch was of you?" Marian asked.

"Who else would it be? Rita said it was."

"Was it *recognizably* you?"

He waved a hand impatiently. "Yes, yes, it was me."

The interview was ended; Marian told the two Galloways they'd be in touch and left. In the car on the way back, Perlmutter said, "That's guy's bleeding."

"You believed him?"

"Yeah, I think I did. You didn't?"

"He tells a reasonable story. The problem is, so does she."

"I didn't hear her tell it," Perlmutter reminded her. "Any vibes?"

"The same ones we just got at Sutton Place. Sincere outrage, resentment, worry about what the other half will do next. She's bleeding too."

"But if Galloway's right that she's the biggest liar on the face of the earth—"

"*One* of them is. He gave us enough that we might be able to pin this down. I wonder if the graphics tech got a face for us?"

The computer's visualization of Bobby's kidnapper was on her desk waiting for her. A rather ordinary face—beefy, clean-shaven. The only unusual feature was an overlarge bottom lip; it made the face look as if it was pouting. It was the face of a man who had not yet reached early middle age; Marian put him at early to mid-thirties.

"It's already gone out," Detective O'Toole told her.

"Every bluesuit in the city will have one of those by six o'clock."

"Good, good. Perlmutter, fill him in." While Perlmutter briefed O'Toole on what they'd learned from their interviews with Rita and Hugh Galloway, Marian made a list of what needed to be done. When they'd both finished, she said, "Okay. O'Toole, go see Rita Galloway. Try to pin her down as to the exact date her brother found the housecleaner going through her checkbook. Get a description, and find out if she reported the incident to the cleaning service. Then go to the service's offices and check their payroll records—see if they had any substitutions on the day in question. If not, come back with the names and addresses of the entire crew that was in the house."

O'Toole was scribbling instructions. "You say the husband accused her of sleeping around?"

"Hold off on that. She wouldn't admit it, not in the midst of a custody fight. And you'd just put her on her guard."

"Right."

"Perlmutter, go to the preschool where Rita Galloway takes Bobby. Talk to the director. Rita says her husband tried to take Bobby out of school three times, Hugh says it was only once. Find out which one of them is lying."

"Yeah." Perlmutter was flipping through his notebook. "The therapist?"

"He's next. He's not going to tell you anything about Rita's alleged promiscuity, but he might unbend far enough to let us know whether the lady has a problem with telling the truth or not."

"Find a judge?"

Marian shook her head. "We can't get an order forcing him to break doctor-patient confidentiality. His patient's no danger to herself or others." She thought of something. "Ask him if he knows whether Hugh Galloway is in therapy too."

Perlmutter looked up from his notebook and grinned. "We could get a court order for his therapist. If Hugh's a suspect."

"I could ask Mrs. Galloway," O'Toole said.

"Do that," Marian replied. "We'll decide whether Hugh's a suspect when you both are finished. Call in when you have something. You've got a couple of hours left today—get hopping."

Perlmutter checked his watch. "How late do preschools stay open?" The two detectives left.

Marian sat and thought about Hugh Galloway in a tutu. In her mental image of him, he looked ridiculous—which, of course, was the whole point. Rita had diminished him by sketching him that way, yet she claimed Hugh had always belittled *her*. But the sketch could have been a way of reducing his menace, of making him less threatening; the sketch might have been done for its therapeutic value to the artist.

Did Hugh really look closely at the face of the figure in the sketch? It would have been the tutu he'd focused on. Marian heard Rita's voice in her head, saying she wasn't very good at catching likenesses...right before she left to work with the tech on a computer portrait. Was that a lie? Or did Hugh say the sketch was of him because he knew it was *supposed* to be of him?

An hour later Perlmutter called in.

"I talked to the school director. She told me how many times Hugh Galloway tried to pick up Bobby."

Milking it. "All right, Perlmutter, how many? Once as Hugh says or three times as Rita says?"

"Twice. As the director says."

"Sheesh!"

"Yeah. And we can believe the director, Lieutenant. You should see the security at this place—nobody gets in or out without three people knowing about it. Lots of wealthy kids here, the parents are very kidnapping conscious. The director keeps a log of everything that happens. She was even able to tell me the exact dates Hugh came for Bobby. Two dates. Twice.''

''Oh…damnation!''

''Yep. They were both lying.''

FIVE

MARIAN SLIPPED INTO the ladies' before going into the bar, the Galloways and their problems firmly locked away until eight o'clock the next morning. Just as she was about to leave, two women came in, laughing and talking.

"Did you see that dark, broody guy in the last booth?" one of them said.

"Yes!" the other one answered. "That one looks like Trouble with a capital T."

"I wonder if he's waiting for someone."

"I don't know. I can't tell from the way he's sitting whether he's saying 'Hands off!' or 'What are you waiting for?'" They both laughed.

Marian left the rest room and cautiously peered around a long floor planter toward the last booth. The "dark, broody guy" was sitting sideways in the booth, his back against the wall and one foot up on the seat. His left forearm rested on his knee and his right hand gripped a glass on the table. He stared straight ahead, motionless. The two women in the rest room were right; you couldn't tell whether his posture meant invitation or rejection.

Marian eased over toward the booth and stood with her fingertips resting on the tabletop. "May I?"

He didn't look at her. "May you what?"

She slipped out of her jacket and sat down opposite him. "May I take off my jacket?"

"You may take off whatever you like."

He still hadn't moved. Marian studied his profile: a good one, even with the slight sag under the chin. His clothes were expensive, and unusual; the open-necked, collarless silk shirt could have been spun from silver. "You look like a toyboy," she said slowly. "Are you?"

He looked at her for the first time. "I like to think I'm not any kind of boy."

"Hmm. Well, it's the 'toy' part that interests me."

He gave her the same sort of close examination she'd just given him. "You like to play, do you?"

"Sometimes."

He shifted his position so he was sitting normally in the booth, facing her. "And is now one of those times?"

"I think perhaps it is."

Almost langorously he reached across the table and slowly began working at the top button of her shirt with one hand. When he had it open, he slipped two fingers inside, where he began a gentle massage of the spot between her breasts.

"In public?!" Marian exclaimed, an octave higher than usual.

He didn't move his hand until the waitress appeared to take Marian's order. When she'd come back with a scotch on the rocks and left again, he said, "You're very warm in there."

Marian took a swallow of her scotch. "I'm very warm all over," she muttered.

He laughed then, a laugh that lit up his face. He took her hand between both of his and continued the gentle massage he'd started elsewhere. "I'm so glad you have a job that makes you horny."

She dipped a finger of her free hand into her scotch, licked it. "It's not the job that makes me horny, Holland, and you know it—you vain creature."

He looked amused but said nothing. He dipped two of her fingers into the scotch—which he then proceeded to lick.

"Arrgh!" said Marian. "I can't stand it! Let's go." She stood up and shrugged into her jacket.

"What about dinner?"

"What about it?" She headed toward the door; Holland left money on the table and followed.

Marian found she'd caught some of his langorous mood; it stayed with them all the way to his place. She took her time undressing him, taking pleasure from the mere sight of the body she'd come to know as well as her own. Their lovemaking was slow and sweet, just as it should have been.

Almost two hours passed before they began regretting missing dinner. Marian showered while Holland called a Greek restaurant that delivered. Then while he was in the shower, Marian called her own number to check for messages. There was one.

"I've been in the land of suntan panty hose and white shoes for exactly three hours," said Kelly's voice, "and already I'm homesick. Like you wouldn't *believe*, I'm homesick. The studio sent this self-important little nudnik to meet me, talked about himself all the way from the airport to this hotel, whatever it is." Marian could hear a rustling of papers, and Kelly read off the name of the hotel and a phone number. "I haven't seen Abby James and Ian Cavanaugh yet. The studio found a bungalow for me, but it won't be ready for another two days. Exactly what is a bungalow anyway? A log cabin without plumbing and electricity? At least I won't have to chop wood for the fire—it's hot as blazes here. Call me when you get home, Toots."

Holland came out of the shower as Marian was punching out the number of Kelly's hotel. The voice on the other end of the phone said Ms Ingram had gone out; Marian left a message that she'd call tomorrow.

"Shouldn't she be prostrate from jet lag about now?" Holland asked, toweling his hair dry.

"I don't think anyone ever told Kelly about jet lag. She probably found herself a dancing partner."

He grimaced. "There is such a thing as too much energy."

"Not for Kelly. When she's in in her eighties and on Medicare, she'll still be dancing."

Their food arrived. They took it out on the balcony; the lights in the park had come on, and they were high enough up that the sounds of traffic were muted. When they'd finished eating, Holland moved his chair next to hers and sat with one hand resting lightly on her thigh. They were both silent.

The thought occurred to Marian that this was a time she'd someday look back on as one perfect moment in her life, as she lazed there on the balcony of an expensive Central Park West apartment on a mild summer night. She was sated with food and drink and sex. She had good friends and good, meaningful work. Her health was good.

And Holland was with her. *Everything* was better when Holland was with her.

She was happy.

THE NEXT MORNING she opened "her" closet and found only one outfit left. "You know, I haven't been to my place in over a week," she said to Holland. "I'm out of clothes."

"We'll do laundry tonight," he replied. "A nice, 'sharing' kind of domestic chore. And such fun."

"Hmm. No, I need to go home."

He placed one hand on his chest in a theatrical gesture. "You wound me to the quick. I thought this was your home."

"It's my other home. But I haven't even checked my mail lately." She looked at her one remaining outfit critically, a lightweight summer suit that came with a skirt instead of trousers—the reason she'd left it to last. Marian still thought of the suit as new; but in the sunlight it was obvious that the suit's new days were long gone. The

NYPD had a dress code for its detectives, a fact that had never been any particular problem before. But now that she was a lieutenant, she had to pay more attention to her clothing than she really cared to do. Marian hated shopping.

She dressed and started the coffee while Holland hacked a melon in two. His day didn't start as early as hers, but he never slept in when she was there. They'd almost finished eating when one of their pagers went off in the bedroom.

"Yours," said Holland.

"How can you tell?"

"Higher pitch."

Marian the Tone-Deaf sighed and went into the bedroom. She clicked off the pager and called in.

When she went back to the kitchen, Holland said, "There's been a break in a case and you have to go in right now."

She laughed and said, "Again, how can you tell?"

"Your walk. You have a Marian walk and a Lieutenant Larch walk. You're walking like a cop now."

"God, I hate being so transparent." They exchanged no casual good-bye kiss; that would have been a little too domestic.

Time to shift gears back to the Galloways.

IT WASN'T a break in the case, but instead one more ugly incident: a fire at the home of Rita Galloway. During the wee hours someone had heaved a brick through the dragon window and followed it with a Molotov cocktail. The alarms going off had awakened everyone on the street. Heron Security had been there within minutes and summoned the Fire Department. The explosion was small and the damage minimal; the fire had been quickly contained to the dragon window room and part of a connecting hallway. The gasoline in the wine bottle had been a minimum amount needed to cause ignition—an act of harassment rather than arson or attempted homicide.

"Bring him in," Marian ordered.

No Heron Security man had been watching the house at the time it happened; their orders were to remain until the lights were turned out for the night. Right now Rita Galloway and Bobby were staying at her brother's place on the West Side until repairs could be completed and the smell of smoke no longer lingered. Alex Fairchild had hired bodyguards to stay with his sister and nephew around the clock; brother and sister both were frightened and angry and demanding Hugh Galloway's arrest. Bobby had been told only that the house had caught fire, but nothing about the cause.

Perlmutter and O'Toole had gone to the headquarters of Galloway Industries and told Hugh he could either come in for questioning voluntarily or they could arrest him as a material witness. He called his lawyer and came voluntarily.

The in control man Marian had interviewed the day before had given way to one in the grip of a titanic rage. "Do you really think I would set fire to a house where my son is sleeping? Don't you see? Rita did it herself! That woman is *evil*, evil to the core!"

"Why should she set fire to her own house?" Marian asked, knowing the answer.

"What was the first thing you did? You hauled me in here. *That's* what she wanted. She doesn't give a damn about Bobby's safety—just so she can get *me*. Why can't you see that? Because women don't *do* things like that? Because Rita's poor-little-me act convinced you she's the victim here?"

"I'd say Bobby is the real victim. Where were you at 3 a.m.?"

"In bed asleep, of course. And before you ask—yes, I was alone. I've slept alone since before Rita and I separated. My father was asleep in his bed, and I assume the servants were asleep in theirs. Now, Lieutenant—are you going to arrest me because no one was sitting there watching me sleep while my house was being firebombed?''

"You still consider it your house, Mr. Galloway?"

"Damned right I do. The deed's in my name. I offered to give Rita the house if she'd agree to let me have Bobby. But she wants more than a house. She wants everything. Most of all, she wants to see me ruined and humiliated. Prison would take care of that. Have you brought *her* in for questioning?''

"How many times did you try to take Bobby out of preschool?"

"What? Oh…just the once. I told you that yesterday.''

"The school director said you tried twice.''

"Once, twice, what's the difference? No—the director's wrong. It was only once. Why the hell are you asking me about that at a time like this?''

Marian left the questioning to Perlmutter and O'Toole. She walked down the hall to Captain Murtaugh's office. "Jim? Got a moment?''

He waved her in. "How's it going?''

"About as expected. She accused him, he's accusing her.'' She sat down and took a deep breath. "I don't think he did it.''

"Reason?''

"I don't believe he would endanger his own son. The little boy's just too important to him. Hugh Galloway is probably every bit the son of a bitch his wife says he is— he's tried to *buy* Bobby from her, for one thing. He offered her the house and god knows what else if she'd give the boy up. But if he was going to heave a Molotov cocktail through the window, he'd do it at a time Bobby wasn't there.''

Murtaugh nodded. "Sounds reasonable. What about the wife? Could she have done it?''

Marian shifted in her chair. "I don't think so. And for just about the same reasons. Even if she is the coldhearted liar Hugh claims she is, Bobby provides the only leverage she has over her husband. She wouldn't risk losing that."

"You've seen them together, Rita and Bobby. Anything there?"

She shook her head. "Looked like a normal mother-child relationship to me. Bobby's a sweet kid. He doesn't know what's going on between his parents—Rita has shielded him from that."

"If we rule out both of them," the captain said, sitting up straight, "then it looks as if old Walter Galloway was right. Kidnapping for ransom."

Marian agreed. "And it's somebody who's new at the game. An amateur. The man who grabbed Bobby on the street...an experienced criminal would have dropped the kid and run the minute he heard the police siren. But this guy not only held on, he even struggled with the bluesuit over possession of the boy. A pro would never have run that risk."

"Why set the house on fire?"

She shrugged. "Planning to grab Bobby when he and his mother came running out of the burning house? But he didn't figure on the alarm system being so noisy. It woke up the entire neighborhood...witnesses all over the place. Another amateur mistake."

"Yeah," Murtaugh mused, "it could have happened just like that."

"There's only one piece that doesn't fit," Marian said. "There are lots of little rich boys in New York. After the first attempt failed, why didn't the kidnapper just move on to an easier target? Why did he come back a second time for this particular little rich boy?"

"I think you'd better find out," the captain said.

SIX

"MRS. GALLOWAY WASN'T sure of the exact date her brother caught the cleaning woman going through her checkbook," O'Toole said. "But she's sure it was a Tuesday either two or three weeks ago."

"Why Tuesday?" Marian asked.

"Because Bobby wasn't home when it happened. The cleaning service comes twice a week, Tuesdays and Fridays. And Bobby doesn't go to preschool on Fridays."

She nodded. "Go on."

"The cleaning woman was Puerto Rican, first name Consuela. About five five, hundred-fifty pounds, in her forties. Mrs. Galloway doesn't remember ever seeing her before. Mrs. Galloway didn't report the incident to the cleaning service herself—she said her brother took care of it."

"What about the cleaning service?"

"Maids-in-a-Row, on Lex," O'Toole said. "They've just been bought by Galloway Industries, and they're gonna be merged with two other cleaning services. The owner, name of Gordon Egrorian, says he don't know nuttin' about no complaint, his words. Could be lying, but he cooperated in checking the payroll."

"And?"

"And Tuesday three weeks ago he had a new employee on the crew that went to Mrs. Galloway's house, a Consuela Palmero with a home address on West 177th Street. I haven't had time to check it out yet, I'll get to that next. Egrorian said one of his regular crew quit without notice, and the Palmero woman showed up looking for work that same day. He put her on the Galloway crew without checking her references."

"Whoa. Aren't those cleaning services all bonded?"

"He said she already was—she had the papers. That was good enough for him, in a pinch. He'd planned on adding her to his own bond later, but he never saw her again. He tried to call when she didn't show up the next day, but the phone number she left wasn't a working number."

"Uh-huh. And what do you want to bet that her name isn't Consuela Palmero and she doesn't live on 177th?"

O'Toole grimaced. "Not even a penny. But I'll check it out anyway."

"Talk to the others on the Galloway cleaning crew. See if this Consuela let anything drop about herself. Slim chance, I know—but this woman's our only link to whoever's behind the trouble. Let's get that owner of Maids-in-a-Row...Gordon Egrorian? Get him in here for a session with the graphics tech. Set it up, O'Toole."

"Okay." He scribbled a note to himself. "And I asked Mrs. Galloway if her husband was in therapy, like you said. She says no, Hugh looks upon needing a therapist as a sign of weakness. She says that's one reason he insisted on *her* going into therapy. An insult. That lady's very bitter, Lieutenant."

"I know."

"What about her therapist?"

"Perlmutter's at his office now. I don't expect he'll tell us much. All right, O'Toole, go check on the elusive Consuela."

"Right, Lieutenant." He hurried away.

Marian looked in the case file and found the West Side address for Alex Fairchild that Perlmutter had put there. She had legitimate police business with Fairchild and his sister, but mostly she wanted to see how Bobby had weathered this newest trauma in his young life.

ALEX FAIRCHILD was standing there waiting for the elevator as the doors slid open to let Marian out. "Lieutenant

Larch!'' he said, surprised. "I hope you've come to tell us that Hugh Galloway is safely under lock and key.''

"I'm sorry, no. How's Bobby doing?''

"Oh, Bobby's doing fine. He's the only one of us who is. He told his bodyguard that he's staying here while his own house gets 'fixed.' He doesn't understand what happened.''

"He must know there was a fire.''

"Only because we told him. All he remembers is that his mother woke him up before he was ready and carried him out-of-doors in his pajamas. He didn't see much of anything.'' Fairchild peered into the elevator she was holding open. "Where's the professor?''

He meant Perlmutter; with his wire-rim glasses and bush of wiry black hair, the detective did have a scholarly look to him. "He's at home grading papers. Are your sister and Bobby in?''

"Yes—Rita's afraid to go out. Look, I'm due at a shoot. If you want to talk to me, do you mind coming along?''

"Just one question and I'll let you go. Who reported the cleaning woman to the service, you or your sister?''

"I did. Why?''

"The owner denies ever getting the complaint.''

Fairchild made a *tsk* sound. "The charitable interpretation of that would be to say he forgot about it. But he's lying, Lieutenant. He's going to deny any of his employees ever did anything wrong.''

Everybody lies. "What's the owner's name?''

A smile played around his mouth. "A test?'' But he concentrated on remembering. "It was an odd name.'' He frowned. "Why am I thinking of a calendar…Gregorian?''

Marian nodded. "Close enough. It's Egrorian. All right, Mr. Fairchild, I won't hold you any longer.''

He stepped into the elevator. "Don't forget Thursday,'' he said just as the doors closed.

Thursday? Then she remembered: a private showing of

his photographs at the Something-or-Other Gallery on Fifty-seventh Street. Marian walked down the hall and rang the doorbell of apartment number 1404.

A male voice came through the door. "Who is it?" One of the bodyguards.

Marian held her badge up to the eyehole and waited. The door was opened by an unsmiling man in a conservative business suit. "I'm Lieutenant Larch, Midtown South. I need to see Mrs. Galloway."

He stepped back to let her enter, and then led her down a white staircase to an open area on a lower level where a television was playing with the sound low. Rita Galloway sat looking at the set with a glassy-eyed stare that suggested she wasn't seeing what was on the screen. She jumped when Marian spoke her name.

"Oh, Lieutenant!" She clicked off the TV. "Any news?"

"A little." She sat down on what looked like a pile of deep-blue pillows but turned out to be a chair. Alex Fairchild's apartment was so ultra-modern it looked like the set of a futuristic movie. Airy and open, no clutter. The bodyguard took another chair near the foot of the stairway; he hadn't spoken once. "Where's Bobby?"

"In the next room, with his guard. What's the news?"

"It looks as if you were right about the cleaning woman being a plant." Marian went on to explain about Consuela Palmero. "It's not her real name. But she's a lead."

"To Hugh?"

"Or to someone who's after Bobby for the ransom. I know—you're convinced it's your husband. But until we find something that links him directly to these things that have been happening, we can't arrest him."

"This is insane! Hugh tried to kill us last night and—"

"Mrs. Galloway, stop and think. Does your husband want Bobby dead?"

"No! He wants *me* dead!"

"So how could he expect the same homemade bomb to get you but not Bobby? It doesn't make sense. Fire is always dangerous, but neither of you was hurt, were you? That bomb was meant to badger you, not kill you."

Rita Galloway was silent a moment and then said, "That stained-glass dragon is irreplaceable, you know. It was one of a kind. The artisan who fashioned it died last year."

A door opened and Bobby rushed in, followed by another unsmiling man in a business suit. "Mama! I wrote my name!" He held up a sheet of paper on which "Bobby" had been drawn in green crayon.

"Why, honey, that's wonderful!" Rita fussed over him a few minutes and then shot a questioning look at Bobby's bodyguard.

The man spread his hands. "He wanted to know."

Rita gave him a big smile, the first Marian had ever seen on her face. Marian leaned forward toward the boy. "Hi, Bobby. Remember me?"

He turned shy. "Mary Ann," he said in a tiny voice.

"Hey, you remember!" She leaned back in her chair: less threatening. "Good for you."

"I drew a cow," he volunteered.

"You did? Cows are hard to draw."

He nodded soberly. "I never see a cow."

"That should make it even harder."

"I see monkeys, and goats, and, and, and snakes—"

"Bobby," his mother interrupted gently. "Ah, Mary Ann and I need to talk right now. Okay?"

"Okay." Bobby dropped to his hands and knees and started chugging away like a choo-choo.

Rita watched a moment to make sure he was absorbed in his play and then turned back to Marian. "Are you having Hugh followed?" she asked in a low voice.

Marian had been afraid she'd ask that. "There's no point. He spends most of his day at the office, doesn't he? There are a dozen ways out of the Galloway Building. We can't watch them all. And if he is guilty, he's hiring some-one to do his dirty work for him. He didn't…ah…'' She remembered just in time that Bobby was in the room. "He didn't do the job outside the church himself. And it's un-likely he ran the risk of being seen in your neighborhood last night."

Rita sighed. "That's true." Bobby had crawled under an end table that looked like an exhibit from the Museum of Modern Art, playing hide-and-seek with himself.

"But accomplices…that's another matter. We have a line on one of them, the Palmero woman. And we have the face of the other, the man you described for the com-puter portrait. And you seem well protected here." Marian glanced over at Bobby's guard. "What agency are you with?"

"Vinni Security," he said.

Marian nodded. A reliable rent-a-cop outfit; no elderly retirees armed with guns they could barely lift. "Mrs. Gal-loway, I'd like you to consider seriously the possibility that your husband isn't behind this."

"What do you mean? Of course he's behind it! How can you—''

"Please, hear me out. Your husband's feeling as belea-gured as you are, and you're both accusing the other of being responsible for what's happening."

Rita Galloway made a sound of disgust. "*Hugh* wasn't the one who was firebombed last night!" Then she sud-denly remembered Bobby was there and jerked her head around to see if he was listening.

The boy was paying no attention to them; he was too busy trying to pull open a shallow drawer in the art mu-seum end table. "It's stuck," he complained.

"No, Bobby," his mother said. "It's locked."

"Why?"

"Uncle Alex always keeps it locked."

"Oh. Okay." Back to being a choo-choo.

Rita returned her attention to what Marian had been saying. "Look, I know how convincing he can be. I fell for his line once myself. But I'm telling you—"

"Mrs. Galloway, please listen. We have to investigate the possibility that an outsider is responsible." Marian's eyes traveled back to the locked end table drawer. "It might even be someone you know." The other woman frowned. "He's made two attempts. I'd like you to think over all the people you know—not just your friends but casual acquaintances and enemies too, if you have any. Try to isolate those who need money, those who might want to hurt you." The end table drawer was shallow, not more than four inches deep.

"Excuse me, Lieutenant, but that would be a waste of time. I *know* who's responsible."

What could be kept in a drawer that shallow? A few papers. A gun. Marian raised her voice and said, "Bobby?"

He peeked out at her from behind a sofa.

"Bobby, that drawing of the cow you made? I really would like to see that. Will you show it to me?"

His face lit up. "Sure!" He ran out of the room, followed by his guard.

Marian stood up and walked over to the end table. "Quickly, Mrs. Galloway. What's in the drawer?"

"Oh, well, ah, this is Alex's place—"

"Answer the question. Is there a gun in there?"

Rita Galloway slumped. "Alex got it for me. I refused to take it—I didn't want a gun in the house with Bobby. But after what happened last night, I've changed my mind. Oh, it's legal—Alex has a permit."

"Where is it?"

"Ah...in the drawer with the gun, I believe."

"Let me see it."

Rita got up and moved over to something hanging on the wall that looked like a comet with a long tail; only then did Marian realize it was a clock. Rita reached behind the clock and took out a key.

In the drawer was a .38 revolver and a box of shells, resting on top of a piece of paper. Marian slid the permit out and read it; it was in order, licensing Alex Fairchild to keep a weapon at his place of habitation. "This permit was issued only two weeks ago."

"Yes. Alex had no reason to think I was in danger before that."

"What if Bobby finds the key?"

"Lieutenant, we just moved in here a matter of hours ago. Alex and I haven't had time to childproof the place yet. We'll work something else out."

She was just locking the drawer again when Bobby came bursting into the room, waving a piece of yellow construction paper. "Cow!"

"Let me see." Marian took the paper. Bobby had used a purple crayon to draw his cow; Gelett Burgess would have been pleased. The cow was recognizably a cow, even though the udder had nine teats. Marian wasn't sure, but she thought the drawing was unusually detailed for the work of a four-year-old; perhaps the little boy had inherited his mother's talent. "Bobby," she said, "that is just about the best cow I have ever seen."

He grinned and hugged himself.

Marian nodded. "It's a *wonderful* cow. You take good care of this drawing." She held the paper out to him.

Bobby wouldn't take it. "It's for you!"

She felt flattered. "You're giving it to me? To keep?"

"Yes!" He was jumping up and down. "To keep!"

Marian hugged the little boy and thanked him. "I'm going to put this up in my office. A lot of people will see it."

"There you go, Bobby," his mother said with a smile. "Your first exhibition."

Marian said good-bye. "I hope you'll do what I asked,

Mrs. Galloway. Try to think of people you know who need money or might act out of malice.'' She started up the white staircase.

"It would be a waste of time, Lieutenant.''

Marian stopped halfway up the stairs and looked down at her. "Help us out here. Cooperate.''

Rita Galloway shrugged and turned her back.

SEVEN

MARIAN USED her pocket phone to call the Ninth Precinct station; she asked for Detective Sanchez. "Gloria? It's a little early, but can you get away for lunch? I'm buying."

"I can always get away for a free lunch," Gloria Sanchez replied lazily. "Your precinct or mine?"

"How about meeting halfway?" They agreed on San Remo's on Eighth Avenue in half an hour.

As it turned out, Gloria was late; Marian had already ordered by the time the detective from the Ninth sat down across the table from her. "Sorrree," Gloria said with a lilt in her voice. "DiFalco call' me in at the las' second."

"And how is dear old DiFalco?" No love lost between Marian and her former captain.

"Gettin' kinda twitchy, if you ask me, and you jus' did."

"Twitchy how?"

"Pre-paranoid. He don' *quite* thin' the worl' is out to get 'eem, but he gettin' there. What did you order?"

That *'eem* for *him* told Marian that Gloria had gone into Hispanic overdrive, something she did when she was irritated. Unless she was being African-American that day, in which case her speech would become mo' po' boy the more annoyed she got. Gloria switched between Hispanic and black as the mood suited her, one legacy of a mixed parentage.

Gloria gave the waiter her order and then asked Marian, "When's Kelly leaving for California?"

"She flew to L.A. yesterday. Hates it already."

Gloria grinned. "A true Noo Yawker. I thought she lived there once?"

"A long time ago. She didn't like it then either."

"She'll adjust. She always does."

Marian waited until their pasta arrived and they'd both taken the edge off their hunger. Then she said, "Gloria, I know you don't like me to talk about this, but I have to. I want you to reconsider your decision never to take the Sergeants Exam."

"I'm goin' to take it."

"If there's anyone qualified to— What did you say?"

Gloria laughed. "I say I'm goin' to take the Sergeants Exam."

Marian almost dropped her fork in surprise. "Well, I'll be damned! You really are?"

"I really are."

"Gloria, I've been after you for over a year to take that exam, and all I ever got from you was *I don' wanna talk about it.* You want to tell me why you changed your mind?"

"I was afraid if I passed the test I'd get transferred out of the Ninth."

Marian blinked. "You *like* working for Captain Di-Falco?"

"Shit, no! I don' like workin' for DiFalco any more'n you did. But I had my Gran livin' with me, Marian. She's old and frail, and I needed to run home and check on her whenever I could. I could do that from the Ninth Precinct stationhouse."

"Which you might not be able to if you were transferred." Marian nodded. "I see. Why didn't you tell me this before?"

"It dint seem right, usin' Gran as an excuse."

Marian could see that too. "Where is she now?"

"I took her to Alabama, where she was born. She don' have much time left, and she say she don' wanna die here. Her great-niece is takin' care of her."

"You miss her, don't you?"

"Yeah, I do. She's the only family I had. But she's better off where she is. At least she doesn't have to stay locked in all day the way she did here," Gloria said flatly.

Marian grinned. "Do you realize you just switched from Rosie Perez to Nichelle Nichols?"

"I did?" Gloria laughed. "Gran's black, and I was thinkin' 'bout her." She tossed her head, making her gold loop earrings dance. "But I look like zee nice Puerto Rican gel, yes?" The lilt was back in her voice.

"Oh, yes," Marian agreed. "Well, this is great news, Gloria. You know we're short one sergeant in Midtown South."

"You thin' Captain Murtaugh put in a request for me?"

"I'm sure he will. Especially since Sergeant Buchanan is retiring at the end of the year. We'll be needing two sergeants."

"Whass wrong with Midtown South detectives? They no take the test?"

"Six of them are going to. But, frankly, only one of them has any real chance."

"Don't tell me—Perlmutter?"

"Got it in one. So you see, we have to find another sergeant somewhere…and I'd just as soon it be you."

"'Sokay wi' me!" Gloria agreed cheerily.

They finished their lunch and went their separate ways. Marian was feeling exhilarated; Captain Murtaugh had seen Gloria at work on two cases that had involved both Midtown South and the Ninth Precinct, and he knew what she could do. Marian loved the idea of having Gloria to work with every day, the way they'd once worked together in the Ninth. Gloria was not only a good detective, she was also a friend, someone Marian could trust in a way she could never trust, say, Sergeant Buchanan.

At the stationhouse, she stopped by the captain's office. "How do you feel about putting a little pressure on Personnel?"

He raised an eyebrow. "Give me a good enough cause and I'll put pressure on anybody."

"Gloria Sanchez." She went on to explain that Gloria would be taking the Sergeants Exam. "And since Midtown South has gone with only two sergeants for…how long now? A year and a half? Surely Personnel should be willing to give you first choice, don't you think?"

He smiled. "Sounds reasonable to me. But didn't you once tell me Sanchez refused to take the exam?"

"She had a family situation that was holding her back, Jim. But that's resolved now, and she's champing at the bit."

"Good. Okay, I'll put in a name request, both for her and for Perlmutter. Now all they have to do is pass the test."

"Yeah, that's all."

He scratched the side of his nose. "Perlmutter has a good chance. Does she?"

"She does if she studies—and she's motivated. Remember who her boss is."

Murtaugh half-laughed. "DiFalco's going to raise holy hell if I take another of his detectives."

"Oh, let him. He doesn't deserve Gloria."

"Meaning I do? Careful, Marian, that sounds like flattery."

"Ah. Gotta watch that."

When she reached her office, she found a phone message from O'Toole saying that Gordon Egrorian, the owner of Maids-in-a-Row, would be in that afternoon to help build a computer face for Consuela Palmero. Perlmutter was back from talking to Rita Galloway's therapist. But first Marian took Bobby's crayon drawing of a cow and taped it to her file cabinet. A cow! What did city kids know of cows? Bobby had seen pictures, of course; bovines probably seemed like exotic animals to him.

"A purple cow?" Perlmutter's voice said over her shoulder.

Marian sat down at her desk. "Bobby Galloway's work."

"Yeah?" He peered at the drawing closely. "Not bad for a four-year-old. Not quite anatomically correct, but careful otherwise. The kid thought about what he was drawing."

"So, what did you get from the therapist?"

Perlmutter took a chair. "Not a whole lot. Rita Galloway's been seeing Dr. David Zukan for fourteen months. He says she consulted him for help in dealing with her frustration and anger generated by a stressful marriage. Her anger was affecting her work as an artist, but she had made great strides in learning to deal with the anger."

Marian growled. "'Learning to deal with'—that's one of those phrases like 'come to terms with'...they don't *mean* anything. Is she overcoming her anger or just co-existing with it?"

"I don't know, Lieutenant. Zukan wouldn't get any more specific than that. When I asked him if she was a pathological liar, he objected to the word 'pathological.' But then he added that all his patients lie to him at one time or another."

"So Rita Galloway does lie, but Hugh Galloway over-stated the extent of her lying?"

"That's the way I read it, yeah."

"Who made the arrangements for therapy, Hugh or Rita?"

"Rita. Zukan has never met Hugh, and knows him only through Rita's eyes."

"Yet it was Hugh's insistence that she go into therapy—or was it? Did he say that, or do we just have Rita's word for it?"

Perlmutter took out his notebook and flipped through it. "He said only that she was in therapy. And that he'd been paying the bills for over two years—but it's been only fourteen months.''

Marian discounted that. ''That's the sort of exaggeration any aggrieved husband would make. He did say she was in therapy for her lying and her nymphomania, though. And Zukan said she came to him for help in dealing with her anger.''

''Those could be the same thing,'' Perlmutter pointed out. ''Zukan wouldn't tell me how her anger expressed itself. Patient confidentiality.''

Marian mulled that over and conceded the point. ''God, these are slippery people! Impossible to pin down.''

''Talk to friends, associates?''

''Not yet. If it looks likely that the kidnapping and the bombing are the work of neither Rita nor Hugh—which I suspect is the case—then I don't want to waste any more time on the Galloways' domestic problems. Let's wait and see what O'Toole turns up about the cleaning lady who isn't a cleaning lady.''

It was over an hour before O'Toole brought the news that he'd run into a dead end. The address on 177th Street was a garage. He'd asked there and in a few other places nearby, but no one knew a Consuela Palmero. O'Toole had volunteered the opinion that they wouldn't have told him even if they had known. But the owner of Maids-in-a-Row was downstairs right then working with the graphics tech to reconstruct Palmero's face.

Someone was going to a lot of trouble to cover his/her/their trail. There were three incidents that marked Rita Galloway and Bobby as targets: the spying cleaning lady, the attempted kidnapping, and the small-scale firebombing of the house. But the first didn't fit with the other two.

Kidnappers didn't disguise themselves as housecleaners, for whatever reason. Kidnapping was not a subtle crime; those who attempted it were blunt and crude and frequently quite stupid. And kidnapping was not a criminal 'career,' the way burglary or counterfeiting was—except in Italy, and even there kidnapping-as-profession had pretty much been brought under control. But most kidnappers hoped to score enough from one kidnapping to keep them in clover the rest of their days. It was an outrageous crime, the trading of a human life for money—if indeed the trade was made. Too many kidnap victims never emerged from their ordeals alive.

Kidnappers would certainly spy out the land before attempting to snatch Bobby Galloway, but what could be gained by placing a spy inside the household? The fact that Consuela Palmero (whatever her real name was) had been checking Rita's finances rather than the layout of the house made Marian think that that incident was not linked to the other two. Hugh Galloway could have engineered the placement of the Palmero woman in his wife's household and still be innocent of the crimes of attempted kidnapping and firebombing.

Marian found herself wondering how much Walter Galloway really knew about his son's affairs. She'd pegged the elder Galloway as a stubborn old man who'd never budge from his position that Hugh had made a bad mistake in marrying the evil Rita but that Hugh himself was a good boy. And Alex Fairchild was every bit as biased in favor of his sister. Those two would be no help.

Thinking of Alex Fairchild reminded her of the private showing of his photographs scheduled for Thursday night—which was tomorrow, she suddenly realized. And still she couldn't remember the name of the gallery. Fairchild had given her a printed invitation; what had she done with it? Probably left it at Holland's. Or thrown it out.

Hoping she'd recognize the name if she saw it, Marian pulled the *NYNEX Yellow Pages* directory off the shelf. To her dismay she found page after page after page of galleries, all listed in tiny type. No way she was going through all that looking for Fifty-seventh Street addresses.

She reached for the phone and called the computer department. A woman answered by saying something that sounded like *Mahjelblmph*. Marian identified herself and said, "I want to locate a gallery on Fifty-seventh Street. I think I'd know the name if I heard it."

"What kind of gallery? Art gallery?"

"It's a gallery showing an exhibition of photographs."

"Yeah, that's an art gallery. I guess."

"Do we have a database of galleries?"

"We don't...but hang a sec." Marian could heard the soft click of a computer keyboard. "Yeah, here we are. Whooee—lotsa galleries on Fifty-seventh."

"Could you just read off the names, please?" Marian stopped her when she got to *Albian*, the sixth name on the list of Fifty-seventh Street galleries. "That's it, Albian Gallery. What's the exact address?" She made a note of the number. "Thank you very much! But if we don't have a database of galleries, where'd you get the information?"

"On the Internet. NYNEX maintains a Web site."

Oh. Marian thanked her again and broke the connection. Next she called Holland and told him they were going to go look at photographs tomorrow night.

EIGHT

A SARDONIC SMILE was on Holland's face as he hung up the phone. This sudden passion for photography on Marian's part could only be the offshoot of a case she was working on. Something in the pictures she wanted to check out? Or was it the photographer? Suspect, eyewitness, potential victim? It would become clear tomorrow night.

Sometimes she brought her work home with her, sometimes not. Tonight she wasn't even bringing herself home. On the phone she'd forestalled his offer to come to her place, saying she had a lot of things to take care of— getting clothes ready for work, checking her mail, stocking the fridge. It was an excuse, of course. She still needed time to herself.

Time away from him.

He understood *that* message. But what *she* didn't understand was that what was privacy for her was like being in solitary confinement for him. *My natural state,* he thought without self-pity or irony. He had been alone his entire life and in fact had preferred it that way; he felt nothing but contempt for those who whined about being lonely. It *was* man's natural state, standing or falling alone. But it had never hurt so in the past, before a cop named Marian had crossed his path.

Once she'd stayed with him ten days, the longest stretch ever. Perhaps one day she would not leave at all.

The phone sounded. Mrs. Grainger's voice said, "André would like to see you. He says it's important."

"Send him in."

The door opened and a well-groomed young man with a baby face entered. André Flood was not yet twenty, but he looked even younger. "Mr. Holland, we need to talk," he said soberly.

How ominous. "Do you talk better sitting or standing?"

"Uh, standing, I think." Nervous: he kept shifting his weight.

Holland had stayed seated. "So? What's the problem?"

"Well, I, uh." He blurted it out: "I've been offered a job by Chris Carnell."

Holland smiled his sardonic smile again; he'd known this would happen sooner or later. It was just his good luck that Carnell happened to be the first. One of the world's aging computer whiz kids.

No computer system was truly secure; any system in the world could be broken into, given time and enough ingenuity on the part of the hacker. Businesses around the world hired systems designers to make their own computers impregnable; then they'd contract Holland's agency to test them. There hadn't been one yet his staff had been unable to crack. So then the businesses would hire a different designer, they'd call in Holland, the cycle would repeat. And the money kept rolling in.

Chris Carnell was one such systems designer. He'd bragged in print that he'd finally come up with the foolproof computer security everyone had been looking for since the invention of the modem. It had taken André Flood exactly eight days to break in.

And now Carnell was after André. "What did he offer?"

"A third more than you're paying me. Plus stock options, of course."

Of course. André was already well paid, and he knew it. "That's a great deal of money," Holland said noncommittally.

André cleared his throat. "I thought I should ask you if you'd care to make a counteroffer...before I give him an answer."

Holland propped his head up on his fist and stared at André, letting the silence grow. Chris Carnell was an erratic, temperamental genius who unfailingly drove his employees nuts. One reason he didn't own the world was that he couldn't keep a staff together long enough for any meaningful continuity to develop. André, on the other hand, was a precise, orderly person—almost anal with his list keeping and preoccupation with detail. He and Carnell were not a marriage made in heaven.

Holland sat up straight. "All right, here's my counteroffer. I'll hold your job open for you for one week. One week, André—not a day longer."

The younger man's eyes bugged. "What?"

"Same salary, same perks, same office. Same job. Take Carnell's offer, if you must. You'll have five working days to decide whether you want to stay with Carnell or come back to your job here."

André looked dumbfounded. "That's it?"

"That's it." Holland waited a beat and asked, "Was there anything else?"

"Er, uh, no." The young man backed out of the office.

Holland paid all of his people well, more than he needed to; it was the time-honored way of assuring employee loyalty. But André had a lesson to learn about loyalty, and Chris Carnell was just the one to teach him.

Holland got up and left his office. In the reception area, Mrs. Grainger looked up from her desk to see if he wanted something; he shook his head. Today she was wearing one of her pearl gray outfits with the white collar; Marian called her The Pilgrim.

He went down the hall to the last office. The door was open; inside, Bill Tuttle stood giving instructions to a new employee—a young woman not much older than André Flood.

Tuttle broke off in mid-sentence. "Mr. Holland?"

Holland held up a hand. "Finish what you're doing." He perched on a high stool to wait.

Bill Tuttle was a skinny, clumsy, balding man who wore Sergeant Bilko glasses and had a nose for business Holland had come to respect. It was Tuttle who'd approached Holland, when the agency was only a month old, with a plan for a way a team of hackers could check out the credentials of job applicants. Holland's first inclination was to pass; it sounded penny-ante. But he'd given Tuttle a provisional go-ahead, warning him his team would have to show a profit fast. It did. Once the groundwork had been laid, Tuttle's gang of hackers could find out anything about anybody, and it didn't take them days or even hours to do it; Holland had had to take on extra staff to handle all the business Tuttle had generated.

But the credentials checking was one aspect of his agency that Holland never talked about to NYPD Lieutenant Marian Larch. The Computer Abuse Amendments Act had been expanded to cover not only federal agencies but all PCs online; Holland could be prosecuted for what Tuttle was doing. The new law had not put an end to hacking; it had merely made hackers more crafty about covering their tracks.

Tuttle wrapped up his instructions quickly; the young woman cast a shy sideways glance at Holland on her way out. "Okay, boss," Tuttle said. "What's up?"

"I'm here to give you a mini-promotion," Holland said.

Tuttle grinned and flopped down in a chair, which rolled back on its casters a few feet. "How mini?"

"An extra thousand a month."

The other man rolled his eyes heavenward. "Thank you, lord!"

"Don't thank him, thank me."

"Thank you, boss. Why, may I ask, am I the beneficiary of such unexpected largesse?"

"I want you to act as my backup. For those times I have

to be away. Mrs. Grainger does a good job of managing
the office, but she can't make decisions about the work we
do. Someone needs to be in charge when I'm out of the
country or if I get hit by a bus or something equally cat-
astrophic happens. That means we'll have to find some
time each week when I can brief you about pending
cases—you'll need to have a rough idea of what everyone
is working on. Do you think you can handle that?''

Tuttle snapped his fingers.

''Good,'' said Holland. ''I'll send around a memo.
Sorry, but you don't get your office redecorated as part of
the deal.''

Tuttle gazed around at the office in which every available surface was covered with paper. ''Looks fine to me.''
Then he leaned forward and turned serious. ''Change of
subject. I got a phone call about fifteen minutes ago from
the CEO of Raiker Corporation in St. Louis. We checked
the credentials of all their employees, not just job applicants—found quite a few college dropouts claiming to be
MBAs. The CEO wants to know if we'd design a program
that would allow them to do some preliminary background
checking themselves.''

''Certainly not. We are investigators, not programmers.
Doesn't the man know those are two different profes-
sions?''

''That's what I told him, but he thinks we're holding
back so we can keep on charging him an arm and a leg. I
don't think he's going to take no from me.''

''Switch him through to me the next time he calls. And
come to my office Monday morning for your first briefing.
Ten o'clock.''

''I'll be there. And thanks, Mr. Holland.''

Holland stopped by Mrs. Grainger's desk on his way
back. ''I'll be leaving in a few minutes,'' he said. ''If
anyone wants to sneak off early, let them.''

''I'm always the first to leave,'' she said with a sigh.

"The others...they all get so involved in what they're doing they never know when it's quitting time."

He knew that, but he enjoyed hearing her say it.

In his office, he typed up the memo announcing Bill Tuttle's new status and e-mailed it to all his staff. Five minutes later he was in the elevator on his way down. He had no urgent business to attend to; in fact, he didn't even have any place to go. It was just that sometimes he had to get out of that office.

Not that there was anything wrong with the office; it was a good office, as offices go. The problem was with Holland. After having been on the go his entire adult life, he was bound to find the office confining at times. He knew it would be, when he first decided to open an agency; but it was a price he was willing to pay for the stability the agency could bring him. He needed stability, now.

But even before he'd found Marian, he'd been feeling a need to put down roots somewhere. His young Turk days were over; he didn't *want* to go adventuring anymore. That kind of life was too insubstantial. It wasn't...enough. He needed to build something, to leave a mark that said "Holland was here." *A monument to my own ego,* he thought wryly.

He walked the streets, heading downtown for no particular reason. Nearly eight million people in this burg, and the only one of those eight million he had any link to had to do her laundry tonight.

A little after five o'clock he tired of his aimless walking and ducked into the next bar he came to. Years of habit made him check out the place quickly before taking a seat. A tall, lean man sitting at the bar almost made him turn and leave. But... *Oh, what the hell.* He took a stool two seats away from the tall man and said, "Murtaugh."

Captain Jim Murtaugh looked up from his drink. "Oh...hello, Holland." He peered around to Holland's other side.

"She's not here."

"Um. I'm on my own tonight too. Edie's out of town."

Holland didn't care for that "too"; and Edie, he presumed, was Mrs. Murtaugh. The bartender, a woman wearing a badge that said "Maisie," came up and asked for his order.

"Do you have Lagavulin—no? Laphroaig, then, with very little ice. And is your name really Maisie?"

"My mom was an Ann Sothern fan."

"Then why didn't she name you Ann?" But Maisie was away looking for the Laphroaig.

Murtaugh was chuckling. "I asked her the same thing."

"She probably hears it a lot." A pause. "Who is Ann Sothern?"

Murtaugh looked surprised. "An actress. She played a secretary named Maisie in an old TV series. I remember watching reruns when I was a kid."

"How fascinating."

"Well, you asked."

"So I did." Maisie came back with his scotch; Holland fished out one of the two ice cubes and dropped it on the drain behind the bar, waiting for the remaining cube to dilute and cool the whiskey just the way he liked it.

She asked, "Why didn't you just say one ice cube? All you said was 'very little.'"

He smiled, mouth only. "You could have been using shaved ice."

Maisie looked surprised. "Oh, we've always used ice cubes instead of the shaved stuff. My boss says shaved ice melts too fast. Then you get customers complaining we're watering the drinks. But everybody knows we don't use the shaved kind. We always use ice cubes."

Holland closed his eyes, opened them again. "Until ten minutes ago, I was unaware of the existence of this sterling establishment dedicated to the dispensing of libations. This lack of knowledge quite naturally precluded any perception on my part of the morphology of frozen H_2O favored by your vice president in charge of ice."

She gave him a funny look and moved away to tend to a another customer.

"I think you offended her," Murtaugh remarked.

"That evens things out, then. She offended me."

"How? She was just being friendly."

"That's what offended me."

A pause. "You enjoy baiting people, don't you?"

Holland smiled. "I find it a great deterrent to inane chatter."

At that moment a small group of people came in, making enough of a stir that every head in the place turned in their direction. At the center of the group was a stunningly beautiful young woman, fashionably thin, expensively dressed and made up. She listened with a little smile on her face as the three men and one woman with her all talked at once, each one trying to get her attention. Just as they were sitting down in a semicircular booth, she locked eyes with Holland.

"Who's that?" Murtaugh asked.

"I have no idea," Holland murmured.

Murtaugh motioned Maisie back and asked her.

"Oh, that's Shari Tyce," she said. "You don't recognize her? She's just about the hottest supermodel in New York!"

"This week," Holland commented. "Cherie? C, h, e, r, i, e?"

Murtaugh said, "Probably S, h, e, r, r, y."

"No, it's S, h, a, r, i," Maisie told them. "But she's on a billboard in Times Square right now, and you can't go to a newsstand without seeing her face on a magazine cover. Or three or four, more like it. She has her own calendar, and I hear she has an exercise video coming out. Do you think she'd mind if I asked for her autograph?"

"I'm sure she'd love it," Murtaugh said. The bartender

looked around for a pen and piece of paper and made her way over to where Shari Tyce was sitting. Murtaugh shot one more look at the celebrity table and turned back to his drink. "If models get any skinnier, they're going to vanish altogether."

"And what a loss to the world *that* would be," Holland said sourly.

The police captain laughed. "You're in a helluva mood today."

"Oh? You know me well enough to gauge my moods?"

"I don't—"

"Do share your penetrating insights. I'd be fascinated."

Murtaugh finished his drink and asked Maisie for a refill. "Look, Holland, don't try that with me. God knows you've made your dislike for me clear enough every time we've met. I'm not going to ask why, because I don't give a damn. But I don't like being needled, or baited, or anything else you feel like doing to keep yourself amused. So, back off. Back all the way off. Are you hearing me?"

Holland smiled. "At least we know where we stand. Shall we agree to be friendly enemies? I think 'inimical friends' is beyond us at the moment."

Murtaugh sighed. "I'm not going to play your game."

"But you already are playing it. And not badly at that."

The empty bar stool that separated them was suddenly occupied...by none other than Shari Tyce herself. She sat sideways, facing Holland, oozing glamour and healthy young sex. "Don't I know you?"

He was annoyed at the interruption. "No," he said shortly.

"I think I do know you. Do you know me?"

"Your name is Shari Tyce and you live by selling your looks."

"Oh, you do know who I am!"

Holland aimed a forefinger at Maisie. "She told me."

"Then you asked about me."

"*I* asked," Murtaugh said.

She didn't even spare him a glance. "Well, then, I should know you," she said to Holland. "What's your name?"

"Impeccable logic," he replied dryly. "I know your name, therefore you should know mine. Surely you have enough people dancing attendance? Look at the consternation you've caused among your devotees. Go on—look." The three of them seated at the bar—and Maisie—all looked over at the booth Shari Tyce had just left. Her four followers sat there unspeaking, watching the model anxiously. "You see how distraught you've made them?" Holland continued. "Be content with that."

She turned back to him. "Oh, they're just people I work with." She began stroking his arm. "But you—you look like someone I want to know."

He sighed. "No."

"What?"

"I said no. Go back to your minions. You'll be happier there."

She kept stroking his arm. "I'm not used to being told no."

Holland cocked his head to one side and looked at her through half-closed eyes. "Yes, you do have a pampered look to you. You always get your way, and someone else does your thinking for you? Or perhaps you simply lack the intelligence to understand 'no' when you hear it. Concentrate, now. Are you concentrating? N, o. No."

She jerked her hand back as if it were burned. She glared at him a moment and then called him a prickless mama's boy. Back to her booth she went.

"Jesus, you're nasty," Maisie said.

Holland leaned both elbows on the bar. "Maisie, I regret my earlier churlishness. I should have saved it all for that anorexic pop icon over there."

"You should have shoved it up your ass is what you

should have done." She moved down to the end of the bar, disassociating herself.

Murtaugh stood up with a sigh. "Holland, you have a real talent for driving people away. You must genuinely enjoy your own company." He walked out without a backward glance.

Holland finished his drink alone, all he had wanted in the first place.

NINE

THURSDAY BEGAN with a homicide.

The call came from a detective in the Thirteenth Precinct. A man's body had been found in the East River, two bullets in his chest. The body had snagged against one of the pilings supporting the Department of Sanitation's dock jutting off Roosevelt Parkway. The corpse hadn't been in the water long enough for bloating to occur and the features were recognizable. The detective said the dead man looked very much like the computer simulation of Bobby Galloway's attempted kidnapper that Midtown South had circulated.

Marian called in Perlmutter and O'Toole. "O'Toole, go pick up Rita Galloway and take her to the morgue—let's see if we can get a positive ID. Perlmutter, call her and tell her what's happened. Tell her O'Toole's on his way and to be ready. Wait forty-five minutes and then call Hugh Galloway and tell him the same thing. Then go get him."

"He's not going to admit knowing the kidnapper," O'Toole scoffed.

"Just covering all the bases. Then we'll have it on record that he lied if it turns out he did know him."

Perlmutter looked at her quizzically. "You don't think he did it, do you, Lieutenant?"

"No, I don't. But let's get him in there anyway. I'll be waiting for you at the morgue. Well? Go!" They went.

Marian thought about reporting to the captain before she left, but there was nothing to report unless Rita Galloway could identify the dead man. If she couldn't, then the murder was the Thirteenth's problem. The detective from the

One-Three who'd called—Krantor, his name was—had said he'd get to the morgue as soon as he could.

Traffic wasn't yet heavy at eight-thirty in the morning, so Marian drove down to the City Mortuary on First Avenue—*down among the dead men*. She made the arrangements for the body to be shown and asked to see the deceased's personal effects. The plastic storage bin contained precious little: a few bills wadded together by river water, a few coins, a pack of gum, a key ring with only one key. No billfold, no scrap of paper with anything written on it. The clothing was off-the-rack, commonplace.

Then Marian went to the viewing room to wait. She watched through the glass partition as the morgue attendant wheeled the body into the small adjoining room and turned on the lights.

Only five minutes passed before O'Toole arrived with a fearful Rita Galloway in tow. Marian spoke to her soothingly, apologizing for the grim chore she had to perform but emphasizing that she was the only one who could identify Bobby's kidnapper. Mrs. Galloway straightened her shoulders and held her head up: *ready*.

Marian nodded to the morgue attendant. He pulled down the sheet covering the dead man's face and stepped back.

Rita Galloway reluctantly approached the window. After a moment she said. "I can't be sure, just from his profile."

Marian said to the speaker mounted near the glass partition, "Has rigor passed? Can you turn his head to face us?"

A blast of static was her answer, but the attendant used gloved hands to move the head as requested. The face was rather nondescript except for the overfull bottom lip.

"Oh!" Rita Galloway took a hasty step backward. She turned her back to the window. "That's the man. He's the one."

"Are you sure?" When she didn't answer, Marian said, "Mrs. Galloway, I know this is a gruesome business, but you must be absolutely sure this is the same man. Please. Look one more time.''

She turned reluctantly but this time managed to stare at the dead man without flinching. ''Yes. That is the man who grabbed Bobby. I am positive of it.''

O'Toole said, ''Looks just like the computer picture.''

''Did you say he was shot?'' Mrs. Galloway asked.

''Yes'm,'' he replied. ''Twice, in the chest.''

She shuddered. ''How can people do things like that to each other?''

Marian thought of the .38 revolver Rita Galloway now felt she needed, but didn't mention it. Instead, she thanked her for her help. ''There's a little paperwork to be taken care of, and then Detective O'Toole will drive you home.''

''This way, Mrs. Galloway.'' Just as O'Toole was reaching for the door, it opened from the other side. A man Marian didn't know stood back and let the other two leave before he came in.

''Lieutenant Larch?'' he asked. ''I'm Detective Krantor, Thirteenth Precinct. We spoke this morning.''

''Yes, I'm glad you could make it.''

''Did you get an ID?''

''Yep. You've got a good eye, Detective,'' she said. ''Looks as if we'll be taking this one off your hands.''

He grinned. ''You're welcome to it. Was that the kid's mother who just left?''

Marian said it was. ''The father's going to be along in a few minutes. I wanted them brought in separately because they both tend to go for the jugular every time they're under the same roof together.''

''Ouch. Do you need two IDs?''

''This is just a long shot. The father wasn't even there when the attempt was made. But we need to check.''

''Then the father isn't a suspect?''

''Not officially, no.'' She looked again at the dead man. ''Were fingerprints taken?''

"Yeah, we're running them now. If we got anything on him, I'll fax it to you."

She nodded. Then she tapped on the glass partition to get the morgue attendant's attention. "Who's doing the autopsy?"

He checked the toe tag. "Dr. Wu" was the staticky answer.

The door opened and an angry Hugh Galloway charged in, followed by Perlmutter. "Now what, Lieutenant?" Galloway demanded. "What do you want of me?"

Marian introduced Detective Krantor, but only Perlmutter acknowledged the introduction. Hugh Galloway was staring through the partition at the dead man, a sobering sight for guilty and innocent alike. Behind his back Perlmutter looked a question at Marian. She nodded; positive ID.

"I have never seen that man before," Galloway said with certainty. "Is that what you brought me in here for? To look at some poor stiff I don't even know?"

"Mr. Galloway—"

"Is that going to be the pattern from now on, Lieutenant? You're going to drag me down here to look at every dead man that comes along? You're really going to put me through the wringer? This is nothing but harassment, and if you think you can get away with that—"

"Oh, stop it," Marian said sharply. "We're not harassing you and you damned well know it. We're doing our job, and you just helped us do one small part of it. Therefore, thank you very much. Now—go away."

Perlmutter took his arm. "Let's go."

Galloway shook off his hand. "I'm calling my lawyer!"

"You do that," Marian said as the door closed behind him.

Detective Krantor grinned. "And he's *not* a suspect?"

"Unfortunately." She thanked Krantor for his help. On her way out, she left word for Dr. Wu that she'd like to know the caliber of the bullets as soon as he had them removed.

Marian stopped for a quick cup of real coffee on her way back to Midtown South. Jim Murtaugh wasn't in his office; she left a note on his desk. When Perlmutter and O'Toole returned from delivering the Galloways to their separate homes, the three of them huddled in Marian's office.

"Let me tell you what I'm thinking," Marian said. "I'm thinking the spying cleaning woman might not have anything to do with the kidnapping and firebombing. Hugh Galloway could have put Consuela Palmero into his wife's house but still have no connection to the guy in the morgue and the kidnapping."

"So we forget about Palmero?" O'Toole asked.

"No. We pin her down. If we can finger that particular bit of chicanery as part of the Galloway marital wars, then we drop it. That's for the divorce courts. But I want to *know*."

"How? She used a phony address."

"Think back. The owner of Maids-in-a-Row, Egrorian—what's his first name?"

"Gordon."

"Gordon Egrorian said that this Consuela Palmero showed up looking for a job *on the same day one of his regulars quit*. Doesn't that strike you as just a little too convenient? Who was this regular, why did she quit without giving notice, where is she now?"

Perlmutter was nodding. "Yeah, that's right. We missed that."

"I want you both on it. Get hold of a picture of both Galloways, and take along the computer likenesses of Consuela Palmero and the guy in the morgue. Find that employee who resigned, and find the connection. O'Toole, did you talk to the rest of the cleaning crew?"

"Yeah, but they don't know nothing," he said. "They

just met the Palmero woman that day, and Rita Galloway's house was the first one they cleaned. The brother threw her out when he caught her snooping, and that's the last the crew ever saw of her. They knew her maybe an hour is all."

"Yet she was bonded in the name of Palmero," Marian mused. "Could her bond papers have been faked? Well, leave that for now. Find the employee who quit. And do it fast. The One-Three is running the dead guy's prints and once we get an ID, I'm going to have to put you on that. So let's move."

SHE HEARD FROM Dr. Wu in the medical examiner's office first. "I got only one bullet," he said. "The other one passed right through the body and presumably is still at the location where he was shot, wherever that is. The Crime Lab boys tell me it's a nine-millimeter. Makes a big hole."

Not Rita Galloway's .38, then. "Can you tell me anything about him?"

"Nothing that will help you." Marian could hear the shrug in his voice. "I haven't finished the autopsy yet, but so far there's nothing unusual. Male caucasian, mid-thirties, six two. Slightly overweight, but not seriously so. General health was good. The only thing wrong with this guy is two bullet holes in him. One of them caught the heart."

"If you do find anything else, will you call me?"

"Sure, but don't hold your breath."

"Okay. Thanks, Doc."

"Don't call me Doc," he said crossly and hung up.

It was another two hours before the promised fax arrived from the Thirteenth Precinct, and it told Marian what she was waiting to hear; the dead man's prints were indeed on file. The man identified by Rita Galloway as the one who'd attempted to kidnap Bobby was named Nick Atlay. He'd done short time twice, once on a burglary rap and once for grand theft auto. He'd been questioned but not charged in two petty burglaries and one B and E. The name of the arresting officer in the burglary case was a familiar one.

Marian stepped out into the squadroom. Sergeant Buchanan was at his desk typing up a form while a young black man sat handcuffed to a metal chair. Marian went up to the desk and said, "Sergeant, I'd like to see you when you finish here."

"I'm finished now," he said, pulling the form out of the typewriter. "Just let me put this loser in the tank." He unlocked his prisoner and led him away.

Marian sat on the metal chair and waited.

Buchanan was back in a few minutes and sat down with a wheeze. "Okay, Lieutenant, I'm all yours."

"Four years ago you arrested a perp named Nick Atlay. Stole some TV sets and other appliances. Remember him?"

Buchanan half-grunted, half-laughed. "Nickie Atlay. Is he in trouble again?"

"You could say that. He's been killed."

The sergeant's bushy gray eyebrows came together in a scowl. "Nickie? How?"

"Shot twice in the chest, then dumped in the East River."

Buchanan shook his head. "Why would anyone want to kill Nickie Atlay?"

"Tell me about him," Marian said.

A deep sigh. "Nickie wasn't none too bright, Lieutenant. He couldn't hold a steady job, so he took any kind of work that came his way. Most of it was legit—I'm not sure he always knew the difference. He'd deliver groceries, wash dishes, like that. Then some little shrimp wants to heist a few TV sets, he gets Nickie to come along and do the lifting. No difference to Nickie. You seen his rap sheet? No *violent* crimes. Tell you the truth, Lieutenant, I felt kinda bad about sendin' him up that one time. Prison's no place for a guy who can't take care of himself.''

"He survived prison twice. Short time.''

"He musta had help. Somebody the other prisoners feared made him an errand boy or something. But Nickie wasn't the sort of guy who gets killed. He didn't know nothing, he didn't understand nothing.''

"Are you telling me he never initiated a crime?''

"Naw, not him. He didn't have the smarts. Besides, Nickie was a natural-born follower.''

"So he couldn't have planned a kidnapping?''

"Kidnapping!'' Buchanan looked surprised, then made the connection. "This the Galloway case?''

Marian said yes. "Mrs. Galloway identified the body this morning.''

He shook his head. "No way Nickie could have planned that. And I'll tell you something. He was fed a line of bull to make him take part. Like, the real perp coulda told him the woman the kid was with had stolen him from his real mother. Nickie coulda thought he was *saving* the boy.''

She thought that over. "It fits. Even the part about no smarts. He didn't check to see if there was a prowl car cruising the street. And when the cops caught up with him, he struggled at first instead of just dropping the boy and running.''

"Yeah, that sounds like Nickie.''

"Do you know if he ever worked as a janitor?''

"Coupla times, 'til he'd get fired. Why?''

"The Galloway boy said he had a strange smell, something like cleaning solvent.''

"Then he was probably moppin' floors somewhere.''

A new voice called out "Lieutenant!'' She turned to see Detective Dowd holding up a phone. "Perlmutter. Line one.''

Marian took the call in her office. "You got her?''

"Not exactly,'' Perlmutter said. "Her name's Annie

Plaxton but she's no longer at the address we got from Maids-in-a-Row. We tracked down her nephew, and he says she's moved to Hoboken. And get this, Lieutenant. She's opened a laundromat there.''

"Bingo. New money."

"Yep. Looks as if our Annie was paid to quit Maids-in-a-Row. Do we go to New Jersey?"

"No, you and O'Toole come on in. We've got a name for our dead kidnapper—Nick Atlay, and he may have been working as a janitor. Buchanan arrested him once. Ask him for known associates."

"Atlay—strange name. I'll bet it was 'Atlee' at one time. Lieutenant, traffic's pretty bad—it'll take us a while to get back."

"Okay, do the best you can." She broke the connection and went to Captain Murtaugh's office.

This time he was in, talking on the phone. He hung up and snarled, *"What?"*

Marian grinned. "Do you want me to come back later?"

"No, no. Sit."

She sat. "Progress." She summarized for him what they'd learned. "I've put Perlmutter and O'Toole on the homicide, so I want to go to New Jersey tomorrow, to Hoboken—to talk to this former cleaning lady who now suddenly and mysteriously owns her own business."

"You're doing the divorce lawyer's work for him."

"Probably. But if I can pin down the missing Consuela Palmero as Hugh Galloway's way of playing a dirty trick on his wife, then we won't have to spend any more time on it."

"You're still convinced he's innocent?"

Marian sighed. "No, I'm not *convinced.* I'm hoping Annie Plaxton in Hoboken will convince me one way or the other."

"All right, then, go talk to her. It's a loose end that may

have nothing to do with either the kidnapping or the killing. But tie it up.''

''Right.''

''On a related matter,'' the captain said, ''earlier today I got a phone call from Alex Fairchild. He wanted to come here and take pictures. I told him no.''

''Good.''

''We can't have someone connected with a case under investigation running loose in the station. I told him to wait until the case is settled and then call me again.''

''Bad.''

A smile flitted across his face. ''You don't want your picture taken by a world-famous photographer?''

''*Is* he world-famous?''

''Oh yes, he's quite well known. He takes these stark, stunning photographs that make you come back and look again. You should see his work.''

''I'm going to,'' Marian said. ''Tonight.''

TEN

WHEN HE PICKED HER UP that evening, Holland noticed that Marian had dressed up for the occasion: she was wearing a gold chain around her neck. Everything else was the same.

On the way to the Albian Gallery, she told him about how she'd misplaced the invitation Alex Fairchild had given her and she could remember only that the gallery was on Fifty-seventh Street. But the computer department had gone to something called a Web site and had been able to pick out all the Fifty-seventh Street galleries from the *NYNEX Yellow Pages*.

"It's called a search function," he said, "and it's old news. Don't you think it's about time you got wired? You could have looked that up for yourself."

She shuddered. "Learn all that stuff? Uh-uh. Besides, I don't need a computer."

"Everybody needs a computer," he said flatly. "You especially. Here you are, a lieutenant in the country's largest police force, and you don't even have an e-mail address!"

This time she laughed. "You sound scandalized."

"Well, I am. If you don't join the twentieth century soon, you're going to miss it altogether."

"Hey. That was a put-down. Don't be so damned superior."

"I'm sorry."

"No, you're not."

"No, I'm not."

She hit his shoulder and he smirked.

There was no place to park near the gallery, so they had

to walk back a few blocks. He didn't know whether to bring the subject up or not, but he couldn't leave it completely alone. "How's Murtaugh?"

"Murtaugh?" She was surprised. "Since when are you interested in Murtaugh's health?"

"I'm not. But you haven't mentioned him lately."

"Hmm. Well, he was a little grumpy today. I think his wife's out of town."

So he hadn't told her about the incident in the bar. Holland was content to leave it at that. He knew from past experience that Marian didn't have much patience with his *im*patience with other people. "Arrogant" she'd called him, more than once.

Suddenly he pulled her to him and kissed her.

She didn't pull away. "That was nice." But he could hear the puzzlement in her voice.

He kissed her again. Holland didn't understand his own need for the reassurance that physical contact with her brought, and it troubled him. But not overmuch.

"Get it *awn!*" Three teenaged boys passed, cheering.

They smiled and broke out of their clinch. Another half block took them to the Albian Gallery.

All Marian had told him was that the photographer was the uncle of a small boy who'd been the target of a foiled kidnapping attempt. And that the kidnapper had turned up dead that morning...but the case was not closed. Fairchild's name was known to him; Holland had once looked through a book of the photographer's stark, memorable images.

Only one photograph was on display in the window, blown up to poster size. Black and white, details crisp in the foreground but fading to a teasing fuzziness in the back. Shot in one of New York's grubbier streets. The entire left half of the foreground was taken up by the bleary-eyed, unshaven face of an old wino looking into the lens, some spark of curiosity left after years of selfravagement. But his curiosity was misdirected; what he didn't see behind him in the background were the figures of a man and a woman on a fire escape who seemed earnestly trying to kill each other.

"Strong picture," Holland remarked.

Marian agreed. "He told me all his pictures had to have a compelling face in them. This one certainly does."

They went inside. Holland automatically checked the place out, knowing Marian was doing the same thing. Albian Gallery was a long, white, narrow rectangle with a balcony running around three walls and with two doors in the rear wall, one above and one below. No music was playing and no food table was in sight, but most of the twenty-odd people there were holding wineglasses.

They strolled along one wall, looking. No photographs were of *just* faces, but the faces were always the focal point of a larger picture. And the faces were almost invariably grim, reflecting fear, anxiety, hopelessness. There were a few exceptions; they stopped in front of one, an elfin little boy laughing with delight as a baby goat in a petting zoo nuzzled his ear. On a greeting card, the picture would have been cute, even coy. But the shot had been taken on a gloomy, overcast day; food wrappers and other trash littered the ground; and a bored zoo attendant was looking on. The child's laughing face was a moment of sunshine in a drab world.

"That's his nephew," Marian said. "The little boy who was almost kidnapped."

The next shot was of an older boy standing at a urinal in a men's room, while a silver-haired man fondled the boy's neck and smiled insinuatingly into his face.

Holland felt only contempt for this blatant bit of manipulation. "Not exactly subtle, is it? Moving from the innocence of childhood to the corruption of childhood in one easy step. The picture of the boy and the goat was only a setup. Preparation for shock value."

"Some people say," a new voice proclaimed, "that my pictures are easier to take when you have a slight buzz on." A man with reddish brown hair and large moist eyes handed them each a glass of white wine.

Marian introduced Holland and Alex Fairchild to each other. "It's the man's face that dominates that picture," she said. "Not the boy's."

Fairchild nodded. "The boy's face is still amorphous— no character showing yet. But the man's face—ah, just look at the depravity there! Marvelous."

"How did you get that picture?" Holland asked. "Did the pederast pose for you?"

"Hardly. He didn't even know I was there until the flash went off. Then he tried to take my camera away from me." Fairchild smiled a slow smile. "The kid skedaddled. I undoubtedly saved him from a Fate Worse Than Death."

Holland smiled; he liked the picture of Fairchild sneaking shots in men's rooms better than the picture hanging on the wall. "You were hiding in one of the booths?"

"I was coming *out* of one of the booths. You take your opportunities where you find them." Then Fairchild shifted his position slightly so he was facing Marian and effectively cutting Holland out of the conversation. "Rita said the kidnapper is dead."

"We have an ID for him now," Marian replied. "Does the name Nick Atlay mean anything to you?"

He looked blank, then shook his head. "Who is he? Or *was* he, rather."

"Small-time crook. *Very* small-time. But without the brains to plan a kidnapping."

"So you haven't closed the case?"

"Not by a long shot. It's the one who hired Atlay that we're looking for."

"You know who that is."

"I know who you *think* it is," Marian said mildly. "But we still need evidence."

"Do you have any leads?"

"Yes, now we do. One of them I plan on following up myself tomorrow morning."

"Which is?"

She just smiled. "Sorry."

He smiled back. "No, I'm sorry. I don't mean to ask you to give away police secrets...Mary Ann? Isn't that what Bobby called you?"

"It's Marian, actually. And there are no secrets as such. But I can't disclose details of an ongoing investigation."

"Of course not. And that reminds me—I'd love to get pictures of you on the job. But your Captain Murtaugh won't let me come in until the investigation is finished. I'd like to photograph you in a variety of settings."

Holland stepped in closer. *Is this guy hitting on her?*

"We can talk about that after the case is closed," Marian said noncommittally.

Fairchild was working at being charming, his moist eyes holding hers in contact. "I can be very discreet, Marian. After the first hour, you'll forget I'm there. It's how I get my best pictures—by becoming invisible myself. I think you'll enjoy the experience."

Holland felt himself scowling. There was an ingratiating sort of intimacy in the photographer's manner that bothered him. Slowly and deliberately, Holland put one arm around Marian, resting his hand on her shoulder. He'd catch holy hell later for *claiming* her like that, but Fairchild needed to be warned off. "You don't take any posed pictures at all?"

"Oh, sometimes I still do celebrity heads. When I can find an interesting face." His eyes flickered toward Holland and away again; he'd gotten the message. "But almost no showbiz people. And never, ever professional models."

"No showbiz people?" Marian repeated. "What about Kelly Ingram?"

He thought a moment. "Yes, I think I would like to photograph Kelly Ingram. There's some real personality in that face. But most of them in her profession look as if they all came from the same plastic mold. Models are even worse."

Holland thought of the model in the bar the night before and had to agree.

The chat continued in a neutral vein for another few minutes until one of the other invited visitors came up and drew Fairchild away. Holland and Marian inspected the rest of the photographs on the walls and then slipped out.

"You got a little possessive in there, didn't you?" Marian asked on the way back to the car.

"Only a little," he answered, and waited. But she said no more about it, surprising him.

They went to her place. Marian headed straight for the bathroom, and Holland wandered into the kitchen. He found the refrigerator filled almost to capacity; when Marian stocked up, she really stocked up. He fixed them a plate of cheeses and white grapes and took it into the living room.

Her apartment seemed smaller than the last time he'd been there. A cop's salary apartment. The place had been his haven, once. Back when he barely knew Marian, he'd gone to her for help and she'd taken him in. The apartment had looked magnificent to him then.

She came back from the bathroom and sat beside him on the sofa. "That looks good," she said, taking a piece of cheese.

"You have enough food in there to feed an Olympic Village," he said. "I take it you're planning to stay here for a while?"

She swallowed a bite of the cheese. "When I stay at your place too long, I begin to feel like a kept woman. Why don't you stay here for a while and feel like a kept man?"

"Very well," he agreed. "And you may pamper me as much as you like."

"Ha."

Then he did something he'd never done before. He asked her to tell him about the case she was working on.

She told him without hesitation. Marian frequently talked over her cases with Holland, not so much because he'd once been an FBI agent but because explaining sometimes helped her think things through. It was also a sign of trust, and Holland appreciated that.

Now she explained about the vicious custody battle being waged by Rita and Hugh Galloway over young Bobby, about the spying cleaning woman with the false name, the attempted kidnapping, the firebombing that did minimal damage, and the murder of Nick Atlay.

"So you're proceeding on the assumption that whoever hired Atlay to snatch Bobby...killed him to shut him up?" he asked.

"Right. He's covered his tracks every step of the way, even to the point of crossing the line to murder."

"And this lead you mentioned you were following up tomorrow morning—that's in connection with the phony cleaning woman?"

"More specifically, the legitimate cleaning woman she replaced. A woman named Annie Plaxton who now suddenly has enough money to open a laundromat in Hoboken, New Jersey."

"Ah. I see. Follow the money. Good lead." He thought a moment. "Where does Alex Fairchild fit in? Innocent bystander?"

"Well, he's definitely on Rita's side in the Galloway fight. He even bought her a gun to protect herself from Hugh. But I don't think Hugh's behind the kidnapping. And Hugh says Rita arranged a fake kidnapping to discredit him and I don't think that's true either."

"So?"

"So, what if I'm wrong? The duel is between Hugh and Rita, and each of them has a second, so to speak. Hugh is backed up by his father, and Rita by her brother. But if Hugh is behind what's happened, he's on his own with no help from dear old dad. Walter Galloway is an old man— and, I think, infirm. I can't be sure because he never got out of his chair the time I talked to him. He looked frail to me. But if it's Rita doing these things, I can see Alex Fairchild helping her."

"And that's the only way Fairchild might be involved?" He mulled that over. "It's a bit of a reach."

"Granted. I think someone else is just exploiting a volatile situation. Rita and Hugh were bound to suspect each other. Rita is so sure Hugh is guilty that she won't even give me a list of friends and associates we could investigate. Those two really hate each other."

They were both silent for a moment. Then Holland stretched both arms along the back of the sofa and asked casually, "Do you find him attractive?"

"Hugh?"

"Alex Fairchild."

"Oh, he's okay, I guess."

"He's interested in you, you know."

"He wants another face for his collection."

"Perhaps. Perhaps he wants more than that."

"Oh, don't be silly."

"I am never silly. He's after you, Marian. And he'll come after you again, some time when I'm not there."

She sat up straight, astonishment written all over her. "You're serious, aren't you?"

"Dead serious. *Are* you attracted to him?"

Her face said *I don't believe this.* "Why would I be attracted to Alex Fairchild?"

"Why? Well, let's see. He's good-looking, in an offbeat sort of way. He can turn on the charm when he wants to.

You can tell from the way he moves that he's a sensual man. He— *What?*"

She was laughing so hard she almost fell off the sofa. "You just described yourself!"

He thought back over what he'd just said...and decided he was not displeased. He watched Marian hungrily as her laughter died down. Then: "You're overdressed."

"Huh. You're oversexed."

"Incompatible opposites. One of those two will have to go. Which shall it be?"

She stood up and started taking off her clothes.

ELEVEN

FRIDAY STARTED the same way Thursday had. With a homicide.

"I wish your killer would stop dumping his victims in *my* precinct," Detective Krantor complained on the phone.

Marian grunted. "I'll speak to him about it as soon as we catch him," she replied, simultaneously resenting and understanding the need to treat violent death flippantly. "Are you sure it's Consuela Palmero?" The phony cleaning woman's body had been found in the East River at daybreak.

"Sure looks like her to me. Spitting image of the computer picture. Same M.O. as yesterday—two shots to the chest."

"'Palmero' isn't her real name."

"Yeah, I know. And before you ask, yes, we're running the prints. I'll get back to you if there's anything on her."

"Okay. Thanks, Krantor."

After she'd hung up, she just sat there a few moments, letting it sink in. She'd been wrong. The spying cleaning woman was not an episode separate from the kidnapping, as she'd suspected. The Palmero woman was more than just an agent for Hugh Galloway in his fight against his wife, more than simply one more piece of nastiness in that nasty quarrel. She'd been hired by the same person who'd hired Nick Atlay to kidnap Bobby, and that person was eliminating everyone who could identify him.

Was there anyone else? Had Nick Atlay been the one to heave the gasoline bomb through Rita Galloway's dragon window—or would there be another body in the river tomorrow morning?

Someone who knew that Rita and Hugh would blame each other was behind this. Someone who'd seen both attempts to grab Bobby Galloway fail and was now desperately trying to cover all trails that could lead to him. Desperately, because he'd had to resort to murder to assure his continuing anonymity.

This time Marian called Alex Fairchild to come identify the body. Yesterday the sister, today the brother.

She went out into the squadroom where Perlmutter and O'Toole were waiting. "First," she told them, "pick up Hugh Galloway and take him to the morgue to see the body. Then tell him we want a list of everyone he knows who needs money, or bears a grudge against the Galloways, or in any way is capable of planning and executing a kidnapping. Then find a judge and get a search warrant naming only Rita Galloway's address book, nothing else. Give her a choice of turning the address book over or of making out a list of possibles. If she chooses to make out the list, stay with her until she finishes."

Perlmutter raised an eyebrow. "Long shot."

"Yes, it is. But somebody who knows the Galloways planned the kidnapping and killed two people. And we don't have a suspect."

"No suspect except Hugh Galloway," Perlmutter stated.

"Naw," O'Toole said. "Not Hugh. Rita."

"You two are a big help. Go on, get going."

She hurried over to Captain Murtaugh's office to tell him of the new homicide and that she was headed toward the morgue. To her surprise, he said he'd go with her.

"You bring in Hugh Galloway two days in a row," he pointed out, "you can bet your bottom dollar he's going to have a legal cannon with him the second time."

Marian was annoyed. "And I can't handle that?"

"I know the Galloways' lawyer—man named Bradford Ushton," Murtaugh replied. "He's the one who gave my name to Walter Galloway, that time Galloway called to say the attempt to kidnap Bobby was for ransom. Perhaps I can ease things a little.''

Well, maybe he can at that, she thought. Murtaugh wanted to drive, so they took his car.

Detective Krantor from the Thirteenth Precinct and Alex Fairchild were already at the morgue by the time they got there. The glassed-off room held the body of a slightly plump Latina in early middle age. She'd been a pretty woman, Marian noted sadly.

"He's identified her," Krantor greeted them. "That makes it official. This one's yours."

Marian introduced Murtaugh to the other two. To Fairchild she said, "This is the woman you caught going through Rita's checkbook? The one you threw out of the house?"

"She's the one," he said positively. "I'd know her anywhere."

Marian turned to the detective. "All right, Krantor, that lets you off the hook. Our case. Did you look through her personal effects?"

"Naw, I left that for you."

Murtaugh spoke up. "She was found the same place in the river as the one yesterday?"

"Pretty close." Krantor went on to describe the exact location, and then the captain wanted to know who'd found the bodies. Dockworkers, in both cases.

While they were talking, Alex Fairchild eased over to Marian and murmured in her ear, "I'm sorry we meet again under such unpleasant circumstances."

"I'm sorry the circumstances exist at all."

"I'd like to see you in a different setting. Le Vert-Galant, for instance. Are you free for lunch?"

Marian was disgusted. "Mr. Fairchild, look where you are. There's a dead woman lying on the other side of that glass."

He made a face of regret. "Yes, my timing is not the best, is it? I'll try later. And please—call me Alex."

She just looked at him. "Thank you for helping us out. You're free to go now."

He smiled a slow, easy smile. "I'm dismissed?" But he left without saying anything more. Marian watched him go, remembering that Holland had said this would happen.

Krantor left too. Marian asked the morgue attendant to wait; there'd be one more coming to see the body. Then she and Murtaugh went to look at the personal effects belonging to Consuela Palmero a.k.a. somebody else.

"No purse," Murtaugh said when they'd emptied the storage bin onto a table.

Clothing that was a better quality than what Nick Atlay had been wearing. Nothing in the pockets of the jacket. Some costume jewelry. And that was all. "The killer ditched the purse," Marian said.

The captain growled. "Sometimes I think we should all be tattooed with an ID number at birth. There's nothing here—let's go." They went back to the viewing room and waited.

Hugh Galloway was much calmer this time when he showed up a few minutes later. And Captain Murtaugh had been right: he had a lawyer in tow. Perlmutter stuck his head in the room long enough to say he and O'Toole were leaving unless the lieutenant had something for them? Marian waved him away, barely hearing. She couldn't take her eyes off the lawyer.

Bradford Ushton was surprised to see Murtaugh there. "Jim? You're investigating?"

"Hello, Brad." The captain indicated Marian. "Lieutenant Larch is in charge of the case. This is a formality, you understand. We're not charging your client. The lieutenant wants his help."

"And she'll get it." Ushton turned to Marian. "Please understand, Lieutenant, that Mr. Galloway is here voluntarily. He *wants* to help. A phone call would have brought him here. It's not necessary to send two detectives into his office to take him away whenever you have a new body for him to look at."

"I'm hoping this is the last body, Mr. Ushton," Marian said, keeping her face impassive."

"It's standard procedure, Brad," Murtaugh interposed. Ushton nodded.

Without being prompted, Hugh Galloway stepped up to the viewing window; Ushton must have pounded it into him that yelling at the police and making threats was not the way to help his case. But all the time Hugh was looking at the body, Marian kept watching Ushton out of the corner of her eye. That silver hair, that face she'd seen only the night before in one of Alex Fairchild's photographs...

Hugh Galloway spread his hands. "I don't know this woman. I don't remember ever seeing her before."

Marian asked, "You didn't hire her to infiltrate your wife's household?"

With an effort, he kept his reaction mild. "No. I've had no contact with her whatsoever."

"And that should settle that," Bradford Ushton said emphatically. "Lieutenant? Are you satisfied now?"

"Yes, I am." She signaled to the morgue attendant that they were through. "Thank you both for coming in."

They all went out into the hallway, where Ushton and the captain chatted about other matters. Marian took Hugh Galloway aside.

"For what it's worth," she told him, "I don't think you're behind any of this."

His eyes widened, and then narrowed again in suspicion. "Why are you telling me?"

"Because you've got it in your head that Rita has persuaded us you are a monster. I don't want you doing anything rash."

He grinned wryly. "Ushton has pretty much taken care of that. Then you believe me about Rita?"

"I don't think either one of you is responsible. Mr. Galloway, there's a third person involved here, someone who knows you and Rita would go for each other's throats at the first sign of trouble."

He licked his lips. "Detective Perlmutter asked me to make up a list of possible suspects."

"Everyone who knows about your marital situation."

He nodded. "I'll do it."

After another moment lawyer and client left together. Marian waited until she and the captain were in the car to bring up her discovery.

This could be tricky. "Jim, how long have you known Bradford Ushton?

"Brad? Oh, a good twenty years, I'd say. Why?"

"Is he a close friend?"

He smiled. "Cops and lawyers are never close friends. But Brad doesn't practice criminal law, so we've never been in an adversarial relationship. I'd say we were friendly rather than friends. Again…why?" She was silent so long he had to prompt her. "Marian? What is it? Spit it out."

She took a deep breath. "He's a pederast," she said. "Fairchild has an exhibition of photographs in a gallery on Fifty-seventh Street, and one of those photographs shows Ushton propositioning a young boy in a men's room."

This time Murtaugh was the one to let the silence grow. When he did speak, it was to say: "You're certain it's Brad."

"Let's go take a look at the photograph. You can see for yourself." She looked at her watch; almost eleven. "The gallery should be open by now."

"All right." He shook his head disbelievingly. "Brad Ushton. Married and with grown children."

"And he's a new player."

"What?"

She sighed. "Right when I'm so hungry for a suspect I'm ready to grab someone off the street, along comes a man who fills the bill exactly. Isn't that convenient? Ushton certainly is in a position to know how the battling Galloways would react if Bobby were kidnapped. Oh, I know, I know—the fact that he's a dirty old man doesn't make him a kidnapper. But I shudder to think of Bobby alone in a room with that man."

Murtaugh was thinking along another line. "It seems to me that anyone in possession of a photograph like that would be in a good position to go in for a little blackmail. Yet Fairchild hung the picture on a wall for all the world to see. Surely he must know Ushton is Hugh Galloway's lawyer?"

"I don't know. He might not. We can find out from Rita."

Murtaugh found a fireplug on East Fifty-seventh to park by and they hurried into the Albian Gallery. No one was there except a fashionable young woman who backed off when they showed her their badges.

The captain looked at the photograph once and turned away in revulsion. "That's Ushton, all right," apparently not noticing that his old acquaintance had stopped being the more friendly *Brad*. "No question. Open a new case file the minute we get back and put someone on it." He glanced back at the fashionable young woman and said, "I suppose we'll have to get a warrant before she'll let us take that picture."

"That may not be necessary." Marian asked the young woman who had the negatives for the photographs on display, and was told Mr. Fairchild retained all the negatives. "I'll call him before I leave," she said to Murtaugh on their way back to the car. "He can make up prints for us."

"Before you leave?"

"I still have to get over to Hoboken today."

The drive back to the Midtown South stationhouse was silent and brief. Once back in her office, Marian called in Sergeant Campos and told him she had a new case for him. She explained about Bradford Ushton and said, "Put your best men on this one, Campos."

His jaw was clenched and his mouth a thin line. "I'll put myself on it," he said tightly. "These smug old men...I know what they do to young boys. I'll get him."

Marian wondered the obvious, but didn't ask. Himself? Someone he knew? God, how common this form of abuse had become! No, not true; it had always been common. It was just that everyone avoided talking about it.

And she was doing the same thing. She changed her mind and said, "Campos? How do you know what they do to young boys?"

He radiated an anger that made her flinch. "My brother. It was a teacher at the school. My brother, he was ashamed to tell anyone. He felt guilty. Then another boy talked, but the school just hushed the whole thing up. They didn't do nothing but ask the teacher to resign. That's when I first thought about becoming a cop. I was fourteen years old and I couldn't protect my kid brother. Nobody would *do* anything."

Oh lord, what a thing to live with. "I'm sorry, Campos. What about your brother? Was he all right afterward?"

"No. He has never been all right."

This was bad. She hesitated, and said, "Look, I didn't know about this. If it's going to be too—"

"Lieutenant, don't take this case away from me. I couldn't get the teacher, but I can get this lawyer. And I can do it without beating the truth out of him, if that's what you're afraid of. Don't take it away."

She considered, evaluating him. And decided. "All right. It's yours." He nodded once, abruptly. She decided to let Campos call Alex Fairchild for prints of the damning picture; she'd had enough of the photographer for a while. "We can get Ushton for solicitation of a minor on the evidence of that photograph alone," she said, "but it would be better if you can catch him in the act. That's going to be tricky. You mustn't let a child be put in danger."

"Don't you worry about *that*," he said positively. "Do I show him the photograph?"

"Up to you. Do what the situation calls for. Even if we get him only for solicitation, his picture in the paper might prompt some earlier victims to come forward. God, I hate putting kids on the stand!"

"Yeah. But it's the only way to get a conviction."

"Unfortunately. Use as many men as you need, but don't lose him, even for a minute. And Campos—proceed with caution. There's a slight chance Ushton could be a killer. Very slight, but keep your guard up just the same."

His eyes glistened. "Which case?"

"The Galloway kidnapping." She told him about the two bodies that had been fished out of the East River. "There's not a shred of evidence linking Ushton to the killings. But he's Hugh Galloway's attorney, so he had certain inside knowledge. I'm not sure if that means anything or not. Probably not. But don't take any chances."

He said he wouldn't and left, eager to get started. Marian called Holland to tell him she'd be getting home late.

Then she left for Hoboken, New Jersey, to find out what Ms Annie Plaxton could tell her.

TWELVE

MARIAN DIDN'T KNOW her way around Hoboken, so she had to ask directions twice before she found Meegat Street. She was surprised at the size of Annie Plaxton's new laundromat; she counted six rows of ten washing machines each. Dryers lined the wall, along with five of the huge washer/dryers for large jobs like drapes and bedspreads. There was a waiting area with tables and chairs and vending machines. And the place was packed; almost all the machines were in use.

A young man was mopping up suds from the floor and explaining to an embarrassed woman that she mustn't overload the washer. When Marian asked where Annie Plaxton was, he pointed with his head toward a door in the rear.

Annie's office was a small square partitioned off in one corner of the main room. Marian knocked on the door and held up her badge when it opened. "Lieutenant Larch, NYPD. I need to talk to you."

The other woman tried to shut the door, but Marian already had her foot in place. "What do you want?" the woman demanded.

"Information. You know something I need to know. Open the door, Annie."

Reluctantly, she did. Annie Plaxton was a wiry-stringy little woman with some gray in her hair and a chip on her shoulder. "You got no jurisdiction here. This is New Jersey."

Marian smiled. "Do you really think police don't help each other across jurisdictions? I didn't go to the Hoboken police because I saw no reason to bring your name to their attention. You have nothing to worry about.''

She was still suspicious. "A New York police lieutenant comes all the way here to find me and I'm not supposed to worry about it? Now tell me another. I spent thirty years cleaning other people's houses and now I got a business of my own and nobody's gonna take it away from me!''

Marian put on a look of surprise. "Well, of course not! Is that what you think I'm going to do? I'm not here about your business or even about *you*. Just answer a few questions and I'll be gone. May I sit down?" She sat down.

Annie slowly took her own seat behind her desk, still not convinced. "What kind of questions?"

"Where did the money come from to open this laundromat?"

She flared. "You said this wasn't about me!"

"And it's not. It's about the source of your money. We want the man who financed your laundromat, but we don't want him *for* financing you. What we want him for is murder.''

"Murder?" Her face changed. "Holy Mother of God." She thought that over but then shook her head. "I can't help you.''

"You don't have to testify. Your name won't even come into it.''

"That's not it. I don't *know* who sent me the money.''

Marian sat back in her chair. "What?!''

"I'm tellin' you true. Some man called and said he'd set me up with my own laundromat on two conditions. First, I had to quit my job with Maids-in-a-Row right away, like, the next day. And second, I had to get out of town, open the laundromat somewheres except New York. He didn't say how *far* out of town, so I just crossed the river and set up here.''

"Did you ask his name?"

"Course I did. He said I didn't need to know that.''

"And you didn't smell anything fishy?"

"I smelled a lot fishy. But I figured it was none of my business."

And you wanted your laundromat. "What about the voice on the phone? Did it sound familiar?"

She shook her head. "It sounded mechanical, like. Like he was using an amplifier or something."

Not an amplifier, but Marian knew what she meant. "How was payment made?"

"In cash. He sent some guy with a briefcase full of money. Dint even ask for a receipt."

"You're sure it was a different guy?"

"Yeah. Guy on the phone sounded educated, like. The delivery guy talked like a kindergarten dropout."

Marian opened a folder she'd brought with her and placed the computer-generated pictures of Nick Atlay and the pseudonymous Consuela Palmero on Annie's desk.

"That's him!" she said excitedly. "That's the guy what brought the money!"

"You're sure?"

"Oh yeah. See that big lower lip? Made him look like a pouty little boy in a man's body. Who's the woman?"

"She took your place at Maids-in-a-Row. Annie, both of these people are dead now. They were killed by the man who sent you the cash."

She jumped out of her chair. "Jesus Christ!"

"Take it easy," Marian said. "They were killed because they could identify him. You, on the other hand, never saw his face and you don't know his name."

Annie slumped back down in her chair. "Still."

"Yes. It's best that you know the kind of man he is. Have you heard from him since you made the deal?"

"Nope. And I don't *wanna* hear from him."

Marian thought a moment. "How did he know you wanted a laundromat in the first place?"

Annie snorted. "That's easy. Everybody who knows me

knows how much I wanted my own laundromat. It's all I been talking about for the past ten years.''

''And he heard you. So you could have cleaned this man's home at one time?''

She shrugged. ''I could have.''

''How many homes have you cleaned in the past thirty years?''

Another shrug. ''Hundreds.''

Marian handed her one of her cards. ''If he calls again, let me know immediately. I don't think you'll be hearing from him, though. He wants as little to do with you as you do with him.''

''That suits me just fine,'' Annie said emphatically.

Marian stopped for a bite to eat before heading for the Lincoln Tunnel. She fought the Friday afternoon traffic all the way to West Thirty-fifth Street, wishing—as she always did when she drove—that there was a shorter way from *here* to *there*. When she reached her office, she found a fax on her desk. The spying cleaning woman's prints had been on file and had yielded a quick identification.

Her real name was Julia Ortega, and she was a licensed private investigator.

Whoo. Marian sat down to read. Ortega had been thirty-eight years old, a native New Yorker, and a cop in Brooklyn for nine years. She'd retired from the force four years ago and had received her private investigator's license shortly after that.

Back to the *NYNEX Yellow Pages*. No Julia Ortega listed, so she was working for someone else.

Marian went out to Sergeant Buchanan's desk in the squadroom. He was talking on the phone but covered the mouthpiece and looked a question at her. ''I need two men,'' she said.

''Take Walker and Dowd—they just wrapped up a case.''

"Right." She looked over toward Walker's desk: no one there.

"They're on their way in."

She left notes on Walker's and Dowd's desks; Perlmutter and O'Toole ought to be getting back soon as well. Enough time to fill Captain Murtaugh in, though.

He was sitting on the edge of his desk, arms folded, long legs stuck out in front of him, staring at nothing at all. *Thinking about Bradford Ushton?*

"We have an ID on the fake cleaning woman," Marian said. "She was a private detective."

Murtaugh looked up and focused on her. "Now, *that* is interesting. Hired to do exactly what?"

"That's the part I can't figure. Why would the killer need to check into Rita Galloway's financial records? It makes no sense. He seems to have hired Nick Atlay as a general dogsbody. Atlay delivered the cash to pay Annie Plaxton for quitting her job at Maids-in-a-Row, he tried to abduct Bobby, and he probably threw the gasoline bomb into Rita's house. We got positive IDs on two of those— the attempted kidnapping and paying off Annie."

"This killer," Murtaugh said with a scowl, "why didn't he kill Annie too? Cheaper than setting her up in business."

"He hadn't crossed the line yet, Jim. He bought off Annie weeks before the kidnapping went sour and Atlay became a liability instead of a helpful errand runner. The killer was still trying to do everything with money then."

"Which tells us he isn't hurting for cash. Still think it's a kidnap for ransom?"

She raised her arms to the side, let them drop. "Nobody ever has enough money. But maybe it isn't ransom. The problem of why he went after the Galloway boy twice instead of looking for a child not so well guarded...maybe, well, maybe he just wants Bobby."

Murtaugh looked at her, hard. "You mean Brad Ushton."

She was uncomfortable. "You know we have to consider that. It *is* a possibility."

He sighed unhappily. "Who'd you put on Ushton?"

"Campos. And I'm putting Walker and Dowd on Ortega. Will you authorize overtime?"

"Absolutely," Murtaugh said. "Don't let this case drag out. Nail it down, dammit."

"Yessir." *Dammit.*

"I HOPE YOU'RE NOT averse to earning some extra money this month," Marian told the four men crowded into her office. "Because you're working through the weekend on this one."

Only Dowd groaned.

Dowd and Walker had been brought up to date on what had happened so far. Perlmutter and O'Toole had returned with the lists of possible suspects drawn up by Rita and Hugh Galloway, and Marian found it interesting that both had listed Bradford Ushton. "We're leaving Ushton to Campos and his team for the time being. If they can bring him in on a child molestation charge, then we'll have a go at him about the killings. But right now we're going to concentrate on Nick Atlay and Julia Ortega. Last known addresses, associates, and especially recent contacts."

Walker asked, "Do we know what agency Ortega was with?"

"No. That's the first thing you'll need to find out. Then contact the owner and see what cases she was working on."

Dowd groaned again. "We're going to have to call every private in the city!"

"No, we won't," Walker said. "Ortega's friends or family can tell us. Someone will know where she worked."

Marian nodded. "Ortega will be easy. It's Atlay who's going to cause difficulties. Perlmutter, have you talked to Buchanan?"

He had. "He gave us a list of those Atlay associates he could remember. But Lieutenant, these are people Atlay hung with four, five years ago. They may not have even have seen him since then."

"Yeah, that's true. Do you have a better suggestion?"

He pursed his lips. "No."

"Another thing. One of you ask Rita Galloway if her brother had ever met her husband's attorney."

Perlmutter said, "Why not ask the brother?"

"He might lie."

He thought that over. "You mean Fairchild may have hung that picture knowing it was Bradford Ushton? Why?"

"I don't know. Find out from Rita—it may be a blind alley." She looked at the fourth detective in the room. "O'Toole, you're being mighty quiet."

"Thinking," he said. "How would Rita ever find someone like dumb bunny Nick Atlay to do her dirty work for her? Where'd they meet?"

"Rita isn't the killer," Perlmutter said disgustedly.

"Maybe, maybe not."

Marian said, "But it's a pertinent point. How did the killer initiate contact? Remember, Atlay may have been working as a janitor. If we could find the building where he worked last, that would give us a real lead."

Dowd asked, "When does our overtime start?"

"Right now. The man Julia Ortega worked for—find him tonight if you can. He takes precedence. Okay, anything else?" No one had any other suggestions. "All right, then, let's get started. Call in as soon as you have something. They'll page me, wherever I am."

When they'd left, Marian settled down to a job she'd neglected for the last few days. The rest of the detectives under her command hadn't been sitting on their hands while she was working the Galloway case; a stack of reports awaited her attention. She got to work.

It was eight-thirty before she started her car for the drive to her place. She was tired, and her fatigue had created an ache in her neck and between her shoulder blades; she'd ask Holland for a massage tonight. He'd done it before, on other nights she'd worked until she ached. The thought of those strong hands caressing her tense body into a state of complete relaxation made her press down on the accelerator a little harder.

But when she reached her floor of the building, she uneasily noticed the smell of smoke in the hallway...a smell that grew stronger as she approached her own apartment. The thought of the firebomb in Rita Galloway's house flashed through her mind. Alarmed, she unlocked the door.

And was faced with a thick cloud of smoke that made her start coughing. "Holland!" she cried. "Holland!"

He came out of the kitchen, wearing only the briefest of black silk briefs. His eyes were streaming. "Don't worry, it's under control. I have the ventilator going."

"But...what happened?"

"Oh, I was frying some peppers and had the fire too high. Grease fire, no damage beyond some black streaks on the wall. And I turned off the smoke detectors before someone called the Fire Department. The smoke will clear out in time."

Marian's own eyes were watering. "Oh, this is awful. What are you doing eating fried peppers anyway? Those things will kill you."

"Then why did you buy so many of them when you stocked the refrigerator?"

"I don't know. Because they looked nice? Holland, I can't take much more of this."

"No, we'll have to stay at my place until the smoke clears. Let's go now."

"Yes, let's. But put some clothes on, stud. You'll get arrested if you go out like that."

"Just living up to my role of kept man." He dressed hastily and they hurried out, locking the door behind them with relief. The smell of smoke still lingered in the hallway.

"My neighbors are going to love me," Marian muttered.

"Do you know your neighbors?"

"No, but that's not the point. Dammit, Holland! What a mess."

He placed the back of his hand against his forehead and proclaimed, theatrically, "Alas, I am guilty! Guilty, I say! I confess! Chain me to the wall! Bring out the whip!"

"Dern. I left the whips and chains at the office."

"Are you *very* mad at me?"

She smiled at him. "No."

They drove to his place separately, as Marian would most likely be needing her car the next day. The first thing they did when they got there was take a long, sudsy shower; Holland especially wanted to get the smell of smoke out of his hair.

Then, at last, Marian got her massage.

THIRTEEN

MARIAN HAD TO GO back to her apartment Saturday morning, to get some clothes. The night before she hadn't thought of her now empty closet at Holland's place; then, all she'd been concerned about was getting out of that smoky apartment. She left the ventilator running in the kitchen; the smoke had cleared, but the smell still lingered. Marian's sinuses were burning as she gathered up what she needed.

Back at Holland's, she hung her clothes out on the balcony to air. "Promise me you'll never fry peppers again," she said.

"I give you my word," he replied with a shudder.

"If you really wanted to come back here that badly, you didn't have to stink up my place to do it."

"Well, now. Let us examine the sequence of events. If you had done your laundry here as I suggested, you would not have returned to that other apartment. If you had not returned, you wouldn't have needed to stock the refrigerator. If you hadn't stocked the refrigerator, I wouldn't have been tempted by the peppers. And if I—"

"So it's all my fault?"

He smiled. "I knew you'd see reason."

She rolled her eyes. Marian picked up a sleeve of a jacket and sniffed. "I wonder how long this will take. I don't like wearing the same clothes two days in a row."

"If we stay in all day, you won't need to wear any clothes at all."

"Fat chance. I'll have to go into the station sometime today."

A big sigh. "When was the last time we had a full weekend together?"

Marian laughed. "*Last* weekend."

Her pager had sounded last night, just as she was drifting off to sleep. It was Detective Walker; he'd learned that Julia Ortega had worked for a detective agency in Spanish Harlem run by a man named Hector Vargas. The place had been locked up tight, but Walker said he'd try again in the morning.

She'd asked if they had a home address for Hector Vargas.

"Not yet. He's probably in the yellow pages, but there's no directory here where I'm calling from. I can get that in the morning too."

"Okay. Good work, Walker." But the detective's uncharacteristic use of "I" instead of "we" aroused a suspicion. "Put Dowd on for a minute."

"Uh, he's in the men's room."

"I'll wait while you go get him." A long silence from the other end, but she could still hear Walker breathing. "He skipped out on you, didn't he?" No answer. "All right, Walker, call it a day. We'll settle this later." She hung up.

"Trouble?" Holland asked sleepily.

"One of my detectives is dogging it, that's all. Go back to sleep."

Dowd was the first one she heard from Saturday morning; Walker had wasted no time in telling him the bad news. But at least Dowd had called her instead of skulking in the background and hoping she'd forget about him. "Look, Lieutenant," he said in a tight voice, "I'm real sorry about last night. It was just, uh…am I in hot water?"

"Damned right you are. What do mean, ducking out on an assignment like that?"

"Well, you didn't give us much notice, and I had this date, see—"

"Oh well, gosh. You should have told me. Your social life is more important than any puny little murder investigation."

"Aw, Lieutenant. Is this going on my record?"

"Of course it's going on your record, what do you think?" She let that sink in for a moment, and then added, "Unless…"

He was quick to jump on it. "Unless what?"

"Buchanan told me you were going to take the Sergeants Exam but you weren't going to study for it. Is that right?"

"Uh, yes. So?"

"So now you're going to study for it. You're going to study *hard*. Remember, I've taken that exam and I'll have access to all the scores—so I'll know if you've been dogging it again. And Dowd, that is the *only* way you're going to keep a dereliction-of-duty report off your record."

"I'll study," he said hastily. "I'll ace the damned test."

"Good. I'm sure you'll make an outstanding sergeant." She didn't even try to keep the sarcasm out of her voice. Change of subject: "What are you doing now?"

"We got a home address for Hector Vargas. We'll try there if he's not at his agency."

"All right. Have me paged when you've got something." She hung up and noticed Holland was watching her with an amused look on his face. "What?"

"I see you're not above a little judicial blackmail when it suits your purpose," he said. "I can't tell you how that delights me."

"Yeah, well. Dowd's a good detective when he puts his mind to it, but he tends to get lazy now and then. He'll be on his toes now for a while. Look, as soon as my clothes are wearable, let's go out. It's a gorgeous day and I don't want to stay cooped up."

"We could go to Belmont Park. Sit in the sun and watch the horsies run."

She considered it. "No, that's too far. I've got three teams of detectives working on three different lines of investigation, and any one of them could break at any moment."

"Three? Nick Atlay would be one, and I assume your spying cleaning woman is another. What's the third?"

"The picture we saw at Alex Fairchild's exhibition—the one of a man caressing a young boy's neck in a men's room?"

"Yes?"

"The pederast is Hugh Galloway's attorney."

His eyebrows rose. "Well, well. What a *remarkable* coincidence. And we are firm believers in coincidence, are we not?"

"Right, it's just a little too convenient."

Holland thought a moment. "If you're thinking he's casting a lustful eye on young Bobby Galloway, forget that. It would be far too dangerous. Seducing the son of a client? He's not going to run a risk like that. He'll stick to boys who don't know his name."

"I know. Dammit."

"You don't have a real suspect, do you? What's the attorney's name?"

"Bradford Ushton. Jim Murtaugh knows him."

"Cozier and cozier. Did Fairchild know who Ushton was when he hung that picture?"

"That's one of the things we'll find out today."

"The answer you'll get will be no, I'll wager. Notice how Fairchild keeps popping up all the time? And always he's pure as the driven snow. He's the one who discovers the cleaning woman spying. When the kidnapping fails, he's right there at his sister's side. After the firebombing, he's the one who provides Rita and Bobby with a home. He's the one who hangs a picture in public exposing Ushton's perversion. But is he *involved?* Oh, no. Mr. Innocence himself."

Marian smiled. "You just don't like him. There's nothing in any of that to make him a suspect."

"Has he made a move on you yet?"

"He asked me out to lunch, if that counts as making a move."

"Did you go?"

The question annoyed her. "No, I did not. Holland, stop this. You're making Fairchild into a rival when he isn't one."

He was silent a moment. "Yes, I am making him important, aren't I? But I can't pretend indifference when I see him trying to move in on me. Ah...that came out sounding more territorial than I intended. But don't expect me to remain detached when another man shows interest in you. I won't even try."

She looked at the grim set of his jaw and decided this conversation was going nowhere. "Oh well," she said with mock regret. "He probably doesn't wear black silk briefs anyway."

Holland stared at her—and then burst out laughing. The awkward moment passed.

IT WAS ALMOST one before Marian heard from Perlmutter. She and Holland were having lunch at an outdoor café near Lincoln Center when her pager went off. She called in from the table.

"We're not having much luck tracing Nick Atlay's known associates, Lieutenant. But we finally found an old con named Lippy Sarkoff who's seen him once since they both got out. And Lippy says Atlay was working as a janitor."

"Aha. Does he know where?"

"No, but he said Atlay was running errands for one of the tenants."

Marian sat up straight. "Find that building, Perlmutter. Residential or office?"

"Lippy didn't know. But he did give us a few leads, people Atlay mentioned. We're going to look for them now."

"This Lippy is very helpful. Sure you can believe him?"

"Oh yeah. Lippy's one of those old criminals trying to go straight because they're scared to death of the new breed of younger prisoners we're sending up—you know, the punks who'll stick a knife in you if they don't like the way you look at them. Lippy'll do anything to stay out of prison. Even tell the cops the truth. What about Walker and Dowd? They get anything?"

She told him about Julia Ortega and that she'd worked for a detective named Hector Vargas. "Vargas is in Atlantic City today, working a case. So right now Walker and Dowd are talking to Ortega's neighbors and friends to see if she told anyone about the case she was on."

"How'd they find out about Atlantic City?"

"Mrs. Vargas. His office was still locked up when they checked this morning, so they went to his home address. Back to Lippy a minute. Is he the only one you've found who's seen Nick Atlay lately? The *only* one?"

"Afraid so. It's June, the weather's nice, no one's staying inside if they don't have to. We got some repeat calls to make."

"Find that building," Marian said and broke the connection.

Holland was looking at her quizzically. "'Lippy'?"

"Good name for a snitch, don't you think?"

They spent the next couple of hours wandering, not fully relaxed because of Marian's mood of anxious expectancy. At any moment her pager could go off; which of her three lines of investigation would bear fruit first?

Eventually the park beckoned. They stopped to watch a man with a camcorder taping the impromptu performance of a street mime. The camcorder man was more entertaining than the mime; he was constantly on the move, always looking for a better angle, hunkering down and shooting upward, climbing onto a bench and shooting downward, thrusting the lens up close in the performer's face, then backing rapidly away for a long shot. After a few minutes of this, the mime began to get a little disconcerted. Other people watching yelled at the camcorder man to knock it off.

"Too bad," said Holland. "I don't like mimes. I was cheering for the man with the camcorder."

"You don't like mimes? Why not?"

"Oh, they play at being coy and wistful, but that's only to put you off guard so they can slip in a zinger. Mimes like to embarrass people."

"This one didn't."

"Only because that budding film director over there never gave him a chance. Perhaps I should pick up a camcorder," Holland added as they strolled away.

"What for?"

"For when we're old and jaded. Taking dirty pictures of ourselves might spice things up."

"Uh-huh. Well, let's just hold off on that for a while, if you don't mind."

They walked a little more…and then Marian suddenly stopped. "Holland. I'm just too fidgety for a stroll in the park."

He wasn't happy about it, but he understood. "I'll drive you to the station."

It took them twenty minutes to get back to where he'd left his car, and it was after four by the time they pulled up in front of the Midtown South station on West Thirty-fifth. Someone else had had the fidgets as well: Captain Murtaugh was just getting out of his car.

"Jim?" Marian said. "You didn't need to come in."

"I know," he answered. "But I wanted to be here if something breaks."

She smiled. "And Edie is still out of town."

"That too." He looked at the other man. "Holland."

"Murtaugh."

A silence developed; the chill between the two men was too strong to pretend it wasn't there. Marian was annoyed; the two most important men in her life, and they couldn't get along. But she knew whose fault *that* was. She turned to Holland and said, "I don't know how long I'll be."

He spread his hands. "In that case, I'll put a candle in the window." He looked at Murtaugh and his voice took on a taunting tone. "You will let her out eventually, won't you, Captain?"

"She can let herself out." Murtaugh turned and strode into the stationhouse.

Marian waited until he was out of hearing and said, "What *is* it with you two? And what was that crap about letting me out?"

He sighed. "That's exactly what it was. Crap. I can't seem to avoid locking antlers with that man every time I see him."

"Well, that's a great pity, because he's a big part of my life. And you're not helping any by sniping at him."

"I did not snipe."

"Only because he walked away before you could start. And I don't like the idea of being, well, *let out*—as if I were some sort of pet that needs looking after. You can get pretty damned possessive at times, Holland."

"Have I ever really 'possessed' you?"

"We'll talk about this later." She went into the station-house, leaving his question unanswered.

FOURTEEN

IT WAS Campos who broke his case first.

Bradford Ushton, highly respected attorney and child molester, had followed a ten-year-old boy into the men's room of a movie house. When the two detectives tailing him saw him go into a children's Saturday matinee, they'd split up. One sat three rows behind Ushton in a theater full of noisy, popcorn-munching kids. The other went into the men's room and stood on the toilet seat in one of the booths; anyone checking for feet under the closed doors would not know he was there.

He hadn't had to stand there long; Ushton had simply followed the first boy who'd needed to pee. The detective watched over the top of the booth as Ushton had petted and sweet-talked the boy, offering to let him play with the latest electronic gadgets geared to the under-twelve set. Ushton had promised to have the kid back in time for the next showing of the movie.

That alone would have been enough to nail him for solicitation, but Sergeant Campos had said to get as much on the attorney as possible without endangering the child; Campos wanted to hit this guy with every law in the book. So the detectives had followed the man and the boy, on foot, to a nearby apartment building. Ushton and his new young friend had gone in the back way, so the boy wouldn't see the street address prominently displayed on the front of the building. None of the mailboxes in the lobby had Ushton's name on it; the cops had described Ushton to other residents until one of them identified him as the man in 410. Instead of crashing in, they'd gone outside and climbed the fire escape. Through a window they saw Ushton taking off the boy's T-shirt. *Then* they went crashing in.

"We've got him cold," Campos told Marian and Captain Murtaugh. "You should see that place. One-room apartment, within walking distance of several different movie houses. He kept it just for a place to take the boys. Packed with stuff for kids—video games, action figures, like that. In case they needed persuading. And the old fool took pictures. Look at this." Campos fanned out a stack of Polaroid shots on Marian's desk, all of naked boys. "He kept those displayed on a big bulletin board. I guess he figured if a new boy saw other boys undressed, he wouldn't think it was so weird."

"Where's the boy he picked up today?" Murtaugh asked.

"I had a bluesuit drive him home and explain to the parents what happened. The kid still don't understand what was going on." Campos grinned crookedly. "Those parents are gonna get a real talking-to. The bluesuit was pissed that the kid didn't know no better than to go with Ushton. He kept saying the parents shoulda taught him better, they shoulda warned him."

"Perhaps they did," Marian said mildly. "Kids don't always listen. Where's Ushton now?"

"Interrogation room. Waiting for a lawyer he called. I was hoping the old buzzard would represent himself, but he's too shrewd for that."

"I want to talk to him," Murtaugh said. "Has he been charged yet?"

"Yeah, he's been charged."

Campos and Marian went to the small room on the other side of the interrogation room and watched through the one-way glass. Ushton sat with his hands folded on the table in front of him, face impassive, aware that he was being watched.

But when the door opened and Murtaugh stepped in, his

face showed something like relief. "Jim! Will you be handling this…misunderstanding?"

"Is that what it is, Brad?" Murtaugh asked tonelessly. "A misunderstanding?"

On the other side of the glass, Campos said, "Jesus Christ! They're *friends?* You shoulda told me, Lieutenant."

"No need," Marian replied. "The captain didn't want us to go easy on this guy. What he wanted was exactly what you gave him—an open-and-shut case."

In the interrogation room, Ushton was saying he'd make no statement until he had legal representation. Murtaugh waved that aside and said, "I'm here to tell you something, not ask questions. And what I'm telling you is this: cooperate. Give the investigating officers answers to all the questions they ask and it will go easier for you. Admit what you've done, face up to it, and ask for help. And that piece of obvious advice is *all* the help you're going to get from me. In fact, I'm going to ask the DA's office to oppose bail at your hearing. You're a menace, Ushton, and you ought to be locked away where you can't hurt any more little boys."

"I never hurt them! I—" He clamped his mouth shut and would say no more. Murtaugh looked at him in disgust and left.

A LITTLE OVER an hour later they gathered downstairs in the briefing room, the only closed room in the stationhouse that could hold more than four people comfortably. Marian's two teams of detectives had come in; and the captain was still there.

Marian said, "Campos and his team are interrogating Bradford Ushton, and they're under strict orders to make no mention of the Galloway case or the two homicides connected with it. They're not even to hint at murder. So when Campos is through and Ushton thinks he's finished for the day—that's when we move in. His attorney will scream and holler, but there's not a damned thing he can do about it."

Walker asked, "Do we have anything linking him to the murders?"

"No, but he won't know that. So far his only connection is that he's Hugh Galloway's attorney."

Dowd said, "He was after the Galloway boy. What more do you need?"

"We need a *lot* more," Marian said emphatically. "It's a flimsy connection at best. But I don't see any other suspects standing around, do you?"

Murtaugh grunted. "See if you can get him to talk about Bobby Galloway. He might let something slip." The others nodded.

"All right," Marian said. "That's what's going to happen next. Let's hear what you found today. Walker, you first."

Walker looked unhappy. "We struck out, Lieutenant. Julia Ortega just didn't talk about her work. We spoke to everyone we could find who knew her, but we're going to have to wait until tomorrow when Hector Vargas gets back from Atlantic City."

"What about Mrs. Vargas?"

Walker shook his head. "No help."

Dowd laughed shortly. "She didn't know nuttin' about nuttin'. She was saying what her husband told her to say if anyone ever showed up asking questions."

"Huh. Well, don't push her. See Vargas as soon as he gets back. Now, what about Nick Atlay? Perlmutter?"

He cleared his throat, prefatory to giving a negative report. "We couldn't find the building where Atlay worked as a janitor. We did find someone who knew Atlay's job was in an office building and not a residential one. But we have a few more leads we can follow tomorrow."

Marian spread her hands. "That's it? Why is this so difficult?"

"Couple of things, Lieutenant," Perlmutter said. "Atlay was a loner. There was *no* one he was close to. Not by choice, I'm guessing. But he just didn't have friends. Everyone looked upon him as part of the background, not as a person worth paying attention to. He was slow and didn't understand a lot and people got impatient trying to talk to him."

"Yeah," O'Toole agreed. "They talked about him like he was a piece of furniture."

"And that's what caused the second problem," Perlmutter went on. "We'd ask about Nick Atlay, they wouldn't know who we meant. Almost nobody knew his last name. We didn't get anywhere until we started asking about 'Nickie'—that's the only name they knew him by."

"How'd you find that out?"

Perlmutter grinned. "Lippy Sarkoff. I told you he'd tell us the truth."

"Well, good for Lippy." She frowned. "There was something else—"

O'Toole said, "You wanted us to ask Rita Galloway whether her brother knew Bradford Ushton or not. She says they never met."

Marian was doubtful. "But surely he knew who he was. From court—the Galloway divorce hearing."

"We asked her about that. It was settled in the judge's chambers, only the two Galloways and their attorneys present. It wasn't a real hearing, anyway—that comes, er, next year?"

"Whenever Bobby is old enough to start regular school." Marian looked at Murtaugh. "No blackmail…since Fairchild didn't know whose picture he was taking in that men's room." The captain shrugged; it was a long shot.

"Anything else?" Marian asked the room at large

"Okay, then, grab a bite to eat while you can. We're in for a long siege."

A LONG and fruitless siege, she should have said. Captain Murtaugh left around nine o'clock, when it became clear that they were going to get nothing from Ushton. When Ushton understood that he was being questioned about murder, he became in turn appalled, angry, indignant, and frightened. Even when they reached the fear stage, he had nothing to tell them.

Marian called it quits. They were all tired and were getting nowhere fast. She'd just about convinced herself they were on a wild-goose chase anyway when Walker came to her and helped her decide.

"No motive," he said. "He's not interested in Bobby Galloway. Not that way. We asked him about Bobby. He said, 'He'll be a lovely boy in a few more years.'"

"And that's not interested?"

"Not now. 'He'll be a lovely boy *in a few more years.*' Bobby's too young for his tastes, Lieutenant. Ushton likes 'em around ten, eleven. All the boys he took pictures of are about that age. There's no picture of a boy as young as Bobby."

Marian looked at him tiredly; she should have thought of that herself. "You're right." She'd known it all along: Ushton wasn't their killer. She'd been clutching at straws when she ordered his interrogation. "Good work, Walker, getting him to tell you that."

He grinned wryly. "It was Dowd he told. He directed all his answers to my partner. Ushton didn't like being questioned by me." Walker was the only black man on the team.

She told him to go home and get some sleep. Marian was discouraged. They were right back where they'd started, with no suspect. She wondered if there was anything to be gained from a talk with old Walter Galloway at a time when Hugh was not around. Not tomorrow, though; wait until next week when Hugh would be in the office.

It was almost one when she finally unlocked the door to Holland's apartment. And found the place dark. A wave of disappointment swept over her, followed by a flash of irritation. And then she was ashamed of herself; she hadn't realized until that moment how much she counted on Holland's making himself available whenever she wanted him. Something to think about.

But later. She was too tired even to take a shower. She stripped off her clothes, slipped on an oversized T-shirt, and collapsed on the bed. Within seconds she was asleep.

WHEN SHE AWOKE the next morning, Holland was sleeping beside her; she hadn't heard him come in. She eased herself out of bed carefully so as not to wake him.

She turned the showerhead setting to its most needlelike spray. Marian felt a lot better this morning; that deep, undisturbed sleep had done her good. Yesterday wasn't a washout at all; they'd nailed a child molester and simultaneously eliminated him as a murder suspect. Not a bad day's work.

On the dining table lay a Carnegie Hall program with yesterday's date. Kiri Te Kanawa. So that's where he'd gone last night.

Marian started the coffee. But the concert wouldn't have lasted until 1 a.m.; he'd gone someplace else afterward. She wouldn't ask.

He came in while she was spreading cream cheese on a toasted bagel. Wearing only black silk mini-briefs again. Dark shadows under his eyes; not enough sleep. "Caffeine," he muttered.

Marian poured him a cup. They sat at the table and she waited until he started to look more awake. "So, how was Kiri?"

"Magnificent, as always." He reached over and took the other half of her bagel. When that was eaten, he said, "After the concert, I picked up a couple of chorus girls and we did the town."

She got up to toast another bagel. "Did you have fun?"

"Oh, yes. A ton of fun. We snorted a couple of lines and went to an illegal gambling den on West Forty-fifth."

"Hmm! Living dangerously."

"And when we ran out of money, we sold our bodies. I had more customers than the girls did."

"I'll bet you did."

"Then Sigourney Weaver came along and asked me to marry her."

"Congratulations. When's the wedding?"

"Egad, woman, will *nothing* make you jealous?"

"Not when you're clever enough to tell the truth but treat it as a joke so I won't believe it. But it didn't work. I truly believe you did do all those things."

"I went back to the office and did some work," he muttered. When she laughed, he said, "Well, this has turned into a working weekend, hasn't it? You'll probably have to go in again today."

"Probably." She looked at him with a gleam in her eye. "But not just yet."

FIFTEEN

HECTOR VARGAS, private detective and employer of the slain Julia Ortega, did not get back from Atlantic City until almost noon on Sunday. Parked outside his building and waiting for him were Walker and Dowd.

"Vargas took it real hard when we told him Ortega was dead," Walker told Marian a little later. "She was his niece, Lieutenant."

"Oh jeez," she said. "And he wasn't worried about her? He didn't report her missing?"

"Remember, Ortega was a cop in Brooklyn for nine years? Well, there's a reason she left the force before making retirement. The lady picked up a habit during her years on the street. Brooklyn sent her for treatment, but she didn't stick to it. So they kicked her out."

"And her uncle took her in."

"Yeah. He said losing her job as a cop pretty much put the fear of God into her, and she made a real effort to stay clean." Walker frowned. "But she backslid once, about a year ago—went missing for six days. Vargas just thought the same thing had happened again."

Marian nodded. "So he didn't want to get her into more trouble by filing a missing person report."

Dowd spoke up. "It had to be a pretty big habit. Brooklyn wouldn't have given up on one of their own unless it was. And that has to be why she went to work at her uncle's fleabag agency—nobody else would hire her."

"How fleabag?"

"Vargas, Ortega, one part-time op to do some of the legwork. That's the whole agency. Their cases are all petty stuff—skip-tracing, like that. Office is two tiny rooms in a building one step up from a slum."

Walker said, "Vargas is eager to cooperate, Lieutenant. You ready to see him now?"

She was.

Walker went to where he'd left Vargas sitting in the squadroom and brought him back. Dowd stood up to let the private detective have his chair, and Walker stayed in the doorway after making the introduction.

Vargas was short and stocky; he wore a white shirt that was frayed at the collar and trousers that had a bit of a shine. His hair was coal black: he could have been anywhere from forty to sixty. Vargas didn't immediately meet her eyes; the man was uncomfortable in a police station.

"I appreciate your coming in, Mr. Vargas," she said. "I'm sorry for your loss."

"Thanks, Lieutenant," he replied in a subdued voice. "You think a client killed Julia?"

"It's almost a certainty. I know you've already talked to the detectives, but I'd appreciate your going over it again with me."

"Anything. Tell me what you want to know."

"How many cases was your niece working on?"

"Just one. Things have been a bit slow lately, you know how it is."

"Tell me about that one."

"Well, a guy named Arlen, Tony Arlen, wanted somebody to check up on a woman named Rita Galloway—"

"Mr. Vargas, start at the beginning. How did this Arlen first contact you?"

"Phone call. He said he was disabled and it was hard for him to get around, but he'd send somebody with the cash if I'd take the case."

"Did he?"

"Oh yeah. Not more'n an hour later. A big guy named Nickie brought it."

Marian opened a drawer of her desk and took out a picture of Nick Atlay.

"That's him!" Vargas said. "That's Nickie. Hey, how'd you happen to have his picture?"

"What was it that Tony Arlen wanted you to do? Exactly."

Vargas sat up straighter, suddenly aware that more was going on than just his niece's murder. "He wanted to know if I could provide him with someone to pose as a cleaning woman. To get some information for him." Vargas paused. "He dint *say* she had to be Hispanic, but I figured he wouldna called me if he wanted Snow White. So I gave him Julia."

Marian said nothing about entering private premises under false pretenses. "Did they ever meet? Face-to-face?"

Vargas scratched the side of his nose. "Well, I ain't real sure that they did. I know that first time he just called her at the office and told her where to go and what he wanted her to do. They coulda met later, I guess."

"What did he tell her to do?"

"He said go to this cleaning service, Maids-something, and apply for a job early the next Tuesday."

"Did she have phony bond papers with her?"

"Naw, we don't do no fake paper."

"The owner of Maids-in-a-Row says she was bonded."

"He's lying."

Or you are. "Okay, she gets the job. Then what?"

"Then she's supposed to go through this Rita Galloway's checkbook, looking for deposits of five thousand dollars. Sounded to me like the guy was being blackmailed anonymously, and he suspected this Galloway broad of being the one."

That's what he wanted you to think. "Then what?"

He shrugged. "Then somebody in the house caught Julia goin' through the checkbook and threw her out. But not before she'd found two deposits of five thousand each. Arlen was satisfied, and he kept her on the payroll.''

"Doing what?''

"Tail jobs. She tailed this Rita for a while and then her brother. Photographer, name of Fairchild.''

"How'd she report to him? Did he give her a phone number?''

"Naw, he called the office. Some people won't give their phone numbers out to nobody.''

"What about an address?''

"No address neither.'' Vargas looked at her closely. "And his name ain't really Tony Arlen, is it?''

"You can bet money on it. But whatever his name is, he's the one responsible for Julia's death. Mr. Vargas, the man who killed your niece also killed Nick Atlay—Nickie, the big fellow who brought you your money. He also tried to have Rita Galloway's little boy kidnapped. This guy is bad news from every angle.''

Vargas's mouth dropped open. *"Ay, díos mía!"*

"Is there *anything* else you can tell us?''

"I wish to god there was,'' he said earnestly. "I'da never sent Julia out if I'da known. But why did he have to kill her?''

"He killed Nickie because he could identify him. Most likely that's the same reason Julia died.''

He sat there, stunned. Marian looked at Walker and Dowd. They both shook their heads; no questions. Marian thanked Vargas and told him to call in immediately if he thought of anything else.

Walker moved aside to let the private detective pass. Vargas paused in the doorway and looked back at Marian. "You really are gonna look for this guy?''

"You're damned right we are,'' she said emphatically. Reassured, he left.

Dowd waited until Vargas was out of earshot and then snorted. "He thinks the killer called him because he wanted a Hispanic. He *called* him because he wanted some low-rent outfit that'd do anything for a buck, no questions asked."

Marian barely heard him. "Interesting how he zoomed in on two people with, ah, defects. Nickie with his slow wit and Julia Ortega with her drug problem."

Dowd was skeptical. "He knew about Ortega's drug problem *before* he called Vargas?"

"Oh, probably not. It just struck me as curious. Well, any thoughts?"

Walker said, "Only two possibilities. First, Ortega and the killer did meet face-to-face and he got rid of her to protect himself. Or, second...he panicked. Killed someone he didn't need to."

Marian nodded, pleased he'd caught that. "A chink in the armor?"

"Yeah. Wouldn't that be nice."

"But Ortega's still just another dead end," Dowd said sourly. "Vargas was our only line to the killer, and he didn't tell us nothing we didn't already know. Or not much."

"So we look elsewhere." Marian opened the Galloway case file. "The killer is someone who knows the Galloways. Rita and Hugh both drew up lists of people they know who might be suspects, and I want you to start checking them out."

They both groaned. "Needle in the you-know-what," Dowd said.

"Maybe not." Marian handed one list to each detective. "Make copies and return the originals to the case file. Look for names that appear on both lists—start with those. Ignore any women's names—two people the killer has talked to on the phone have identified him as male."

"Two?" Walker asked. "Vargas and who else?"

"The woman he bribed to quit Maids-in-a-Row so Julia

Ortega could move in. Listen, you two…push on this. Push hard. And push fast. We're running out of time.''

"Yeah, the trail gets a little colder every day," Dowd said. "Okay, Lieutenant, we'll push." He and Walker left.

There was another reason Marian wanted them to push. She was afraid Jim Murtaugh might be running out of patience.

LATE THAT NIGHT, Marian called Kelly Ingram. She needed to hear a cheerful, upbeat voice.

But the news from Hollyweird was gloomy. "These people are *idiots!*" Kelly screamed. "They're doing everything they can to turn a beautiful, original play into a clone of everything else they grind out here! Abby and the director are about to come to blows!"

Abigail James, who'd written the screen adaptation of her own play. "But you've just gotten started," Marian said. "Maybe—"

"I know, that's the worst part! If they show this little respect for the script the first week, think what it's going to be like later!" Kelly went on at length, detailing all the shortsighted changes that had been made, until at last she was able to speak without exclamation points. "They're making changes just for the sake of making them," she moaned. "Ego games, that's all it is."

"Who's making the changes?"

"The director, the producer, the umpteenth assistant director, the set designer, the F/X man—"

"F/X? Special effects in *The Apostrophe Thief?*"

"Yeah, would you believe it, they've got me riding a roller coaster during a fireworks display that gets out of control. Ducking and dodging rockets, that's what I'm doing. The director says that when it's edited, the final cut will be 'real surreal.'" She made an unladylike noise. "*Real surreal.*"

Marian groaned in sympathy. "And Abby can't stop it?"

"Abby has less clout on the set than the guy they send for coffee. Once the script was finished, she was just a fifth wheel. Ian and I back her up every time she objects, but it doesn't help. This movie is going to hell in a hand-basket. Why do they say *hand*basket? What else would you carry it with—your teeth? Anyway, I thought Abby was going to belt the director this afternoon."

"Maybe that's what he needs."

Kelly laughed. "He's six foot six and weighs close to three hundred pounds. Abby's…what, five two? She'd have to stand on a chair." Then, more seriously: "I'm really discouraged, Toots. I had such high hopes for this movie."

They talked for a while longer, commiserating over work gone wrong. Marian told her friend she was stuck on a case but gave no details. They wished each other luck and promised to talk again in a few days.

Marian went into the room where Holland kept his computer. He looked grouchy; he'd spent all of Sunday afternoon and evening at the keyboard without finding what he was looking for. Something was out of kilter at his agency; nothing major, just little things not working the way they were supposed to. The professional breacher of other people's computer systems suspected that someone had breached *his* system.

She went up behind him and rested her chin on the top of his head. "About ready to be interrupted?"

"One moment." The screen changed five or six times before he gave up and shut down. "Every gateway we use is secure. Everyone who's been using them has a legitimate reason for doing so. So where's the problem?"

"In the modem," Marian said.

He moved his head from under her chin and twisted to look up at her. "In the *modem?*"

She shrugged. "It's a word I know."

He grunted. "That makes as much sense as anything else." He stood up and stretched. "Did you talk to Kelly?" Then, without waiting for an answer: "I need to get away from this for a while. Let's go out."

"Do you know it's after midnight?"

"Oh." A pause. "Bed?"

"Bed."

SIXTEEN

MONDAY DAWNED without anything new having been learned. Captain Murtaugh summoned his lieutenant in for an accounting.

"The Ortega line of investigation is a dead end," Marian explained. "Vargas never saw the man who hired them. Presumably Julia Ortega did and that's why she's dead. But Vargas can't give us what he doesn't know."

"What about Atlay?"

"We're still looking for the office building where he worked. It's a tedious process, Jim. Nobody paid much attention to Nickie Atlay. He was just available muscle for hire, nothing else. Perlmutter and O'Toole are following through on every lead they can get."

"Say you find the office building. Then what?"

"Then we take a list of the tenants to the Galloways to see if they know any of them. The killer must have office space there or work for someone who does. How else would he link up with the likes of Nickie Atlay?"

Murtaugh thought that over and nodded. "What else are you doing?"

"Checking out a list of possibles supplied by the Galloways." It sounded like pitifully little. Marian sighed. "If you can think of another line of investigation, I'm open to suggestion."

He was pondering something. "Not a line of investigation—but what about a prod? If we're at a dead end, let's goose this guy a little. Look." He picked up a copy of the *Daily News;* the front page prominently displayed a picture of Bradford Ushton and an article about his arrest on a child molestation charge. "This is a second-day story.

Think what they'd do with a new murder story to milk for all it's worth."

"Now, wait a minute—"

"Hear me out. So far the news media have not made the connection between Nick Atlay and Julia Ortega. Just two more bodies fished out of the East River on different days as far as they're concerned. Say you call a media conference. You announce that Atlay and Ortega are victims of the same murderer, a man who has twice attempted to kidnap the young son of a prominent New York family—don't mention the Galloways by name."

"Jim—"

"Admit the police are still trying to identify the building where Atlay worked as a janitor and ask for the public's help. We'll set up a hot line to handle the calls—most of them will be nuisance calls. You further announce that you have a suspect and you expect to make an arrest shortly. Then make a quick exit without answering any questions."

"That would be a big mistake," Marian said heavily. "Jim, this is a guy who solves his problems by killing people. We can't take that risk—it's just too dangerous."

"Who's left to kill? He's eliminated the two who could identify him."

"Who's left? Annie Plaxton in Hoboken. Hector Vargas. Whoever sold the killer his gun. Someone who might have seen him talking to Nickie Atlay. Other people we haven't even thought of."

"Oh, that's a stretch."

"No, it's not. We don't know for sure that Julia Ortega could have identified him. It could have been a panic killing. What do you think he's going to do when he reads that we've got a suspect?"

They went on arguing about it. Captain Murtaugh could have just ordered Marian to make the announcement. But before it came to that, they reached a compromise. Marian would make the announcement, but she'd omit the part about their having a suspect. She'd say instead something like *We are pursuing several lines of investigation.*

The only part of the plan that Marian really liked was asking the public's help in locating the building where Nickie worked. If the building's owner or superintendent read or watched, they'd be a giant step closer to their killer. "Just one more thing," she said. "I've never made a press announcement before."

"Hmm, well, it can be a little disconcerting the first time, flashbulbs going off in your face and all those TV cameras pointing at you. Just try not to sweat when you're on camera."

"Ah. Don't sweat on camera. What *helpful* advice. Thank you."

"And don't let them rattle you when they start yelling questions. Just make your announcement and then leave the room."

Four hours later, for the first time in her career, Marian Larch faced a barrage of lights and cameras as an official spokesperson for the NYPD.

THE NEXT DAY she put O'Toole on the hot line for incoming calls about Nickie Atlay. By eleven o'clock there'd been nothing but the nuisance calls Captain Murtaugh had predicted: people who only thought they knew Nickie, people who didn't give a hoot about Nickie but enjoyed bugging the police, lonely people trying to insert a little drama into their lives. Plus two confessions to the murders…with more undoubtedly to come.

Marian hated the way she'd looked on TV the night before; but even more than that, she hated the way she'd sounded. Holland said she was a little stiff, but other than that it was a pretty good debut performance. But the next time Jim Murtaugh wanted an announcement made to the news media, she was going to suggest strongly that *he* do it.

"Yes, ma'am," O'Toole was saying patiently on the phone. "Let me see if I got that. Your upstairs neighbor just started working as a janitor, so you think he killed Nick Atlay to get his job?...I see...yes... All right, ma'am, we'll look into it. Thank you for calling." He hung up and turned a whipped-puppy-dog look on Marian. "Why do you hate me? What have I done?"

She grinned and said, "Come on, O'Toole—you know I had to put our smoothest talker on the job."

He muttered something she didn't ask him to repeat.

But a couple of hours later it was Captain Murtaugh who was climbing the walls, not O'Toole. "Doesn't anyone other than nutcases read the paper or watch the news anymore?" he asked rhetorically. "We'll have to ask the TV stations to rerun part of your announcement. We should have used morgue shots."

"No, the computer picture is better," Marian said. "Nickie's recognizable from that."

"Why is it so hard to find out where one man worked? This should be so simple. What's the difficulty?"

"The difficulty is that no one ever really saw Nickie. He was one of those people everyone looks right through. Nickie could disappear from his job and most of the tenants in the building would never even know he'd been there in the first place."

"The tenants, maybe. But somebody hired him."

"Somebody who's out of town right now. Somebody who fell asleep watching the news. Give it a few more days."

He looked her in the eye. "I want this case *closed*," he said harshly.

Normally Marian would have responded *It will be*. This time she said nothing.

The street leads Perlmutter and O'Toole had picked up were dwindling down; Perlmutter alone was following through on those few that were left, with no real hope of finding anything other than the same vague responses they'd encountered so far. Walker and Dowd said the lists of possibles supplied by Rita and Hugh Galloway divided neatly into artistic types on her side and wheeler-dealers on his. Marian told them they might save some time if they took Hugh's list to his father; old Walter Galloway probably had the lowdown on every name there.

A little later she'd just returned from meeting Gloria Sanchez for lunch when the news broke.

Sergeant Buchanan took the call and came straight to Marian's office. "Bad news, Lieutenant," he said bleakly. "Rita Galloway just shot and killed her husband."

Marian was stunned. She asked Buchanan to repeat what he'd said.

He did. "No doubt she did it. Seven witnesses. She barged into a meeting at Galloway Industries and shot him four times before anyone knew what was happening. They're holding her at the office."

Rita? It was Rita all along?

Marian snapped out of her daze and asked Buchanan to find someone to replace O'Toole on the hot line. She told O'Toole to come with her and went to get Captain Murtaugh.

The drive uptown to Galloway Industries was silent except for O'Toole's self-satisfied comment that he'd known it was Rita right from the start. But Murtaugh was as taken off-balance by the news as Marian herself had been.

Three uniformed officers were stationed at the entrance to the Galloway Building, not letting anyone in or out. One TV news crew was already there, and the reporter recognized Marian. She thrust a microphone into her face and started asking questions. "Later," Marian said, pushing the mike away. They asked directions of the bluesuits guarding the entrance.

In the elevator on the way up, Marian said, "How'd that

TV crew get here before we did? Someone in the building must have called them.''

"There'll be more when we come out," Murtaugh replied.

Another bluesuit was waiting for them when they got off the elevator, a woman named Ravella. She led them to a conference room where Hugh Galloway lay sprawled in a chair at the head of a rectangular table on which a gun lay. His face was barely recognizable under all the blood.

Marian found it ugly-ironic that these would be the conditions under which she first saw Hugh Galloway surrounded by his accouterments of power. Before, he'd always been the outraged, beleaguered father trying to reclaim his only child...or else the unscrupulous, manipulative monster his wife claimed he was. Even now, Marian didn't know which was the more accurate picture of the man. But either way, the ending was the same; before the hour was out, what remained of Hugh Galloway would be carried out in a body bag for its journey down among the dead men.

"Ozymandias," Murtaugh muttered.

"What?" she asked. But he just shook his head.

"We protected the scene," Officer Ravella said. "Nothing has been disturbed." She pointed to the gun on the table. "One of the men in the meeting took it away from her."

"It looks like the .38 her brother gave her," Marian told Murtaugh. She asked the officer, "These other people who were in the meeting—where are they?"

"We got 'em in an office down the hall."

"O'Toole, check their stories." The detective followed Ravella out.

Murtaugh was bending over Hugh Galloway's body. "Four shots. She wanted to make sure he stayed dead."

"What could have provoked her to do this?" Marian wondered. "Now, I mean."

"We'll ask her." The captain was silent a moment. "I'll tell Walter Galloway for you, if you like."

"No, I'll do it." Her responsibility. Voices in the hall made her look around. "Crime Scene Unit's here."

She and Murtaugh got out of the way, leaving the photographer and the lab boys to do their thing. Officer Ravella was back. "The ME's not here yet?" the captain asked her.

"He's on his way," she told them. "Guy over there you want to talk to. Says he came here with the Galloway woman."

The man she led them to looked as if he was in shock. Marian recognized him; he was one of the bodyguards Alex Fairchild had hired to protect his sister and nephew. He said his name was Lindor. "What can you tell us?" Marian asked him.

"Nothing, really." Lindor was sweating. "She went out, I tagged along. I rode over here in a cab with her. She didn't say a word to me the whole time."

"How was she? Angry, upset?"

"Just the opposite. I've never seen her so icy calm."

"Then what?"

"Then she demanded to see her husband," Lindor said, "but the secretary told her he was in a meeting and couldn't be disturbed. So Mrs. Galloway just pushed right by her and went on into the conference room. I called out to her to stop and hurried to catch up. Next thing I know, I hear four shots and everyone's yelling and screaming."

Murtaugh asked, "So you didn't actually see the shooting?"

"No, I got there about two seconds too late. I saw the men rush her and take the gun away." Lindor pulled out a handkerchief and wiped his forehead. "Jesus, I thought *she* was in danger from *him*."

Marian pressed her lips together. "Lindor, where's Bobby?"

"With his uncle. Mr. Fairchild took him along on a shoot."

"Where?"

"In the park. At the boathouse. By the lake?"

"Yeah, I know it. Okay, Lindor, we'll need a statement from you. Hang around."

Murtaugh spoke to the officer. "Where are you holding Rita Galloway?"

"Last office, down at the end of the hall."

Marian said, "Let's check with O'Toole first."

They moved down the hall until they came to the room where O'Toole was getting the names and addresses of the witnesses. O'Toole saw them looking in and held up a finger: *one minute.*

It was more like five. O'Toole came out and said, "They're all telling the same story. Rita Galloway came charging into the conference room with Hugh's secretary right behind her, trying to stop her. Hugh said, 'Goddammit, Rita!' and started to get up when she took the gun out of her purse. By the time the others in the room had time to react, she'd fired four times. Two of the men jumped her and a third took the gun away. Then they held her in another office until the bluesuits could get here. And that's it. The secretary and the four men and two women in the meeting all agree."

"No attempt at subterfuge there," Marian commented. "She expected to get caught."

"Or just didn't think far enough ahead," Murtaugh replied. "Her lawyer can make a good case for diminished capacity there."

"Yeah, well, it was a crazy thing to do. Okay, O'Toole, tell those people we'll need statements. Send them on in to the station, and call Buchanan and let him know they're coming. Then you come to the last office at the end of the hall."

"What's down there?"

"Rita Galloway," Marian said.

SEVENTEEN

SHE LOOKED LIKE a dead woman, propped up thoughtlessly on a chair to get her out of the way. Her color was bad, her eyes unfocused, her mouth open. Her hands lay in her lap palms up, motionless.

"She's been like that ever since I got here," the officer guarding her said.

But she stirred when Marian spoke her name. Slowly she came back from wherever she'd been and looked around her. She frowned at the sight of Captain Murtaugh and the uniformed officer and then came back to the one face she knew. "Lieutenant?"

Marian pulled up another chair and sat facing her. "Rita...*why?*"

Her chest started heaving and she gasped for breath. "Because he was *evil*," she finally blurted out. "He was evil and he couldn't be stopped! Not any other way. I had to stop the evil."

Murtaugh said, "Do you suppose you could be more specific?"

"Bobby," she said, her face filled with pain. "I had to protect Bobby." She started when O'Toole stepped into the room. "Who are these men?"

"We're all police here," Marian said, in no mood to make introductions. "What do you mean, you had to protect Bobby? Had Hugh threatened him?"

"Worse than that. He was going to give him to that child seducer. His lawyer. That was the deal they had. One day a week."

"What deal? What are you talking about?"

Rita made an impatient gesture. "If Bradford Ushton

could get Bobby away from me permanently and legally, Hugh promised him he could have Bobby one day a week for…for as long as he wanted him. I saw the letter.''

Marian sat back in her chair, aghast. The three men in the room all had the same appalled looks on their faces. ''Hugh was willing to turn his own son over to a pederast?''

''Yes! That's what I'm telling you! It was in the letter.''

''What letter?''

''It's a letter Ushton wrote to Hugh, stating the conditions of their agreement. It's on his letterhead stationery, and I have a photocopy.''

Ohhhhhh…lots of things wrong here. But before Marian could say anything, Murtaugh spoke up. ''Mrs. Galloway, don't you realize such a letter would convince the courts to award you permanent custody of your son?''

Her head whipped around. ''You don't know Hugh! He'd have me killed before he'd let me use that letter against him! The only way to stop him was to kill him first!''

''Let's back up a little here,'' Marian said. ''How did you get this letter?''

''The private detective sent it to me by messenger. My lawyer hired an agency to see what they could dig up on Hugh…for the divorce. I, I guess she must have stolen it from Hugh's files. I never asked where the papers came from. Just every once in a while she'd send photocopies on to me. My lawyer told her to.''

She, her. ''Rita, what's her name? The private detective.''

She put her hands to her head. ''Oh, I don't remember! I never met the woman. It was something Hispanic.''

''Like, Julia Ortega?''

Rita looked up. ''Yes! That's it!''

Marian exchanged a long look with Murtaugh. O'Toole said, ''Boy oh boy oh boy oh boy oh boy. Mrs. Galloway,

what's your lawyer's name and address?'' He pulled out
a notebook and wrote down what she told him: Dorian
Yates, with offices on Fifth.

"A new player?'' Murtaugh remarked dryly. "This
stage of the game?''

"Uh-huh,'' Marian said. Another new suspect handed
to them on a platter. "Rita, did Dorian Yates actually *tell*
you he'd hired Julia Ortega?''

"In person? No, but there was a letter from him in the
first envelope she sent.''

"Explaining Julia Ortega was working for him? And
you accepted that as valid? Okay, then. This other letter,
the one from Ushton to Hugh about Bobby. When did it
come?''

"Right after lunch today.''

"Was there anything else with it?''

"Just a note from the Ortega woman.''

"Was the note dated?''

"Ah...yes, it had today's date. Why?''

Captain Murtaugh was shaking his head. "Machiavelli
is alive and well and living in Manhattan.''

"Rita,'' Marian said softly, "you *have* met Julia Ortega.
She was the cleaning woman your brother found going
through your checkbook.''

"What?''

"And she couldn't have written that note or sent you
that letter this afternoon. Julia Ortega has been dead for
four days.''

She looked frightened. "Dead?''

"She was murdered.'' Marian let that sink in and then
said, "Tell me—have you ever seen Bradford Ushton's
letterhead stationery before the envelope arrived today?''

The first dawning of doubt appeared in her eyes.

"I...I think so. But who remembers letterheads?''

"Think it through. Say Ushton and Hugh did have such
an agreement as the letter claims they did. Is either one of

them such an utter fool as to put it in writing? And on letterhead stationery yet? Well?''

Rita Galloway's face crumpled. ''It…it isn't true?''

''You never questioned it at all? You never stopped to think how improbable it was? No, you didn't. Instead, your first instinct was to reach for a gun. Rita, you were manipulated into killing your husband, and you followed your cues perfectly.'' Marian stood up, disheartened by the ugliness of what had happened. ''Bobby was in no danger from Ushton. He likes boys six or seven years older than your son. Where's the letter?''

She had to repeat the question twice before the other woman heard her. ''It's in my purse.'' Like a sleepwalker, she got up and started looking for it.

''Where's her purse?'' Murtaugh asked the uniformed officer. He didn't know.

O'Toole said, ''Bring Dorian Yates in for questioning?''

Marian said yes. ''Go to Bradford Ushton's office first and get a sample of his letterhead stationery. When you get back to the station, call in Perlmutter, Walker, and Dowd.''

Rita asked, ''What's going to happen?''

''Right now we're going to look for your purse. Then we're taking you downtown, where you'll be charged with first-degree murder. Your lawyer will be there shortly.''

O'Toole left on his assignments. Marian and the captain started asking the bluesuits about the purse. The Crime Scene Unit had it; they'd found it under the conference table in the room where Rita had shot Hugh. The contents had all been bagged and itemized; Murtaugh held the plastic envelope by the edges while he and Marian read the letter that had sent Rita Galloway off to kill her husband. The letter said exactly what she'd told them it said.

''Ten to one Rita Galloway's lawyer knows nothing about all this,'' Murtaugh said, discouraged.

''No bet,'' Marian responded in the same tone. ''Dorian

Yates is just another patsy that's been offered up to us. Our killer wouldn't write a letter saying 'I hired Julia Ortega'—that's tantamount to a confession of murder. We need to ask Rita Galloway about those other envelopes Ortega is supposed to have sent.''

"Maybe she did send some of them.'' Murtaugh was scowling. "But either using Ortega or acting on his own, the killer kept sending envelopes to Rita until he finally hit on the one thing that would prod her into action. A threat to Bobby's well-being.''

"Yep. Makes you wonder how much of the trouble between Rita and Hugh was real and how much was fabricated by the killer.''

The captain looked at her. "That's a thought.'' He considered for a moment. "Does Rita have a lover?''

Marian shrugged. "Hugh said she slept around.''

"But Hugh can't be considered a reliable source of information as far as his estranged wife is concerned. We know the killer is male, though, so unless Hugh swung both ways, it would have to be *her* lover. A jealous lover—yes, that would fit. A lover who got in over his head with his machinations. A lover who had to resort to murder when things got out of hand.''

"And kidnapping Bobby—that was just one more way to fan the flames? Could be. Okay, we'll get on it.'' Marian checked her watch. "Would you take Rita in and book her? I want to get to Walter Galloway before the news breaks. Oh yeah, that's another thing…what do we tell the news people downstairs?''

"*You* tell them there'll be no statement until the next of kin is notified. Then say there'll be a media announcement at…make it six-thirty.''

"Oh gawd.''

"Part of the job. Go ahead—I'll take care of Rita.''

AT SUTTON PLACE, Marian was told Mr. Walter Galloway was taking a nap and was not to be disturbed. She had to threaten the manservant with arrest before he'd go wake the old man up.

Galloway was out of sorts at having his sleep interrupted. Marian had been left waiting in the entrance hallway; the old man came up to her smoothing down his hair with one hand and leaning on a cane with the other. "What is it, Lieutenant? I already told Detective Dowd everything I know about that ridiculous list of *suspects*." He made the last word into a joke.

"It's not about that, Mr. Galloway. Is there someplace we could sit down?"

"If we sit down, you'll stay longer. What do you want?"

All right, then. "It's bad news, I'm afraid," she said.

The old man paled. "Bobby. Something's happened to Bobby."

"No, Bobby's fine. It's Hugh. I'm sorry to have to tell you—but your son is dead."

He stared at her wordlessly, his mouth open. Then he began to sway; the cane slipped from his grasp and clattered to the floor. Marian stepped over quickly and caught him before he could fall. She half carried him into the first room that opened off the hallway and got him seated on a small divan. "Can I get you something? A drink?"

He shook his head. "How did he die?"

Marian braced herself. "Rita shot him."

Walter Galloway's shock instantly turned into rage. "That *evil* woman! That vampire! She sucks Hugh's blood until she can get no more out of him and then she kills him! And you let it happen!"

"Mr. Galloway—"

"You were told what she was! You sat in that room across the hall and listened to Hugh telling you how dangerous she was. And you did nothing! Nothing! That's what comes of putting a woman in charge—you sided with Rita all along, I know you did."

"I didn't side with either of them, Mr.—"

"I should have made some phone calls the minute you walked into this house! You're in over your head, girlie, and now my son is dead because you waffled and dilly-dallied and didn't take action when there was still time to stop her. Well, you're going to pay for this…*Lieutenant.*" He sneered the word. "You can count on that!"

Don't shoot the messenger. "I'm sorry for your loss."

"You're *sorry?* Get out of my house. Get out!"

Marian knew there was no reaching him before his rage had spent itself. She went looking for the manservant who'd let her in and sent him to the room where she'd left Galloway.

She was on her way to the front door when the old man's voice called out, "Wait!"

Marian went back to see what he wanted.

"Where's Bobby now?"

"He's with his uncle."

Galloway growled. "Him! That picture taker's not going to raise *my* grandson! Go on—get out."

She left.

Whew. Galloway's accusation that she'd waffled and dilly-dallied until it was too late—Marian knew it wasn't true; the law did require evidence before she could make an arrest. But it still hurt.

She wondered if Alex Fairchild had finished taking his pictures in Central Park; the light was still good. Marian checked her notebook and dialed first his home number and then his business number; the same answering service took both calls. *Mr. Fairchild is on a shoot.*

Marian turned the car uptown and entered the park at East Seventy-second. The first thing she saw at the boat-house was Bobby playing on the dock with two little girls, all three of them watched over by Bobby's bodyguard and the girls' mother. But the shoot was more than just Fairchild and a camera looking for interesting faces; he'd brought a couple of assistants and heavy batteries and extra lights to get rid of shadows where he didn't want them. It looked like some sort of commercial job; a small group of onlookers had gathered, willing to be entertained by whatever they came across.

But not one professional model was in sight; Marian remembered Fairchild's mentioning his aversion to working with models. As she watched, he drew a pair of teenagers out from the small crowd watching and put them in the picture. He ran off a series of shots of the girl laughing good-naturedly at the boy's awkwardness as he climbed into a rowboat. The final picture would be natural and charming, a far cry from the photographer's usual street scenes.

"Marian!" He'd spotted her, and motioned her to come over.

She went up to where he was changing cameras on a tripod. "What's all this?"

"All this is paying the bills, that's what all this is. The Parks Commission wants some 'people-oriented' shots of fun things to do, for next year's tourism brochures. They got special funding from somewhere, so the money's good. And this kind of thing is a nice change of pace once in a while."

"Mr. Fairchild, I need to speak to you privately."

An exaggerated sigh. "What do I have to do to get you to call me Alex?"

"All right, Alex. I need to talk to you."

"Okay, I'm almost finished with this setup and—"

"Now. It's urgent."

This time he heard her. He called out some instructions to one of his assistants and led her around the boathouse out of earshot. "What's wrong?"

As gently as she could, she told him what his sister had done.

Fairchild turned into a zombie, plodding a few steps one way, a few steps back, stunned with disbelief. Marian turned away, to give him a little privacy.

Eventually he regained enough control to croak out a question. "Where is she now?"

Marian turned back to face him. "Right now she's at Midtown South, being charged. We're bringing her lawyer in. Then she'll go to Riker's Island to wait for trial."

"But why? Why'd she go after Hugh now? I thought they'd reached a kind of temporary truce." His head snapped up. "Bobby. Oh my god, how am I going to tell Bobby? Both his parents gone—oh god."

"Does he understand about death?"

"He knows things die. I'm not sure he understands that also happens to people he loves. Maybe he does."

"Then tell him the truth. Tell him his father is dead and his mother has to go away for a while. Don't tell him the why of it yet."

He was nodding. "Yes, I'd better not lie to him. Oh, he's so very young! It looks as if I'm going to be mother and father both."

Marian hesitated. "Walter Galloway is going to claim Bobby. He doesn't want you to have him."

Fairchild's jaw set. "Well, we'll just see about that. I'll not let Bobby be brought up by servants—that's what would happen in that old buzzard's house."

She followed when Fairchild went back to where his assistants were waiting with his equipment. He told them to pack everything up; they were finished for the day. Then he rented a rowboat and called to Bobby to come for a ride.

Marian stood on the dock and watched as they rowed out onto the lake. When they were a little way out, Fairchild shipped the oars and started speaking to his nephew.

After a moment, Bobby's thin wail carried across the water, and the boy started flailing at his uncle with his small fists. Fairchild gathered him into his arms and held him.

From where she was standing Marian couldn't be sure, but it looked as if they both were crying.

EIGHTEEN

"SO THE TWO duelists took each other out of the game," Captain Murtaugh said, "and now the seconds are taking up the fight?"

"Looks like it," Marian replied. "Neither Walter Galloway nor Alex Fairchild wants the other to raise Bobby. They're Bobby's only remaining relatives—the courts are going to have to settle this one. Rita will get out of prison eventually, but Bobby will be grown by then."

They were in the cubicle adjoining an interrogation room, watching through the one-way glass as Perlmutter and O'Toole questioned Rita Galloway. "The wisdom of Solomon," Murtaugh murmured.

"What?"

"The story of the two women who came to Solomon, both claiming to be the mother of the same baby? Solomon suggested cutting the baby in two and giving half to each woman. The false mother agreed, but the real mother gave up her claim rather than let the baby be harmed. Didn't Rita Galloway just do something like that? Give up her baby to protect him?"

"Hmm, I always thought that Solomon story sounded a bit phony myself, but I see what you're getting at. But I don't know whether Rita was making a noble sacrifice or just acting on impulse. If she'd stopped to think, she'd have hired a hit man to get Hugh instead of letting a roomful of people watch her pull the trigger."

Murtaugh looked at his watch. "It's six twenty-five."

"Shit." Marian hurried to the ladies' room where she gave her face a good dusting with powder to take away the shine but didn't bother with anything else. Then she went to face the cameras and the reporters.

She told them that artist Rita Galloway had been arrested for the fatal shooting of her estranged husband, Hugh Galloway, president and CEO of Galloway Industries. There was no question as to her guilt, as the shooting was done in full view of seven witnesses. The charge was murder one, as Mrs. Galloway had demonstrated intent by bringing a loaded weapon with her.

As for motive, Mrs. Galloway was acting on false information that made her think Mr. Galloway was a threat to the safety of their son. But the case was not closed. The police were currently seeking the person who provided her with the false information—the same person who was responsible for the deaths of Nick Atlay and Julia Ortega.

That last statement triggered an explosion of questions, all of the reporters yelling at once. Marian ducked the question of whether they had a suspect or not and said instead that they were pursuing several lines of inquiry. She gave no more details than those in her original statement; and when the reporters started repeating themselves, she ended it and left.

Captain Murtaugh was gone from the cubicle adjoining the interrogation room by the time Marian got back. Once Rita Galloway fully understood that someone had been pulling her strings and that she had made a dreadful mistake in shooting Hugh, she'd gone into a blue funk that she still hadn't pulled out of. But she was cooperating, waiving her right to have an attorney present during questioning and trying to answer every query put to her.

Yes, she'd had a lover, last year, a man who'd moved to Seattle seven or eight months ago and whom she hadn't seen since. No, there'd been no one else since him...or before him, as a matter of fact. And yes, Hugh had found out about it. As to Hugh's charge that she slept with everything that wore trousers, she said tiredly that was just

Hugh's bruised ego talking. If he could turn her into a tramp, then he wouldn't feel *personally* betrayed.

The door to the cubicle opened and Dowd stepped inside. "This Dorian Yates don't know nothing, Lieutenant," he said without preamble. "Me and Walker think he was set up." The two detectives had been questioning Rita's attorney, the one the police were now supposed to think had hired Julia Ortega.

"You're sure he's not just a good actor?" Marian asked.

"Naw, this guy's scared shitless. He says he never heard of Nick Atlay or Julia Ortega before he read their names in the paper, and he didn't know who Hector Vargas was. We believe him, Lieutenant. The guy's a rabbit. He'd never have the nerve to plan a homicide, much less carry it through. Besides, Yates just came back from Boston today, got in around noon. Didn't Rita Galloway say the envelope was delivered shortly after lunch? That's cuttin' it pretty close."

Marian nodded; she and Captain Murtaugh both had already more or less discounted Dorian Yates as a viable suspect. He *had* been set up to take the fall for the real killer, a new scapegoat brought in at the eleventh hour to divert the police into a false line of investigation. But the setup itself had too many holes in it; the plan smacked of haste, of desperation. Maybe the police were closer to the truth than they realized?

"What about Bradford Ushton's letterhead stationery? Did O'Toole get a sample?"

"Oh…yeah, he did. And it's not the same as the letterhead on that letter Rita Galloway got about Hugh promising the kid to Ushton. The killer just went to a printer and had something official looking made up. After all that news coverage, Ushton made a good boogeyman."

"All right," she said. "Let's waste no more time on Dorian Yates. Take him into Rita's interrogation room and let him be a defense attorney instead of a suspect."

Dowd grinned. "He don't wanna. He's a divorce lawyer, Lieutenant, he don't know beans about defending a homicide. He says the best thing he can do for Rita Galloway is find her a good criminal attorney."

"Then tell him to find her one fast. We can't get her to sign a statement until she has legal counsel. And I want you to check the messenger service that delivered those envelopes to Rita. It's probably another dead end, but check it out anyway. Where's Walker?"

"In the can."

"Get him and tell him to look in Rita's room at her brother's place for those other envelopes she received. He won't need a warrant—Fairchild will cooperate."

"Right." He hesitated a moment and then asked, "Are we getting close, Lieutenant?"

"I think we may be." Dowd gave a grunt of satisfaction and left.

Marian turned her attention back to the interrogation room. Perlmutter and O'Toole had finished with the accusatory part of their questioning and were now trying to elicit from Rita every detail of the matter she could think of, whether it proved relevant or not. Rita herself looked on the point of exhaustion, but she was still making an effort to give her questioners what they wanted. Marian didn't like feeling sorry for murderers, but she was beginning to feel sorry for Rita Galloway.

"MUCH BETTER this time," Holland said later as he clicked off the eleven o'clock news. "You looked preoccupied with your case and not worried about the impression you were making on the reporters, as if giving them their news was only a small courtesy you were observing. Which is the only way to treat those people. You spoke with authority and to the point. You're getting the hang of it."

Marian groaned. She'd stretched out on her stomach

across Holland's lap to watch the news. "I resented the time it took to tell them even that little bit. I wanted to get back to Rita's interrogation."

"But you did your duty like a good little cop."

"'A good little cop'?" She bit his knee. "Don't you call me a *good little cop*."

"I will if it makes you nibble on my knees. Hey! Ouch!"

Detective Walker had found three envelopes in Rita's room at Alec Fairchild's apartment. One was a "report" alleging Hugh dallied with prostitutes. Another claimed he was free-basing cocaine. The third purported to be some kind of bank report showing Hugh was diverting money from Bobby's educational trust fund to the account of a woman Hugh was supposedly setting up in a luxury apartment. But even that failed to stir Rita to action.

It was only when the papers broke the story of Bradford Ushton's arrest on a charge of child molestation that the killer had hit on the one thing that would send Rita off on her murderous mission.

Detective Dowd had had to track down the day manager of the messenger service, but he came back with some answers. The first three envelopes had been brought in by Julia Ortega, using her own name. The fourth and fatal one had arrived by ordinary U.S. Mail, with a twenty enclosed to pay for the messenger's delivery. The manager said it wasn't his place to wonder why the sender hadn't just mailed the envelope straight to the addressee.

Marian said, "Murtaugh thinks the killer is a disgruntled lover who set out to destroy the Galloways' marriage and then got in over his head and had to kill to protect himself. But the only lover Rita admits to has been living in Seattle since last year."

"I imagine he's heard of airplanes," Holland remarked.

"Yeah, I'll have to check that tomorrow. I suppose it's *possible* to engineer a kidnapping and a firebombing and two murders—three, counting Hugh's—all the way from the other side of the country. But I don't believe it. No, our killer's right here in New York."

"So it isn't Rita's lover."

"Or else she has another lover she hasn't told us about." Marian reached over and turned out the light. "Frankly, I'd just like to forget about all of them for a while, all the Galloways and Julia Ortega and poor dumb Nickie Atlay. I don't want to do anything but sleep."

"Aw," said Holland.

THE NEXT DAY she phoned the Seattle police and asked their help in tracking down Rita Galloway's former lover. The return call came less than half an hour later. The man she was asking about had been hit by some collapsing scaffolding at a construction site and had been in a coma for the past two weeks.

"Well, you can't beat that for an alibi," Captain Murtaugh commented when she told him. "But maybe Rita Galloway tossed us a past lover to keep us from looking for a present one."

"I'll put Perlmutter and O'Toole on it," Marian said, "but I think she was telling us the truth, that the man in Seattle was the only lover she had. She's trying to atone, Jim. I don't think she really regrets Hugh's death, but she does regret killing him."

"A fine distinction. I wonder if the jury will be impressed." He cocked an eye at her. "You don't think it's a lover, do you?"

She made a vague gesture with both hands. "I think it's a very reasonable explanation...*if* we find Rita has been holding out on us. If she does have another lover tucked away somewhere, he'll be our suspect, all right. But right now I'm more worried about what the killer will do next."

Murtaugh scowled. "He's not finished?"

"Well, look at all the elaborate plans he's made to keep

his identity hidden. He did his dirty deeds through Nickie Atlay and Julia Ortega and then got rid of them before they could become a problem. Next Bradford Ushton appears on the scene—although I don't see how the killer could have had a hand in that. But then when Rita shot Hugh, we were supposed to think she was behind everything that's happened. And if that didn't work, he had a backup plan in place that would hand us her lawyer—Dorian Yates—as the big bad killer. So what happens? Last night I go on television and say the case is *not* closed. You think he's going to let it rest there? No, he'll try something more. He has to. He can't leave it alone."

The captain swore. "That," he said heavily, "is bad. But how much further can he go without making a slip? He must be getting desperate by now."

"I wonder. At first I thought all that rigamarole about sending those false reports to Rita was an act of desperation. But now I'm not so sure."

"Meaning?"

"Meaning I think he's enjoying himself."

He looked at her gloomily. "You don't know how *much* I hope you're wrong."

Marian sighed. "Me too. But he's committed two murders and manipulated a third…and got away with all three. He must be feeling pretty pleased with himself along about now."

"The lists of possible suspects that Hugh and Rita drew up—anything there?"

"Not yet. Walker and Dowd have eliminated only one name so far, a man who was out of the country when Nickie Atlay was killed. They're still working on it."

"Dammit, we need a line on him!" Murtaugh growled. "Before he does something else."

But it was not to be. At eleven o'clock Marian got a call from Annie Plaxton in Hoboken, saying her laundromat had been firebombed.

NINETEEN

HOLLAND WRAPPED UP an informal meeting with the two investigators he'd assigned to a fugitive case, an embezzler whom they were tracking electronically through the movement of the money he'd stolen. The embezzler had gone about it the right way, siphoning off relatively small amounts at a time and transferring the funds to new accounts, which he kept moving from bank to bank all over the world. But now two of the accounts had come together in one bank in Mexico City; the embezzler was running short of cash. If he drew upon the Mexico City account, they had him.

On his way back to his office, Holland paused to look in on André Flood. The faint sound of hard rock leaked out of the earphones the young man wore as he worked. André had not taken the full week Holland had given him to decide whether he wanted to stay with Chris Carnell or not; he'd resigned at the end of the first day.

In the reception area, Mrs. Grainger was signing for a package. "This is for you, Mr. Holland."

It was an ordinary mailing bag. Holland took it into his office and pulled the tab on the back: a videotape, no label. He slipped the cassette into the VCR.

And found himself watching Marian. Getting out of her car somewhere in Manhattan. Looking in a store window. One brief shot of her having lunch with Gloria Sanchez. Standing in front of the station talking to Murtaugh. Picking up her dry cleaning. The picture wobbled once in a while and occasionally the top of Marian's head was cut off; but the camera must have had an autofocus feature because the images were crisp and clear. Marian was wearing different clothing in the various vignettes, so the tape must have been made over a series of days.

Holland felt a vein pulsing in his temple. *Marian was being stalked.*

Then Holland was looking at himself. It started with a long shot of the two of them at the outdoor café near Lincoln Center where they'd gone for lunch on Saturday. Then the camera zoomed in on Marian talking on her phone. The lens moved over to Holland, showing him slowly savoring his food as he watched Marian. Whoever had done the taping had followed them into the park, capturing them watching the mime and then, a little later, in a more intimate moment when they thought they were alone.

The last pictures were of Marian coming out of the Galloway Building and telling the reporters gathered at the entrance that there would be no statement until the next of kin had been notified.

Then, after a break, the camera lingered on what looked like a large poster board with a message stenciled on it: *If you want to see her alive again, you're going to have to do something for me. Something big. Take the subway to Coney Island, this afternoon. Do not drive your car, do not take a cab. Be there by five o'clock. Go to The Hurricane and wait by the entrance. If you are not alone, she's dead.*

Holland whipped around and grabbed the phone. He called Midtown South and asked for the captain. ''Murtaugh, it's Holland. Where's Marian? *Right this very minute.*''

''This very minute? On her way to Hoboken. She left about ten minutes ago. What—''

Holland broke the connection and punched out Marian's cell phone number. He got a recorded voice telling him the number he was trying to reach was temporarily outside the service area.

But that was the standard recording used whenever there was no answer; it could mean anything from a dead battery to to a sabotaged handset. And if Marian had left Midtown South only ten minutes ago, she wouldn't have had time to reach one of the tunnels yet; she'd still be inside the service area.

He called Murtaugh back. "Call out your troops—there still may be time to stop it."

"Stop what?"

"Stop Marian from being abducted," he said.

THE TWO MEN stood in Holland's office watching the tape. The patrol cars Murtaugh had dispatched to the entrances of both the Lincoln Tunnel and the Holland Tunnel had failed to spot Marian's car. A phone call to the Hoboken police confirmed that she'd not showed up at Annie Plaxton's laundromat on Meegat Street.

They'd been too late.

"You can't go meet him alone," Murtaugh said when the tape had finished.

"Of course I have to go alone," Holland snapped. "The only reason I called you was that there was still a chance of preventing the abduction. But from this point on, the police are out of it."

The captain shot him an odd look. "Do you really think we're going to step aside because you say so? She may be your Marian, but she's also my lieutenant. I want you wearing a wire—"

"That's the first thing he'd look for. He's not sloppy— he's been planning this for a while. That tape covers several days."

"All the more reason to proceed with caution. But all right, no wire—you may be right. We'll have police inside the booths all the way to the entrance to The Hurricane."

Holland shook his head. "It's a long ride to Coney Island, even on the subway. There's no time to set something up even if that were the right way to go about it.''

"I've already set it up. The minute you told me what was on this tape. They're on their way now."

Holland flared. "Just what we need—a bunch of heavy-handed cops spooking this guy before we find out where Marian is!"

"Give us some credit," Murtaugh answered mildly. "They know not to reveal themselves. And they'll follow him after the meet, whether he drives or takes a cab or rides the subway. We'll get him and find Marian both."

"It's too risky," Holland argued. "Let me meet him and find out what it is he wants me to do. That alone will give us a clue to his identity. And there's always the chance that I already know him."

"What's risky is your going in without backup. This is a police operation now, Holland, and we're going to do it by the book." He popped the tape out of the VCR and slipped it into his jacket pocket. "Just keep in mind that once you leave the subway station, you'll never be out of sight of the police all the way to the roller coaster."

Holland didn't like it, but he could do nothing but accept it. "And where will you be? Selling ice cream to the kiddies?"

"I'll be there, but you won't see me." Murtaugh looked at his watch. "I'm going now. Wait another fifty minutes before you leave. That should get you there close to five o'clock. He started out but turned at the door. "Holland...good luck."

Holland nodded, said nothing.

HE WALKED the entire length of the subway train twice during the long ride to Coney Island, but he saw no familiar faces among the other passengers. That proved nothing, however. Holland didn't know all the detectives under

Marian's command; Murtaugh could easily have put someone on the train with him.

Holland had been with the FBI long enough to come to
understand what was derogatorily referred to as the police
mentality. That need to *nail* a perp sometimes grew so
strong it overrode all other considerations, including the
safety of the innocent; it became a compulsion. He'd seen
it happen time and again, both among federal agents and
municipal police. He simply didn't share Murtaugh's faith
that all the men and women at the stakeout in Coney Island
would keep their cool.

He preferred to rely on his own assessment of the situation, but that didn't mean walking into danger unprepared. In the shoulder holster under his jacket was a .38,
and strapped to his ankle was a .22; it was the first time
since he'd left the FBI that he'd carried a weapon. If the
meet stayed out in the open, he would need neither gun.
If he was frisked elsewhere, perhaps the smaller gun would
be overlooked. But he had no intention of meeting a potential killer unarmed.

The ride seemed interminable, but it did finally end.
Holland stepped off the train and paused, automatically
checking out the ground-level station. It was crowded, but
not overly so. One man was elbowing his way frantically
toward the men's room. Two women were talking in ov-
erloud voices. Two muscular young Hispanic street toughs
stood bracketing the steps leading down to the street.

Warning bells. The two Hispanics were glancing over
the disembarking passengers with a studied casualness that
would fool no one who was really looking. Yet their eyes
slid right over him, as if he weren't even there. Holland
was prosperous looking and he was alone; he should be at
least one object of their attention. They were only pre-
tending not to have noticed him.

He swore to himself. *I don't have time for a mugging
now!* It was almost five. *The Hurricane, five o'clock.*

He fell in with the small crowd pushing toward the exit stairway. He timed it so that at the last minute he could break into a run and dart between the two young Hispanics and on down the stairway. When the moment was right, he made his move.

And got past them! He whirled to face them, .38 in hand. They both froze on the top step, watching him. "That's right," Holland said with ice in his voice. "Stay like that and you won't get hurt."

He started backing down the stairway. A middle-aged man myopically pushed his way between the two Hispanics and on down past Holland, unaware of the gun or anything else. A flicker in the eyes of one of the muggers warned Holland; but by the time he turned, the two who'd been waiting at the bottom of the stairs had jumped him.

Among the four of them, they managed to get the .38 away from him—almost breaking Holland's arm in the process. He lashed out with fists and feet and prayed his assailants weren't carrying knives. The other passengers screamed and jostled one another in their haste to get out of the way. No one rushed to help.

It was hard to get a good footing on the steps, so his four attackers eventually were able to wrestle him down on his back. "Hey, stop fightin', man," one of them panted. "We gotcha."

Holland was aware only of the time ticking away. "All right," he said quickly. "Take what you want. Inside jacket pocket—wallet."

"Why, thank you, man," the talking one said. He took the wallet. He also took Holland's watch. "But we already got what we came for. We got *you*. Get up. You comin' with us."

Suddenly they were all four holding knives.

Holland got slowly to his feet, trying to think. *They could have cut me at any time—what's going on?* He faked a stumble and made a run for it.

They caught him before he reached the street. He couldn't get to his .22, but he twisted his body and used elbows and knees and felt himself making some headway until a searing pain tore through his head, his vision dimmed, and he blacked out.

CONSCIOUSNESS RETURNED slowly. By inches.

At first he was aware only of several blurs of light around him, yellow and indistinct. He closed his eyes but quickly opened them again; the temptation to yield to sleep was too strong. He wondered if he was concussed.

He was lying facedown, his right cheek resting on a hard surface that was rough and gravelly. Something—a pebble?—was pressing against his temple. He tried moving his head; the pain that exploded in his skull forced him to lie completely still for several minutes.

When the pain began to subside, he tried again. This time he managed to pull his head far enough back to free himself of...not a pebble, but something metal that his temple had been lying on. He scraped his cheek on the rough surface but barely felt it. He lay with the small metal object only inches from his eyes, *willing* it to assume a recognizable shape. Eventually it did: a bottle cap. As he watched, it seemed to grow, and grow, and grow...

Despite his best effort not to, Holland slipped away into sleep.

When he woke again, his first thought was: *Marian!* He'd missed the five o'clock meet. His breath came short; had he signed Marian's death warrant? What would Murtaugh have done when he didn't show? Why was he here and where was "here" anyway? Was Marian nearby? Was she still alive? He drifted off again trying to puzzle it out.

The third time he woke his vision had cleared; the bottle cap was only a bottle cap, old and rusty. The blurs of yellow light had resolved themselves into lanterns, four of them, placed in a semicircle around him. Beyond the fee-

ble light cast by the lanterns lay solid darkness. The floor
he was stretched out on was cement, covered with litter
and filth.

He'd been lying on his hands and they too were hurting
now. Slowly and cautiously he eased over onto his side.
But when he tried to use his hands to help push himself
up to a sitting position, he found they wouldn't separate.
He brought his wrists up to eye level, and saw they'd been
manacled.

The manacles were attached to a thick chain. Wonder-
ingly, Holland followed the chain hand over hand to its
other end: an iron ring set in the cement wall behind him.

He opened his mouth and roared out his anger and frustration, setting off another explosion in his head. But in
spite of his pain and the beginnings of despair, one part
of his mind noted the four quick echoes that followed his
cry of rage. *This place is cavernous.*

He used the chain to pull himself shakily to his feet. In
the yellow light he could make out that the iron ring in
the wall was new, and the cement immediately around it
was clean and a lighter gray than the rest of the wall.
Holding on to the chain with both hands, he got both feet
up flat against the wall and pulled with his whole weight.
The iron ring didn't budge.

The effort took a lot out of him. He leaned against the
wall and closed his eyes. When the jackhammer in his
head started to slow down, he opened his eyes and looked
around. From his new vantage point, he could see over the
tops of the four lanterns placed on the ground; and what
he saw was a mound of something behind each lantern.

He moved as close to the lanterns as the length of chain
would let him, but he still couldn't quite make out what
was piled behind them. He used his foot to push one lantern a little farther out. The yellow light finally revealed
what had been concealed in shadow: Holland looked on

the peacefully slack face of the young thug who'd taken his watch and wallet.

As quickly as he could manage, Holland moved the other three lanterns. They were all there, all four of his attackers.

And all four of them had been shot.

TWENTY

"I HAD CAR TROUBLE," Marian had explained to Captain Murtaugh. "*And* my phone wouldn't work. But the garage said the fuel line had been cut, clean through. So I left the car there for them to put in a new one and took a bus to Hoboken."

When she'd finally arrived, late in the afternoon, at the laundromat on Meegat Street, Annie Plaxton told her the Hoboken police had been there looking for her. Annie's phones had been taken out by the firebombing—which was more extensive than that at Rita Galloway's house on East Seventy-fifth—so Marian had gone to the nearest Hoboken police station. A few phone calls and she learned Murtaugh and most of her detectives were in Coney Island trying to rescue *her*.

Even riding the bus, she got back to Midtown South before the others. The garage where she'd left the car was closed for the day, so she had to take a cab for the last leg of her journey.

Murtaugh had shouted *"Where the hell have you been?"* when he first heard her voice on his phone.

"In Hoboken," she'd replied with a touch of irritation, still not knowing what had happened. "Just where I said I was going."

Murtaugh ordered her to stay in the stationhouse, not even to stick her nose out-of-doors until they got back. So she waited until they all returned from Coney Island, arguing among themselves, confusion and tension thick in the air.

Then they told her the bad news.

Marian's stomach started to churn when she heard Holland had been taken. Murtaugh allowed her a little recovery time, but not much; he expected her to act like a cop no matter how much she was hurting. Marian resented his demand even while acknowledging it was the best thing he could do for her. She washed her face with cold water and went downstairs to the briefing room.

"The whole thing was an elaborate setup," Murtaugh was saying. "The firebombing in Hoboken was done for one reason only—to get Lieutenant Larch out of the way during the crucial time. Our Mr. Machiavelli even sabotaged her car and her phone to slow her down, to delay her return to the station even longer. Then he sent Curt Holland a videotape he'd made of the two of them over several days' time, to show he could get close to them when he wanted to. Yes, Sergeant?"

"Is this a new case?" Buchanan wanted to know. "Or is it connected to somethin' we're already workin' on?"

"It's the Galloway case," Murtaugh answered. "The laundromat in Hoboken that was firebombed is connected to the Galloway killings. As I just told you, the firebombing was a diversionary tactic, to draw Lieutenant Larch out of Manhattan so the killer could make Holland and the rest of us think she'd been abducted."

"Who is this guy Holland anyway?" one of the detectives asked.

Murtaugh looked at Marian. She stood up and said, "He's my personal friend. The Galloway killer invaded my private life and took the single most important person there to use as a hostage." She had nothing more to add and so sat back down.

"You must be gettin' close," Buchanan remarked.

The detective who'd asked the question nodded, satisfied now that he had a label for Holland. The other detectives in the room who didn't know Holland—which was most of them—sneaked looks at her back over their shoulders.

Murtaugh continued. "The killer gave instructions on the tape for a meet…phony instructions, as it turned out."

"Ransom demand?" someone asked.

"Of a sort. The killer said, 'If you want to see her alive again, you're going to have to do something for me. Something big.'"

"Jesus." Marian recognized O'Toole's voice.

"Something big…like what?" Sergeant Campos asked. "What kind of work does Holland do?"

"Holland is a former FBI agent who's now a licensed private detective with his own agency, on Lexington," Murtaugh replied. "You'll not have crossed his path because most of his work has to do with electronic crime. Almost all of the investigators on his staff are computer detectives. Holland probably assumed he was needed to perform some computer wizardry—I know that's what I thought. But that was all part of the ploy. The idea was to make Holland think that Lieutenant Larch had been abducted as a way of getting to him, when in fact it was just the other way around."

"So what went wrong?" Marian asked.

A number of things had gone wrong, beginning with a couple of those small unforeseeable incidents that can alter a carefully planned operation in the blink of an eye. Captain Murtaugh had told Sergeant Buchanan to assign two of his detectives to ride the subway with Holland. The meet at the entrance to The Hurricane might be a blind (as indeed it turned out to be); Murtaugh thought that the killer's insistence on Holland's taking the subway might mean contact would be made on the train.

So Buchanan had put a man named Provine and a woman named Grant on the job. But before the train had even left Manhattan, a crazy high on crack boarded, shouting evangelical pronouncements and slashing out wildly with a knife. He'd cut one woman and was going after another when Provine and Grant overpowered him. But even without his knife, the crazy was still dangerous; they couldn't kick him loose, and the woman he'd cut needed medical attention. So Grant got off at the next stop, supporting the bleeding woman with one hand and hanging on to the cuffed crazy with the other.

Holland had known nothing about all that; it had happened four or five cars away from where he was riding. After Holland had checked out the entire subway train twice, Provine moved to the car adjoining Holland's where he could keep an eye on him. But the constant swaying of the train during the long ride began to make the detective feel queasy. The farther they traveled, the sicker he got. Soon Provine was sweating profusely and his skin was hot; then his stomach started cramping.

Whether it was food poisoning or a virus, it effectively took Provine out of the action. The minute the train pulled into the Coney Island station, Provine made a dash for the men's room, where he spent a good five minutes throwing up.

By the time he came out, the station was virtually empty. But two passengers who'd witnessed the assault were still there; they told Provine about the fight on the exit stairway and how four Hispanics had dragged an unconscious man away.

Provine ventured the opinion that Holland must have put up one hell of a fight. He'd found fresh blood on the steps.

Marian bit her lip.

"Tossing your cookies may have saved your life, Provine," Murtaugh said. "It still would have been a two-to-one fight. But the odds against Holland were four to one." The captain let his anger show. And Provine still looked as if he should be home in bed.

When Provine informed Murtaugh of what had happened, the captain immediately launched a search of all the exits and the parking areas. But they weren't in time. Holland and his abductors were long gone.

They were just regrouping after their futile search when Murtaugh got a call from Marian wanting to know what everyone was doing in Coney Island.

"We've got a team still in the Coney Island area doing a house-to-house," Murtaugh said, "looking for anyone who might have seen four Hispanics carrying an unconscious man. They had to have a car waiting somewhere. Also, we're going to put Holland's picture on TV and ask anyone who's seen him since five o'clock today to get in touch with us immediately." The captain looked around the room. "All right, anything else?"

No one could think of anything. The meeting broke up, but Murtaugh motioned to Marian to wait. Perlmutter murmured *Sorry, Lieutenant* as he passed. Walker gave her a grim thumbs-up.

Murtaugh told her, "I'll need a photo of Holland."

"I don't have one," she said.

They used clips from the videotape. A little after eleven that night Marian sat in Holland's living room and looked at his image on the big television. There was the zoom shot of him at the sidewalk café, followed by a section showing him with her in the park. They were standing and watching something off-camera, probably the mime. Holland had one arm draped casually across her shoulders. The last thing displayed was a freeze-frame enlargement of his face alone. He was laughing, and he looked happy.

Every cell in Marian's body ached.

The story got a big play because the abducted man was so obviously the S.O. of a police lieutenant. It would get an even bigger play once the TV reporters had time to discover what a moneymaking machine Holland's agency was.

She got up and wandered through the apartment, frustrated by being so helpless and outraged that such a thing should happen to Holland. She deliberately fed her frustration and outrage; it was a way of avoiding the thought that she might never see him alive again.

Her wandering took her into Holland's computer room—where she spotted something new. A new table, a new chair…and on the table a new laptop with a bright red ribbon tied around it.

He'd bought her a computer.

She sank down on the chair and buried her head in her arms on the table. It was too much; the dam broke, and all the anguish of the day that she'd been keeping pent up came pouring in. She mourned the loss of her lover, even though the killer needed him alive. For a while. And then…

She had never felt so empty.

After a while, the worst of it passed. Marian raised her head and stared at the silly, splendid big red bow. She slipped the ribbon off the laptop and opened the machine.

She saw a button labeled POWER and pushed it. The screen came to life; lines of type scrolled past too fast for her to read. Several windows opened and closed, until only ten words remained on the screen: *There, that wasn't so hard, was it? Now press* ENTER.

She looked at the keyboard. An oversized key there was marked with ENTER and a bent arrow pointing to the left. Marian pressed it.

A few more windows flickered by and then the screen steadied. Across the top was a row of icons that meant nothing to Marian. Immediately under that was a small window where a cursor was blinking. But most of the screen was taken up by a larger window, which was blank.

Marian waited a few moments but nothing else happened; clearly Holland had meant to be with her when she first tried out her new computer. Because she didn't know what else to do, she turned the machine off. After a brief hesitation, she slipped the ribbon back around the laptop.

A shower—that was what she needed. She took a long

one, shampooing her hair twice. Marian had never spent a night alone in this apartment before. She slipped on a big T-shirt and pulled a light thermal blanket from the bed. Out on the balcony she wrapped the blanket around herself and settled down to listen to the occasional, muted sound of traffic drifting up from below.

She did not think she would sleep much that night.

AS IT TURNED OUT, she managed a little over two hours, awaking shortly after six to a kind of edgy need to be up and doing. The garage where she'd left her car opened at seven; she took a cab there and got her wheels back. Since it was still early, she decided to stop by her own apartment and check her mail before going into the station.

Not so much as a whiff of smoke lingered in the apartment; the place was habitable again. Marian went into the kitchen and turned off the ventilator, which had been left running all this time. Two joined black streaks marred the wall next to the stove. In the sink was a skillet with burned peppers still stuck to the bottom in spite of days of soaking. She threw it out.

Several messages were waiting on her answering machine, one of which surprised her. It was Abigail James, the playwright whose play was being made into a disastrous mess of a movie, according to Kelly.

"Hello, Marian, this is Abby James. I'm back in town. They kicked me off the set. I wasn't even allowed through the studio gates anymore. It's probably just as well. Otherwise you'd be reading a headline that said DISGRUNTLED WRITER KILLS MOVIE DIRECTOR or something to that effect. So I've abandoned Ian and Kelly to their fate—I just couldn't stand it out there any longer. Give me a call, Marian. Talking to someone who has both feet on the ground would do me a world of good."

Oh lord, what timing. At any other time, Marian would have felt flattered. But Abby would have to wait. Marian made a note to call her later from her office, to explain they'd have to postpone their get-together until after…until after.

The mail had piled up during her short absence. In the stack was a mailing bag. It held a videotape, with a label that said only *Watch this when you're alone.*

The temperature dropped. With numb fingers Marian fumbled the tape into the VCR. And cried out at what she saw.

There was Holland, in manacles, chained to a wall—pulling at his chain and roaring at the camera like some feral creature captured in a faraway jungle. She could see his hair matted with blood on the left side of his head. At one point he tried a flying kick; his foot came within inches of the lens and the camera jerked back hastily. The last shot was of a piece of poster board on which ten words has been stenciled: *If you want him back, mark the Galloway case closed.*

Marian clenched her fists and screamed in frustration and fury. She'd assumed he'd be locked away in a room somewhere, maybe even tied up. But who would imagine that he'd be *chained* to a *wall*? What kind of person were they dealing with here? This came very close to torture. The killer was playing, enjoying himself. Laughing at them. Kidnapping Holland wasn't enough; the killer wanted her to see for herself how her lover was being treated. What better way to put pressure on her? Holland was chained to a wall like an animal because of *her*.

For one insane moment she considered doing what the killer demanded. Make up some excuse for the captain, close the case, and get Holland back.

But then reason returned. Trust the killer to keep his word? Sure.

It was the ugliest hazard of her hazardous profession; all law enforcement officers risked retaliation against their loved ones, threats against their families to coerce them into doing or not doing something. Marian was not the first it had happened to, nor would she be the last. There was never one answer as to what to do.

Calm down. When her breathing had returned to normal, she called Jim Murtaugh at home and told him of their Machiavelli's latest move.

TWENTY-ONE

MARIAN DIDN'T HAVE a VCR in her office, so they'd gathered in the captain's office. Besides herself and Murtaugh, Sergeant Campos, Perlmutter, O'Toole, and Walker were there. A special Getting Holland Back task force. Neither Marian nor Murtaugh had wanted Buchanan on the team, and Marian still didn't quite trust Dowd. The six of them watched Holland thrashing about and raging at the unseen man behind the camera.

"If he was less defiant," Walker said, "if he'd just cooperate with his captor—"

"Never happen," Marian and Murtaugh said together.

None of the five men would have admitted it, but they felt vaguely flattered that Lieutenant Larch should trust them to find her Holland. That *Watch this when you're alone* printed on the cassette label meant *Don't tell anyone.* Yet here they all were.

Walker asked, "The cassette's been dusted for prints?"

Murtaugh said it had. "Just smears. He wore gloves." They were all silent a moment, studying the tape.

Campos growled. "There's nothing there to tell us where he is. A cement floor, a wall."

"A basement?" Murtaugh wondered. "A warehouse? It could be anywhere."

"An airplane hangar?" O'Toole suggested.

"A *dirty* cement floor," Perlmutter noted, peering at the screen closely. "Let's try it in slow mo."

Murtaugh manipulated the remote; the tape rewound and started forward again, one frame at a time. The picture dipped a couple of times, showing Holland only from the neck down. "This guy hasn't learned how to use a camcorder," the captain grumbled.

"Can you freeze it?" Perlmutter asked.

Murtaugh stopped the tape. On the TV screen, Holland was pulling at the chain, turned away from the camera, snarling back over his shoulder at the unseen cameraman.

"Just look at all that rubble on the floor," Perlmutter said. "That stuff's been there for years. Wherever this place is, it hasn't been used in a long time."

"An *abandoned* warehouse," Murtaugh said.

"Or an old factory building," Marian added. "A factory that shut down years ago."

"Which tells us," Campos said, "that he ain't in midtown Manhattan. Brooklyn looks good to me. Someplace within easy driving distance of Coney Island."

That made sense to all of them. The captain growled, "We'd need an army of searchers to find it. One thing we have to do is consider doing what he wants, announcing that the Galloway case has been closed."

"Closed!" O'Toole protested.

"*Announcing* it's closed, O'Toole," Murtaugh said impatiently. "It won't *be* closed. Wake up. But even making the announcement might prove dangerous for Holland, since the kidnapper would no longer have a reason to keep him alive. Let's hold that as a last resort. What happens to an old building that's been abandoned for years?"

"City takes it over for back taxes?" Campos ventured.

"If back taxes are owed. Sometimes the owners pay the tax just to hold on to the land. But it's a place to start. Get a list of all city-confiscated warehouses, factories, and so on in Brooklyn. Campos, you're in charge. Divide the list and check 'em out."

Campos nodded. "You heard the man. Let's go."

Marian stood up to follow them out. "I'd better get up to Holland's offices. They're going out of their minds there—they started calling the station as soon as they saw the news last night. And Holland's second-in-command has been here twice.''

"A man named Tuttle?" Murtaugh asked. "I've spoken to him."

"He left word he wants to use the agency to help find Holland."

"But you'll discourage that, right? Before you go..." Murtaugh motioned to her to close the door.

She did, and sat back down again.

He said, "Several years back, I was tracking a freelance hit man who called himself Pluto."

Marian nodded. "I read about it."

"Well, what you didn't read was that Pluto threatened my wife if I didn't back off the case. I was getting too close for his comfort."

She hadn't known that. "What did you do?"

"I got her out of town. But even though I'd made Edie as safe as I could, the fear never really went away. What if he found her? It was like an elevator in my stomach dropping out of control."

"Yes." That's exactly what it was like.

He paused. "I think I would have gone crazy if I'd seen Edie chained to a wall. So I do have an inkling of what it must be like for you. Not to mention the self-recrimination. Edie had to abandon her work and hide in fear of her life because of *my* work. I'll bet you've already accused yourself of putting Holland in danger."

She smiled tightly. "I'm still tussling with that one."

"Marian, don't beat on yourself for something that's beyond the control of all of us. It's wrong, all of it—our jobs shouldn't put the people we care about in jeopardy. But accept the fact that there is no remedy for this problem. None. It's an unresolvable dilemma. Don't waste your energy on it."

Thanks for the pep talk, Captain. But he was just trying to help. "You're right, of course. Don't worry about me,

Jim. I'll be all right." Before he could say anything more, she got up and left.

ONCE AGAIN Holland paced off the extent of his new world. A half-circle exactly fifteen feet from its center to the perimeter. Slightly beyond the perimeter, four lanterns. Slightly beyond the lanterns, four corpses. That maniac who'd nearly blinded him with the light for his camcorder—was he just going to leave them there until they decomposed?

The man himself had never stepped into the light, had never spoken. Before he left, he'd pushed in a plastic bucket with his foot. Then he'd gone without a word, the glow of his flashlight shrinking to a pinpoint before it disappeared completely.

The bucket contained a thermos of water and a ham sandwich. Holland knew what the bucket was for and used it. The sandwich was dry, but the water was delicious. He restrained himself from gulping it all down; there was no telling how long he'd have to make it last.

He took inventory. Both of his guns were gone, including their holsters. And of course his billfold and watch were gone. His jacket was missing; his shirt was dirty and bloodstained, and one sleeve was torn. The pockets of his trousers had been emptied.

Holland searched through every inch of rubble within his half-circle, looking for a wire or something pointed he could use on the locks on the manacles. There was nothing. Grit and bits of pebbles and broken cement, not even a real stone. The only thing that had any potential at all as a weapon was the rusty bottle cap. Holland pocketed it.

His captor had approached from the left, his flashlight visible from a long distance away. Holland could see nothing but darkness over his head; but at one point during the videotaping, the maniac who'd put him here had almost dropped his light and had turned it upward as he caught it. Holland had a glimpse of cement ceiling about twelve or fourteen feet up. He was in a long, low place, then, with no electric power or running water.

He could hear only one sound. Occasionally from the darkness around him came a stirring, a rustling. Rats.

A wave of drowsiness came over him. He tried to shake it off; he needed to have a plan for the next time his captor visited. Assuming there was a next time. He needed a way to make the other man approach him...

Holland's body was suddenly so heavy that he sank to his knees. He could feel the heaviness spreading outward from his center even to his fingers and toes. The water...the bastard had put something into the water.

He swayed on his knees a couple of times, and then keeled over.

MRS. GRAINGER had demanded news of Mr. Holland. When Marian had none to give, she reluctantly pointed her toward Bill Tuttle's office. Mr. Tuttle was in charge while Mr. Holland was "away," The Pilgrim said.

Tuttle's office was at the end of the hall. A skinny, balding man with an anxious manner was saying on the phone, "Sorry, Mr. Bayban, but I just can't authorize that big a job... Well, do you have to have an answer right now?...Just as soon as Mr. Holland returns, I give you my word...A few days, a week, I don't know...I'm sorry, Mr. Bayban—that's the best I can do. Yes, I will call you." He hung up and looked worriedly at Marian. "If you're here to apply for a job, you're hired. You can have mine."

"I hope you're joking," Marian said. She introduced herself and Tuttle practically hugged her, he was so glad to see her.

"Any news? Is he all right? Have you heard from the kidnapper? How much ransom will we need?"

She told him that Holland was alive, that they had heard from the man who abducted him, but there had been no ransom demand as yet. She did not tell him there never would be.

"What can we do? How can we help?"

"By not helping. I know you feel you should do something, but you can help us most by staying out of the way."

"We're a detective agency. Me, I do all my detecting at the computer, but we do have operatives on the payroll—"

"Mr. Tuttle—please. You'll only muddy the waters. Keep out of the case, and keep everybody else here out too. You'll just slow us down. You can see that, can't you?" Reluctantly, he nodded. "We are going to get him back," she added with a confidence she was far from feeling. "The best thing you can do for Holland is carry on business as usual."

He ran a hand over his balding head. "But that's a problem too. It's anything but business as usual here. I had to fire one of our investigators this morning. One of the first men Mr. Holland hired when he opened the agency."

"What happened?"

"Well, for a long time we thought someone outside had broken into our system and was indulging in some malicious mischief. Selected files were destroyed. Memos were tampered with—meeting times would be changed so one or two people would always show up late. One woman came in one day to find her hard disk had been wiped clean. It took her two full workdays to restore everything. And phony e-mail was sent out assigning needless tasks. That made it look as if certain people were nonproductive, just wasting time."

"And it was all the work of this man you fired?"

"Yeah. He was deliberately trying to make the other investigators look bad. It was his way of gaining advancement. The problem is, I don't know whether I really have the authority to fire anyone or not."

Marian asked, "What would Holland have done with this man?"

Tuttle thought a moment. "He'd have hung him out of a fortieth-story window by his heels."

She smiled. "Then I don't think you have anything to worry about. Holland trusted you to take care of his agency for him when he couldn't. I'd say that meant you had full authority to make any decision that needs to be made. In fact, you might want to call that Mr. Bayban back and tell him you'll take the job." When he looked dubious, she added, "Holland admires initiative."

"Yeah, he does, doesn't he?" Tuttle suddenly grinned. "All right, I'll be Mr. Initiative himself. Boy, I'm glad you dropped in, Lieutenant. I *will* take care of Mr. Holland's agency for him. I'll take good care of it."

By the time Marian left, they were both feeling greatly reassured.

WHEN SHE GOT BACK to Midtown South, the first person she saw was Abigail James, sitting on a bench and waiting.

The playwright rose and came to meet her. "Since Mohamet won't come to the mountain...or did I get that backward?"

"Oh, I'm sorry, Abby," Marian said. "I didn't hear your message until this morning." She explained about the grease fire that had driven her out of her apartment for a few days.

"Come along home with me and have some lunch," Abby said. "It's almost noon. We can talk without all that restaurant chatter in the background."

Marian hesitated but decided she might as well. They'd page her if anything happened.

They walked to the brownstone Abby shared with actor Ian Cavanaugh, four blocks west of the Midtown South stationhouse on West Thirty-fifth. Ian was still in California, doing his valiant best to keep the movie version of *The Apostrophe Thief* from being turned into utter dross.

"Kelly says tell you that if you know of any hit men currently in Southern California, she'd like to hire one," Abby said.

"He's that bad, is he? The director?"

"The director's the worst, but they're all meddling fools—the producer, the designers, everybody. Do you remember the scene in which Kelly puts on a dress she doesn't like, just to please her mother? Then she sits quietly at her mother's feet, both of them posing for a picture of domestic tranquillity that's phony as hell?"

"Sure, I remember that."

"For that scene, the costume designer put Kelly in a skirt so short and so tight that she couldn't sit down at all. So what did the director do? He wrote new lines for the mother, making her criticize her daughter's choice of attire. He changed the *scene* instead of the costume."

"Oh good god."

They ate their lunch in Abby's big, old-fashioned kitchen with the high ceiling and the generous floor space. Abby spoke at length of what it was like to watch something she had created being casually and carelessly destroyed by other people. She didn't rant; she didn't even raise her voice. She seemed resigned, and sad.

But then she broke off in midsentence to say, "Marian, what's wrong?"

"What?"

"When I see someone forcing herself to pay attention to what I'm saying, I'm either doing a lousy job of talking or something's wrong. And I don't think I'm doing a lousy job of talking."

"No, no, I'm with you, I—"

"Marian. *What's wrong?*"

Marian stared at her a long moment…and suddenly she found herself spilling out the story. How Holland had been made to think she was in danger, and how he'd been lured into a trap at the Coney Island subway stop. How he was at that very moment chained to a wall somewhere. How they were so lacking in clues to his whereabouts that they were actually checking out abandoned buildings in Brooklyn, just hoping to stumble across his place of captivity.

The look of horror on Abby's face grew with every word Marian spoke. She reached out and took Marian's hands, squeezing them helplessly. "He's *chained to a wall?!* That's...that's barbaric! And you saw a tape of it? Oh, that poor man! Oh, Marian, I'm so sorry. Was he taken for ransom?"

"No, the man who took him is a killer. He wants me to close a case I'm investigating. His case."

"Then close it! You can always go after the killer again, after he releases Holland."

"Oh, Abby." Marian shook her head. "He's not going to release him. The minute I announce the case is closed, Holland is dead. The killer will have no more use for him."

A funereal pall descended. They talked a while longer in muted tones, until Marian needed to get back to the station. The original purpose of the lunch—cheering Abby up—had failed miserably.

TWENTY-TWO

BACK IN HER OFFICE, Marian pulled out the Galloway case files—plural, now, three of them. Each file was filled with notes of interviews, names and addresses, witness statements, detectives' reports. Surely in that mass of information there must be some clue, some hint, some million-to-one shot she could follow up that would take her closer to naming the killer. She set herself the task of rereading every word in all three files.

The sun was setting when she finally gave up for the day. The last notes added were those about Rita Galloway's current lover—who was nonexistent, the detectives were convinced. About that, she had been telling the truth. Marian's head was filled with facts, names, numbers. But nothing had jumped out to say *Here! You missed me!* She'd start over again tomorrow morning.

Marian stayed the night with Abigail James. Abby's house was closer to Midtown South than either Holland's place or her own; but the real reason she was there was that both women felt the need of a friendly presence. But the playwright hadn't mentioned the movie once since Marian told her about Holland.

Abby put her in a room with a four-poster bed—the first Marian had ever slept in. Or tried to sleep in, rather. She lay there in comfort with the scent of freshly laundered sheets in her nose and thought about how Holland was spending the night.

Abby was still asleep when Marian left early the next morning. She was at her desk by seven-thirty, pulling the first of the Galloway files toward her. This time she would read every letter of every word, every punctuation mark, every blank space. If there was anything in there to be found, she was determined to find it.

She'd been at it for a couple of hours when she came to her own notes of the interview with Hector Vargas, the private detective who'd given his niece Julia Ortega a job when she was kicked off the Brooklyn police. Vargas was one of the small army of low-rent private eyes squeezing out a living in New York any way they could; but he wanted the police to catch his niece's killer and Marian thought he could be trusted in what he said about Ortega.

Vargas had told them the killer had hired Ortega to pose as a cleaning woman so she could gain access to Rita Galloway's checkbook. She was to look for deposits of five thousand dollars that had been made over the last few months, implying that Rita was a blackmailer and the killer her victim. That would seem a dismissable ploy except for one thing: Ortega had found two deposits of five thousand each before Rita's brother caught her and threw her out.

That's something they hadn't followed through on.

Marian still thought it was a ploy; Rita Galloway wasn't blackmailing anyone. But if the hinting at blackmail was just a smoke screen, how did the killer know there would be those five-thousand-dollar deposits recorded in Rita's checkbook...unless he'd given her the money himself? And if it wasn't blackmail, what was it?

Rita's bank statement wouldn't show whether the deposits were made in cash or not. There was one obvious way to find out: ask Rita. Marian didn't want to pull anyone off the search for Holland; she'd have to go to Riker's herself. A longish trip; better get started.

She took the Riker's Island bus, the quickest way to get there. The inside of the correctional institution itself was every bit as depressing as she remembered it, its gray walls and battered institutional furniture not exactly geared to inspiring hope. As always, the place was crowded; Rita Galloway was only one of hundreds awaiting trial.

Marian was sitting in a small interrogation room. When Rita was brought in from her Tarial cell, she looked better than the last time Marian had seen her in spite of the prison outfit she was wearing. Her color was better, and her posture was no longer that of a defeated woman.

"Hello, Rita," Marian said as the other woman sat down across the table from her. "How are you doing?"

"As well as could be expected, I suppose."

"The other prisoners treating you all right?"

"They gave me a little trouble at first, but now they've stopped." She smiled wryly. "It's amazing, the number of women here who approve of husband killing."

"Hmm." *Best let that go unanswered.* "You have a new lawyer, don't you? What does he say?"

"He says my chances are pretty good. He wants to go to trial rather than make a deal for a reduced sentence."

Her chances probably were pretty good at that, Marian thought. She hadn't tried to get away with the killing by doing it in secret or by hiring someone to do it for her. She'd not resisted arrest and had cooperated with the police. But most of all she was a distraught mother who'd thought she was protecting her child. That would go over well with a jury.

"Rita, I need your help," Marian said. "A matter that may help us identify the man who sent you that phony letter about Hugh and Bradford Ushton. If we can nail him, that will take some of the heat off you."

"Anything. Ask."

"Julia Ortega—the private detective who posed as the cleaning woman? She found two deposits listed in your checkbook, five thousand dollars each. Remember them?"

Rita looked blank for a second but then remembered. "Oh, those."

"Where did that money come from?"

"Those were Alex's checks. He was running short of

cash and I let him have ten thousand. He paid me back in two hunks.''

"*Your brother?*"

Rita misunderstood her tone. "I'm sorry, Lieutenant. You were thinking it would be the man who...who engineered all this, weren't you?" Alex Fairchild was above suspicion, obviously.

"Are you positive it was Alex who wrote those two checks? Five thousand each?"

She was positive. Marian was so taken aback that she had no more questions. She thanked Rita for her help and called the guard.

Alex Fairchild?

On the bus back, she tried to puzzle it out. Fairchild was the one who'd *discovered* Julia Ortega going through his sister's bankbook-and who'd tossed her out of the house. And why would he hire Ortega to look for deposits he already knew were there? It made no sense.

Unless...unless the whole incident was just for show.

A harassing incident, designed to drive the wedge between Rita and Hugh even deeper. Say Fairchild hired Ortega to do something underhanded so he could rush in and play the hero. Ortega could have seen only Nickie Atlay in making the arrangements; she'd have no idea that the outraged brother was the same man who'd called Hector Vargas's number and engaged her services. It would have worked.

And Alex Fairchild would come out smelling like a rose—Defender of His Sister, Protector of the Sanctity of the Home. Alex Fairchild, who created trouble for his sister just so he could rescue her from it. And who watched gleefully when Rita blamed Hugh.

Possible. Entirely possible.

But opposed to that, there was the Alex Fairchild who'd sat in a rowboat on the lake in Central Park, gently comforting young Bobby Galloway after his father's death.

Which was the true man?

But I don't have to guess, Marian thought grimly as the bus hurtled its way through Queens. There was a way to find out.

IT WAS THE COLD that brought Holland back to consciousness. He was still fuzzy-headed from the drug, but awake. The first thing he noticed was that his shoes and shirt were missing.

"Well, Sleeping Beauty, you finally decided to wake up," said a voice he'd heard before.

That was all he needed to bring him fully awake. He rolled over with his back to the other man and fumbled the rusty bottle cap out of his pocket.

"Come, come—this won't do. Stand up and face me."

Holland grasped his chain with his free hand and pulled himself up, feeling the rubble on the ground cutting into his bare feet. "So, you've decided to show yourself, have you, Fairchild?"

Alex Fairchild stepped between two of the lanterns, smiling at him. "Oh, it was too much trouble hiding in the dark. I had to keep watching where I was stepping."

Holland sneered. "Well, we can't have you put to any trouble, can we?"

Fairchild laughed. "Oooh, what sarcasm. Let's see if we can teach you better manners. I have a little surprise for you."

"Where's Marian?" Holland demanded.

"Safe and sound, and probably weeping on her stalwart captain's shoulder. That's a pretty picture for you to contemplate, isn't it? The captain with his manly arms around his lieutenant, comforting her."

"Is that supposed to make me squirm? You—*where are the four bodies?*" Holland had just noticed they were no longer there.

Fairchild waved a hand. "Dispensed with. We can't

have them smelling up the place. I just left them here for you to see what I do to people I no longer need. Right now, I still need you. For a while."

Holland had already figured it out. "To force the police to close the Galloway case. You're deluding yourself, Fairchild. That will *never* happen. The police can't allow themselves to be blackmailed by criminals. It's been tried many times, and it *never* works."

His captor looked irritated. "First of all, I'm no criminal. Do you think I do this sort of thing for a living? And second, you had better pray you're wrong, because the possibility of getting the case closed is all that's keeping you alive. And third, only one member of the police knows you're missing, one person with the authority to close the case. I sent the tape to your lady lieutenant."

Holland kept his face impassive. Fairchild didn't know Murtaugh was clued in and had set up a stakeout at Coney Island. And he sure as hell didn't know Marian. "What have you done with my shoes?"

"Taken them, and you're not going to get them back. You tried to kick my camera!" Accusingly.

"What a pity I missed." Holland looked the other man straight in the eye. "Of course, I do understand why you're so afraid to come any closer."

Fairchild glared at him. "You're an arrogant S.O.B., aren't you? Well, I've got something here that'll take that insolence out of you." He disappeared into the darkness behind the lanterns and returned carrying a bullwhip. Fairchild held the whip out so Holland could have a good look. Then he snickered. "Absurd, isn't it? I had to go into one of those dreadful places around Times Square to get it. But your ladylove hasn't cooperated—the case is still open. We're going to give her a little incentive."

He was going to be *whipped*? What kind of stupid melodrama was this? But the other man raised his arms and Holland tightened his muscles. When the whip came shooting out he jerked his arms up to shield his face; the lash cut into his chest, deflected slightly by the chain. The second blow fell lower, slicing his midriff. Gritting his teeth against the pain, Holland started dodging and weaving; he didn't have to be a *stationary* target. But the next lash caught his raised arms and one ear, setting his head to ringing. He could feel the blood running down his chest, working its way inside his trousers.

Fairchild got in a few more blows…then Holland lunged for the whip with his left hand, the right still gripping the bottle cap. The whip flicked harmlessly away.

"Oh well," Fairchild said easily, "I suppose that's enough." He examined Holland closely. "Yes, that looks good. Bloody ear and arms as well as torso." He put the whip down and picked up his camcorder. "Now you just stand there and bleed prettily."

Holland immediately turned his back and hunkered down into a fetal position, hiding his wounds from the lens.

"Get up!" Fairchild yelled. "You pigheaded fool! Don't you know you can't win? Get up!" The whip lashed out again.

Holland took six more blows across his back before he passed out.

When he came to a few minutes later, the first thing he saw was the nozzle of a gun.

"How long do you think you can resist a bullet, Pretty Boy?" Fairchild said, enjoying himself. "Come on, now. On your feet."

"I don't know if I can," Holland said thickly.

"Oh, do try."

The effort to get up made him dizzy. Holland leaned a shoulder against the wall to keep from falling over. When he'd steadied a bit, he kicked out with his right foot.

But his movements were sluggish and Fairchild saw it

coming. He danced nimbly out of the way and laughed. "Pigheaded."

When the camcorder light came on, something in Holland snapped. His pride was wounded almost as much as his body, to be photographed in such a condition, bleeding and helpless. He roared out a stream of curses, straining toward the camera. "I'd like to tear your throat out with my bare teeth, Fairchild!"

His captor stopped taping. "Oh, that was naughty. Mustn't mention names."

Fairchild rewound the tape and started over, impervious to Holland's roaring. After a few minutes the light went out. "That was very good," Fairchild said, amused. "I'm sure your Marian will love it." He put down the camera and picked up the whip again, hefting its weight in his hand. "I was never into the S-M scene. It always seemed ridiculous to me. But now I have to admit I'm beginning to see the attraction." His moist eyes gleamed in the yellow light.

Holland tensed. When the whip came snaking out, he made a grab for it and got his left hand around the lash. In spite of his surprise, Fairchild didn't let go of the handle. Holland jerked hard, pulling his tormenter in close. Holland quickly dropped the whip and raised his manacled hands to slash at Fairchild's face with the bottle cap.

Fairchild screamed and jumped back out of reach. "You've cut my face!" he cried. "You've cut my face!"

"I missed again," Holland panted. "I was going for your eyes."

"What was that? What did you cut me with?"

"A rusty bottle cap." Holland smiled slowly. "You'll need a tetanus shot."

Fairchild swore and paced back and forth behind the lanterns, one hand to his cheek and his other trailing the whip. "You think you aren't going to pay for this? You think you won't pay?"

Something about the scene struck Holland as comical. He leaned back against the wall and began to laugh. And laugh.

"What's so goddam funny?"

Holland let his laughter die down. "You. You are funny. Here I've been knocked unconscious, abducted, chained to a wall, drugged, and flogged—and you're whining about a scratch on the cheek. I find that hilarious."

Fairchild blew up. "Well, let's see if you find *this* hilarious!" He disappeared into the darkness and came back with a new plastic bucket which he set on the ground. He squatted down beside it and pulled out a bottle of Evian water. "Never been opened—untampered with." He unscrewed the top and took a long swallow. "See? No drugs." Then he pulled out a sandwich. "Roast beef." Next he took out an apple. "I even brought you a piece of fruit." He put everything back in the bucket and stood up. He swung the bucket by its handle a few times and sent it sailing off into the darkness. "Now, go hungry. Go thirsty."

Holland sank to the ground. He didn't even watch as the glow of Fairchild's flashlight grew smaller in the distance.

TWENTY-THREE

THE BUILDING MANAGER was a smallish man with a stiff military bearing; he introduced himself as Major Saurian. He marched Marian into his office on the first floor of the West Side office building where Alex Fairchild maintained his studio. Once he had Marian squared away in a straight-back chair, he stood at parade rest and politely inquired what he could do for her.

The lieutenant asked the major if he had ever employed Nickie Atlay as a janitor in the building.

The major frowned. "Yes, until recently. I'm afraid I'm greatly disappointed in Nickie."

Bingo.

Quieting her excitement, she asked, "Disappointed? How?"

"He proved unreliable. Simply stopped coming to work. No notice, nothing. It was quite a surprise, really. He'd been a steady worker up until then. I took a chance in hiring him...Nickie's not quite bright, you know. But he could handle menial chores."

"Major, do you know if Nickie ever ran errands for any of the tenants here? Outside his regular janitorial duties, I mean."

"As a matter of fact, he did. I had no objection, so long as he confined his errand running to his own time. Since our cleaning crew works late at night, there was no conflict."

"Did he ever perform chores for Alex Fairchild?"

"Mr. Fairchild?" He frowned. "I believe so, but I can't be certain. Why not ask Mr. Fairchild?"

Because he would deny it. "I'm sorry to tell you this,

but the reason Nickie stopped coming to work is that he died. He was murdered.''

The major looked disbelieving. ''Nickie? Someone *murdered* Nickie? Good god. Excuse me, Lieutenant, but are you sure it's murder?''

''Two bullet holes in the chest, body tossed into the East River.''

He nodded slowly. ''Forgive me for questioning you, but it's incomprehensible to me why anyone should want to kill Nickie. He was the most harmless fellow I believe I've ever met.''

Marian sighed. ''Nickie knew something that made him a threat. He didn't *know* he was a threat, but the killer wasn't taking any chances.''

The major sighed too. ''I'm sorry. Nickie wasn't a bad fellow. He just couldn't keep up with the world around him.''

And that, Marian thought, was a pretty good epitaph for poor, dim-witted Nickie Atlay. ''Well, thank you for your help, Major.''

She raced back to Midtown South, hoping to catch Murtaugh before he left. He was just coming out of his office when she got there.

''We have a suspect,'' Marian said.

HOLLAND WASN'T EVEN aware that Fairchild was back until a bottle of Evian water rolled to a stop against his thigh. He uncapped the bottle and forced himself to drink in small swallows. The bottle was still half full when he replaced the cap.

''Oh my, such instinct for self-preservation,'' Fairchild mocked. ''You must be dehydrated but you're still thinking ahead.''

What Holland had been thinking was that the plastic bottle would make a good weapon—not against Fairchild, but against the rats. ''How long?'' he asked huskily.

"Since the last time I was here? Fourteen hours." Fairchild was wearing a bandage on his cheek. "Before that, about ten hours. And since you missed your last meal, we'll just say you've been fasting for twenty-four hours." He slid a brown paper bag toward Holland. "Make it last. I'd love to stay and chat, but I want to be home in time for the news. Let's see if your ladylove takes the hint this time." He started to walk away.

"Bring..."

Fairchild stopped. "What?"

"Bring something for rat bite," Holland said hoarsely. "It's the blood. It attracts them."

Fairchild stared at him a long moment, and then turned and left without speaking.

O'TOOLE WAS the last to arrive at Captain Murtaugh's office. He'd been hurrying and was short of breath. "What's up? Has something happened?"

"Oh, nothing much," Perlmutter replied lazily. "Just that while we were all crawling through dilapidated buildings in Brooklyn, Lieutenant Larch figured out who the killer is, that's all."

"That's all? Well? Who is it, for chrissake?"

"Alex Fairchild," Murtaugh told him. "We still don't have any hard evidence, but Fairchild kept a studio in the building where Nick Atlay worked as a janitor."

"The brother?" O'Toole was stunned. "He did all that to his own sister? But why?"

"He had to be after the Galloway money. Whoever controls young Bobby Galloway controls the money. And at this moment Bobby is living with Fairchild. Right from the beginning, Fairchild was out to discredit *both* parents."

"How'd the lieutenant finger him?"

"She checked with the building manager where Fairchild keeps a studio. Nickie Atlay was working there at the time of his death."

O'Toole looked at Perlmutter. "We never thought to check Fairchild's building. He wasn't a suspect."

Perlmutter spread his hands. "That's why she's a lieutenant and we but lowly toilers in the vineyard."

Sergeant Campos was frowning. "Bobby's grandfather might have something to say about all that. He's not going to let Bobby be brought up by the brother of the woman who shot his son."

"Walter Galloway is old and in poor health," the captain said. "When he dies, Alex Fairchild will be the boy's only remaining relative, since Rita is out of the picture. Fairchild will be in a perfect position to plunder the Galloway fortune at his leisure."

"Where's Lieutenant Larch?" O'Toole asked.

"She went to her place to see if another videotape had been delivered."

Walker spoke for the first time. "Say we nail Fairchild, and then Walter Galloway dies in a couple of years. Who's going to take care of Bobby then?"

No one had an answer to that.

Ten minutes later Marian came in, clutching a mailing bag. "Another one."

Murtaugh loaded the tape into the VCR and worked the remote. The tape began to roll.

Marian cried out and the men all gasped. Holland's wounds were still fresh enough that they could see the blood running down his body. His right ear was a mess, the whip cuts in his body appeared deep, even his feet were bloody.

"Good god in heaven," Murtaugh muttered. "Are we back in the Middle Ages?"

O'Toole yelled, "The son of a bitch! Let's pick him up right now!"

"And what would happen to Holland then?" the captain asked sharply. "Fairchild would leave him to die there before he'd admit to anything."

Marian had both hands pressed against her mouth to keep from screaming. She felt a couple of comforting hands on her shoulders but didn't know whose they were because she couldn't take her eyes off the screen. Bleeding, lacking the energy he'd shown in the first tape, and none too steady on his feet-Holland was still raging at the camera, still defiant.

The tape was short. The poster board at the end said only: *It can get worse than this.*

Marian was afraid, more afraid than she'd ever been in her life. More afraid than the times when she was still in uniform and chasing dangerous perps down dark streets. Holland was in the hands of a madman, a sadist, a ruthless and conscienceless man. And if the police made even one false step...Holland would be gone.

They watched the tape one more time. Marian ached for Holland, feeling every one of his cuts, bleeding with him. The fact that he was being tortured as a way to get to *her* was salt in the wounds. And for a man as proud as Holland, the ordeal he was going through must be doubly difficult.

"We can't announce the case is closed," Campos said gruffly. "That would kill 'im for sure."

The captain agreed. "Tail job—that's the only way. Fairchild has to go to wherever he has Holland hidden to take those pictures."

Walker suddenly said, "That wobbly camera—he was doing that deliberately! So we'd think the guy handling the camcorder was an amateur."

"Hmm, yes, I suppose so. Campos, set up a surveillance schedule," Murtaugh said. "Two-man teams, around the clock. And for god's sake, don't let him make you. I don't know how long Holland can hold out, but our only chance of finding him is to let Fairchild lead us to him."

"I'm on it."

"And make sure your teams are made up of people Fairchild doesn't know. That lets out the lieutenant, and Perl-mutter, and…?'' He looked at O'Toole.

"Never met him."

"Okay. Get a team on him *now,* Campos."

"Right." The four detectives filed out.

Murtaugh looked at Marian. "Try not to worry," he said gently. "They'll find him."

"I'm sure they will," she said.

A polite lie.

HOLLAND POURED the antiseptic over his wounds, welcoming the sting. One place on his chest looked as if it were already infected; he pinched off the crusted blood and re-opened the cut, dousing it thoroughly. There wasn't much he could do about his back. He poured the antiseptic back over his shoulders and hoped for the best.

Fairchild had returned about an hour after Holland had told him about the rat bites. He'd brought a big bag filled with various kinds of antiseptic medicines, and plenty of them. There was one patent medicine ''to combat infection,'' according to the label. Holland swallowed a couple of the tablets without expecting much; what he needed were antibiotics.

Fairchild had also added three more bottles of Evian water and a box of cheese crackers. Evidently he'd just gone into the first drugstore he came to and grabbed up whatever was available.

But if that was the case, why had it taken him an hour? There were drugstores everywhere in New York; you never had to go more than a couple of blocks to find one. How far did Fairchild have to walk from here to get back to civilization anyway? Just where the hell *was* he?

Or maybe it hadn't really been a full hour. Holland could no longer trust his sense of time in this place.

He finished the first bottle of water Fairchild had brought and hefted the empty plastic container in his hand.

Not much weight, but it would give him something to hit with the next time he opened his eyes to see a rat sitting on his chest.

ABBY JAMES took one look at Marian and poured her a drink.

Marian found herself being steered into Abby's big kitchen, where she slumped down at the table, vaguely aware of the aroma of something good simmering on the stove. Her body felt so heavy she could barely keep her head up. She stared at the ice melting in her glass and remembered to take a swallow.

After a few minutes Abby reached across the table and touched her arm. Hesitantly, she asked, "Is he dead?"

Marian looked up at Abby and shook her head. "Not yet."

"Oh!" Abby let out the breath she'd been holding. "From the way you look, I thought...I thought..."

"There's been another tape."

Marian described what was on the tape, in detail. Abby's eyes teared up and she kept saying *Oh... Oh* while Marian talked. "My god, that's...that's *medieval*."

Marian nodded; that's what Jim Murtaugh had said too. "Our killer's enjoying what he's doing. He's been enjoying all the manipulating and the creating of misunderstanding, all the things he's been doing. And now he's enjoying torturing Holland."

"And you still don't know who he is?"

"Yes," Marian said dully. "Now we do."

Abby knew better than to ask a question Marian couldn't answer. "Have you arrested him?"

Marian shook her head. "He'd just refuse to talk. If we let him run loose, he ought to lead us to where he has Holland hidden."

"So he's being watched?"

"Around the clock."

Abby was silent for a long moment. "You know, don't you, that Holland isn't the only one this man is torturing? You're the one he really wants."

"I know."

"Oh, Marian, I'm so sorry! I can't begin to imagine what you must be feeling!"

"Guilt," Marian said. "I feel guilt."

TWENTY-FOUR

THE NEXT MORNING the surveillance teams reported Fairchild had stayed in his West Side apartment except for a quick trip to his studio and an hour he spent with Bobby Galloway in one of the Central Park playgrounds. The team on duty at the time said Bobby didn't seem to want to play with the other children.

Well, of course he doesn't want to play, Marian thought. His father dead and his mother in prison—though how much of that Bobby understood, she didn't know. But if such a traumatic thing had to happen to a child, it was better that it happen at Bobby's age than, say, when he was entering puberty.

Fat comfort in *that.*

Her flesh crawled to think of Bobby in the care of a man who *enjoyed* killing and torturing. But Fairchild was taking good care of his nephew, trying to help him lead a normal life again. Marian remembered the first time she'd met the two of them, the uncle bouncing the little boy on his shoulders and both of them laughing and having a good time.

But no matter how much Fairchild cared for the boy, Bobby Galloway would never be allowed to reach adulthood, marry, and beget children—of that Marian was sure. Sooner or later the last Galloway would have a tragic accident...and Alex Fairchild would be a rich, rich man.

Perlmutter was contact man for the surveillance teams to report to; so when he appeared in Marian's doorway, her heart skipped a beat. Perlmutter held up a hand and said, "He's in his studio."

Letdown. Then: "Is Bobby with him?"

"No, and that's what I came to tell you. Fairchild's

hired a nanny—live-in, name of Verna Muller, forty-three, strictly legit. Somebody stable who's there all the time— that's gotta be good for the kid.''

Yes, that was good. ''Have you thought about what's going to happen to Bobby if Fairchild gets away with this?''

''Yeah, that kid's days are numbered. But he isn't going to get away with it, Lieutenant. If Holland can just hold out until the next time Fairchild goes wherever it is, then—'' He broke off. ''Was that my phone?'' He hurried back to his desk.

Marian waited, tense. Time dragged.

When he at last came back, his face told her the bad news even before he spoke. ''They lost him.''

''Jesus Christ!'' Marian hit at the desk, sending the desk calendar flying to the floor. ''How could they lose him?''

''Freak accident. Campos and O'Toole were following his taxi when they ran into a bottleneck on West Fifty-second. Car and a bakery van collided, traffic backed up for two blocks. Everybody just sitting until the vehicles could be towed. Campos stayed in the car while O'Toole went to check on Fairchild. But by the time he could work his way through the bumper-to-bumper cars, Fairchild had got tired of waiting and had already left his cab.''

''Damn!'' *This wasn't supposed to happen!* ''Where was the cabdriver taking him?''

''Astor Place, O'Toole says.''

''Astor Place? But that's in…'' She thought quickly. ''Perlmutter, go tell the captain what you just told me. It looks as if Holland's being held somewhere in the Ninth Precinct instead of in Brooklyn.'' She unlocked the bottom drawer of her desk and took out her bag.

''Where will you be, Lieutenant?''

''Home,'' she said grimly. ''Waiting for the next tape.''

THIS TIME Fairchild had brought a pull truck with him, piled high with boxes and bundles. One of the wheels was squeaky; Holland had heard it even before he'd noticed Fairchild's flashlight bobbing in the distance. *What in the hell does that maniac have in mind now?*

Among the things Fairchild had brought were two lights on stands, which he set up quickly and expertly. "Since this will be your farewell performance," he told Holland, "we want everything to look just right."

A chill ran down Holland's back. "It's time to kill me."

"Oh, no. At least, not now. No, I meant this will be your last chance to persuade the reluctant lieutenant to put an end to the investigation. So make it good, Pretty Boy. That woman is as pigheaded as you are."

"And if she won't?"

Fairchild made a kissing sound. "Bye-bye!"

Holland knew why Marian was refusing to close the case; the minute she did, his usefulness to Fairchild would be ended. He also knew she'd played the tapes for Murtaugh and was even now drawing upon the resources of the NYPD to locate him. But how could anyone ever find him…*here?*

"All right, I'm ready," Fairchild announced. "Stand up. And strip."

"What?"

"You heard me. Strip. Take off those trousers and whatever you wear under them. Let's get a look at what our lady lieutenant finds so fascinating."

A long silence built. Then Holland slowly got to his feet and spoke one word: "No."

Fairchild tut-tutted. "Ah, but I insist! Your last performance must be done *au naturel*. Take off your trousers."

Holland smiled his nastiest smile. "You take them off."

The challenge hung in the air between them. Fairchild paced back and forth, never taking his eyes off Holland. Suddenly he stopped and commanded, "Show me your hands!"

Holland opened his empty hands. The bottle cap had been lost in the struggle earlier.

"You do understand, don't you," Fairchild said, "that if anything happens to me, you'll die here?"

"I understand."

"Nobody knows where you are. And nobody ever comes here. I found this place by accident. If you injure me—if you even *try* to hurt me—I'll leave you here to rot, I swear I will!"

"Oh, I believe you."

Fairchild licked his lips; still undecided.

All of life is about dominance, Holland thought. If Fairchild could get the trousers off him, he would win. King Alex.

Fairchild made up his mind. He took a gun from his hip pocket and placed it behind one of the lanterns, outside of Holland's reach. "Hold your hands up over your head. Now, stretch back. Farther!"

"That's as far as they go."

Fairchild approached slowly, never taking his eyes off Holland's hands. He fumbled the waistband of the trousers open without looking, and got the zipper open. But then he dropped his eyes for one second...

Holland brought his manacled hands down hard on the back of Fairchild's neck. He twisted him around so that Fairchild was facing outward and brought the link between his manacles up hard against the other man's neck. "The key!" he hissed. "Unlock me!"

Fairchild was pulling ineffectually at Holland's arms. "I...I don't have it on me," he choked out.

"Do you know how easy it would be for me to break your neck? *Where is the key, dammit!*"

Fairchild was coughing and had to struggle to get the words out. "Show you...need flashlight."

Holland's trousers had fallen down around his ankles; he kicked them aside and walked Fairchild toward where he'd left the flashlight. Fairchild had to hook it with one toe and roll it toward them. He shone the light along the wall to the left, looking for something. There it was: a nail in the cement wall, holding a key ring with one key on it. Fairchild coughed. "Can't reach it from here."

"Let's try, shall we?" Holland moved them both as close to the key as his chain would allow. "Now, reach for the key. Stretch, damn you!"

Fairchild stretched one arm out as far as it would go. The tips of his fingers were a good four feet short of the key ring. He made an attempt to laugh; it came out a gurgle.

Seeing the uselessness of it, Holland released him and shoved him away. Fairchild had won.

Fairchild was coughing and holding his throat. He picked up a bottle of Evian water and swallowed some, making a face as the liquid went down. When he'd recovered, he walked over and planted himself in front of Holland. "That was very unpleasant," he said...and slapped him.

Holland bared his teeth but did not retaliate.

Fairchild slapped him again. And again. And again. When Holland did not respond, Fairchild put his fists on his hips and smiled. "That's better. You're learning. Now, take off those fancy black briefs."

Holland felt a surge of adrenaline; it would be so easy to kill him, right now, where he stood. But he fought down the impulse; Fairchild had the upper hand, for now. Without a word, Holland tugged his briefs down over his hips and stepped out of them. Standing naked before his captor, he waited for what was to come next.

Fairchild picked up both briefs and trousers and turned to walk outside the circle of light. "You know I said I'd leave you here to rot if you tried anything," his voice came from the darkness. "But now that you acknowledge I'm in charge here, I just might put that off for a while.'' When he came back, he was carrying the whip.

Holland's heart sank. He disguised his anguish with flippancy. ''A rerun? I thought you'd have some new treat in store.''

''Oh, this is just for aesthetics. All those ugly red cuts above your waist and none below. We'll balance things out by adding a few stripes to your legs.'' He sniggered. ''At least, I'll *try* to hit your legs.'' He waited a moment to make sure Holland got his meaning.

If I'd never met her, this wouldn't be happening.

Then it hit him, what he'd thought. Holland was so sickened that he was unprepared when the first lash landed across his thighs. On some level—oh god!—on some level, he had been blaming Marian. The whip sliced across his knees. He clenched his teeth and stood as still as he could. *I deserve this. I deserve this.*

When Fairchild was satisfied, he said, ''Well, you took that like a little man.'' He tossed the whip aside and picked up the camcorder. ''Show time, Pretty Boy. Do your stuff.''

But Holland remained standing still, teeth clenched against the pain and holding his head high. He followed Fairchild with his eyes as he jumped around, shooting from different angles, fancying it up.

''Very amateurish, what I'm doing,'' Fairchild confided. ''But we don't want them suspecting I know how to use a camera, do we?'' At last he finished. ''Well, I must go see that this is delivered to your ladylove. But first, let's get some antiseptic on those new cuts.''

He went to the hand truck he'd brought and carried back what turned out to be a thin mattress, the kind used for cots or narrow bunk beds. Fairchild told Holland to lie down. Wondering what he was up to, Holland stretched out on his side.

''On your back.''

"I'd rather not. Lying on my back is painful."

Fairchild looked at the lash cuts on his back. "Oh, those do look nasty. All right, I'll get to them in a minute."

He got to work with antiseptic and gauze squares, even holding compresses against the deeper cuts to stop the bleeding. "Do you know what day it is?" he asked chattily. "It's July first. The weather gods must be watching the calendar, because those nice June days are *gone.* It's chilly here, but outside you could be broiled alive." He grinned. "Aren't you glad I didn't put you in a tin hut somewhere?"

Then he started in on Holland's feet. He wiped away the dried blood with antiseptic and brushed the gravel and grit off Holland's soles.

Holland watched in bewilderment. *He's cleaning my feet?*

"I picked up a new antiseptic salve," Fairchild said. "That ought to do the trick on your back. Let's see, now." He started applying the salve, his touch as light as a feather. "It should take some of the sting out as well."

His back did feel a little better already. "Why are you so good to me?" Holland asked sarcastically.

Fairchild smiled enigmatically. "I can be *very* good to you...as long as you behave yourself." He stood up and went to the hand truck. When he came back, he was carrying a thermal blanket which he spread over Holland. "Take a nap, Pretty Boy. I'll be back as soon as I arrange to have the tape delivered."

But Holland lay wide awake as he listened to the sound of Fairchild's retreating footsteps, trying to figure the best way to make use of this extraordinary turn of events.

TWENTY-FIVE

IT SHOULD HAVE BEEN the ultimate humiliation. The tape showed Holland in a state that would have reduced most men to a posture of abject defeat: unshaven, with dark shadows under his eyes, and naked as the day he was born. Fresh cut marks on his legs and thighs were bleeding heavily. But Holland stood straight and still, his head up, only his eyes moving as they followed his tormenter. Holland wouldn't give Fairchild the satisfaction of seeing him cringe.

"Incredible," Murtaugh murmured. "He's been chained, whipped, stripped naked—and he still manages to keep his dignity."

Marian didn't give a hoot about Holland's dignity; it was his *person* she wanted back. But she saw Murtaugh's point, although not sharing his amazement; Holland was behaving exactly as she thought he would.

"Hang in there, dude," Campos muttered to the image on the screen.

The poster board at the end was filled with a stenciled message: *This is the last tape. If the eleven o'clock news tonight does not report that the Galloway case has been closed, then he dies. And he will die horribly.*

"Look at that," Walker said in disgust. "He couldn't just stop after 'then he dies.' Oh, no, he had to twist the knife." He glanced at Marian. "I'm sorry, Lieutenant."

"Run it again," Marian said.

Murtaugh rewound the tape and pressed the PLAY button. The picture was brighter and clearer on this tape, and the camera moved around a bit, shooting Holland from all sides.

"What's he doing?" Perlmutter asked. "Showing off?"

"Wait," said Marian. "What was that white blur on the left?"

"What white blur?"

"When he was swinging the camera around to get a different angle. There's something white at the extreme left side, very narrow—the light just barely caught it. Back it up, Captain?" They all watched closely as Murtaugh ran the tape back. "There. Now, forward just a few frames. That's it!" Murtaugh hit PAUSE.

But the picture was streaked and blurry. "Try the tracking knob," Perlmutter suggested.

Murtaugh looked at the controls on the VCR. "This machine has two."

"Try 'em both."

The captain fiddled with the two knobs and managed to bring the picture into focus. Marian's white blur revealed itself to be the beginning—or ending—of a tiled wall. Graying white tile.

"Bathhouse?" Marian asked. "Subway? A rest room, the locker room of a gym?"

"Hospital, laboratory," Perlmutter added. "The morgue."

Murtaugh said, "A lot of the older municipal buildings have that white tile in them. The stuff's all over this town."

"But it's unfinished, whatever it is," O'Toole pointed out. "They ran out of money before they finished tiling the wall?"

"Yeah, but where?" Campos complained. "It could be anyplace."

They stared gloomily at the tape.

FAIRCHILD HAD BROUGHT a small camp stove that was heated by cylinders of propane gas. "It didn't occur to me that the lack of running water would be a problem," he said. "I thought this would be over by now—I didn't realize how stubborn your ladylove could be. Well, we'll just make do with bottled water. Do you have any idea how heavy those big bottles are? I hope you appreciate all the trouble I've gone to for you."

"Oh, I appreciate it," Holland said dryly.

Fairchild was no longer wearing a bandage on his cheek. The two scratches the bottle cap had made were neither as long nor as deep as Holland would have wished. Fairchild put a pan of water on the stove to heat. "Now, while that's getting warm, I've got something here you'll like."

"Chicken soup." Holland could smell it; his mouth had been watering ever since the other man returned.

"That's right. No, no—you'll spill it. Here, let me." He twisted off the lid of the cardboard carton and dipped a plastic spoon into the soup.

I'm to be spoon-fed? Holland obediently opened his mouth.

Fairchild fed him a spoonful, then another. "There, isn't that good?"

Holland sat wrapped in his blanket, allowing himself to be fed like a baby, sure now of his role in this grotesque game. Fairchild was the dominant one, the source of both pain and pleasure, the one from whom *everything* came. Hrothgar, the ring bestower. Everybody wants to be God. Fairchild could mete out punishment or reward according to his whim, and Holland's task was to be totally subservient to that whim. Fairchild, the all-powerful father, never to be questioned; Holland, the dependent child, to be pampered or spanked as the occasion demanded.

Test it out. "Did you bring just one carton? That's all?"

"Oh, I'm sorry," Fairchild said. "Next time I'll bring two. I didn't know you liked soup so much."

"I love soup. All kinds of soup. I like soup for breakfast."

"I'm thinking you need red meat. You've lost a lot of blood, you know." Reproachfully.

"I'll try not to bleed so much," Holland said through clenched teeth.

Fairchild held out an apple. "Eat that. It's good for you."

Yes, Daddy.

While Holland was eating the apple, Fairchild took a plastic bag and began picking up food wrappers and empty Evian water bottles. "A lot of mess here." He held out the bag for the apple core.

Clean up your room?

After being so finicky about the litter, Fairchild carelessly tossed the plastic bag behind the lanterns. "Let's have a look at those cuts." He pulled Holland's blanket away. "Hmm. Most of them are healing nicely, but there are a few that look like trouble." He made a tsk-tsking sound. "It's too dirty here—too much risk of infection. The water ought to be warm by now."

He went over to the propane stove and poured the water into a bucket. From the hand truck he fetched soap, a sponge, and a towel. He dipped the sponge in the bucket and squeezed out the warm water over Holland's head.

Holland wanted a bath, but not that badly. "I can wash myself."

"No, I'll do it. Hair first." He worked up a lather in Holland's hair, carefully fingering the part matted with blood.

Here I sit, wherever "here" is, chained to a wall, while a madman gives me a shampoo. "Who's watching Bobby?"

"Oh, I found the most marvelous nanny—I was lucky to get her. A big motherly type named Verna. Bobby loves her already."

"It was Bobby you wanted all along, wasn't it? Bobby and the Galloway money."

"Of course. As long as Rita and Hugh were fighting like cats and dogs, I thought I might as well take advantage of it." He patted most of the moisture out of Holland's hair with the towel and started sponging off his back.

"And his grandfather is just going to let you keep him?"

"That'll be the day. He might even convince a court that he's a better guardian for Bobby than I am. But it won't matter. Walter Galloway is old and sickly—he won't be around long. Sooner or later, Bobby and his millions will come to me. Turn around."

Holland turned so Fairchild could wash his face. "So why was it necessary to kill two people?"

Fairchild laughed dryly. "You think you're going to get all the answers so you can tell Lieutenant Marian? Haven't you figured it out yet? You're never going to see her again. What's so great about her anyway?" He lathered Holland's neck and shoulders; the touch of the sponge was almost a caress.

Holland sat perfectly still. "So why did you kill them?"

"Oh, that great fool Nickie Atlay could identify me. And the woman investigator, Julia Ortega—well, she started getting qualms of conscience. I had her writing up reports about Hugh and sending them to Rita. She didn't like doing it, and finally she balked. She actually threatened me over the phone...said she was going to the police. I don't think they could have traced me through her, but why take chances—right?"

"Oh, right." *And that's all that was needed to end a woman's life.* Fairchild was working on his chest now, cleaning around the wounds but being careful not to disturb the scabbing that was forming. The scent of the soap was perfumy and sickeningly sweet.

Holland said abruptly, "That photograph of Bradford Ushton with the boy in the men's room—you knew who he was, didn't you?"

"Of course I knew. I thought he'd make a good suspect for your Marian, but, alas, she rejected my gift."

So even that was part of the plan. "You had it all worked out," Holland said. "You've been very clever."

Fairchild smiled. "Yes, I have, haven't I? You have nice skin. Hold your arms up."

Holland complied. "So if Bobby will come to you eventually, why try to kidnap him in the first place?"

He laughed. "If I'd really wanted to kidnap Bobby, do you think I'd hire Nickie the Nitwit? The only reason I sent Nickie was that I knew he'd bungle the job. Rita got hysterical and accused Hugh. Hugh blew his top and accused Rita. Exactly what I wanted. They were both such fools, reacting to every little stimulus that came along. No restraint, no self-control—neither one of them. Now, stand up."

Holland got to his feet, cautiously watching the other man. Fairchild could have been talking about a dinner party instead of kidnapping and murder, so impersonal was his account of what he'd done. The man had totally detached himself from any kind of moral responsibility. Fairchild was playing his own game, and now he was amusing himself by washing his captive.

He started soaping Holland below the waist. When his hand went between Holland's legs, Holland knocked it away. *"Watch it."*

Fairchild slapped him. His soapy hand slid off Holland's face, but the blow was still hard enough to set his ears ringing. "Must I teach you your lesson all over again?" Fairchild asked. *"You* do what *I* say. Always. Without question."

The two men stood facing each other no more than a couple of feet apart. In the yellow lantern light, with its broad forehead and gleaming eyes, Fairchild's face looked like a skull.

Play the petulant child. "That hurt."

The skull smiled. "Of course it did. When you misbehave, I have to punish you."

"You're not supposed to hit someone who's suffered a blow on the head. You could do serious damage. You're the only one I have to take care of me. You shouldn't hit."

Holland's acknowledgment of the other man's caretaking role pleased Fairchild. "If you'll give me your word not to misbehave, then I'll give you my word not to hit."

"I promise."

"Then so do I."

Holland braced himself, and Fairchild took up the washing where he'd left off. "Well, I see you don't get excited easily. What does that bitch Marian do to get you going?"

Holland didn't answer.

Fairchild washed his legs and told him to turn around. While he was soaping Holland's buttocks, he remarked, "You do have nice skin. Do you put anything on it?"

"Uh, no."

"No creams or lotions or oils?"

"No."

"You mean you and the bitch never heat a little oil in the microwave and give each other massages?"

"Never."

"How boring your sex life must be. What do you see in her, anyway?"

"For one thing, she's not a bitch."

Fairchild laughed and dried Holland off with the towel. "Defending your woman. How noble. And how conventional." He stepped around to face Holland and looked him up and down. "Yes, I can see why she likes you. But you need a shave."

Holland watched as Fairchild went back to the hand truck and returned with a safety razor and a can of shaving foam. He'd planned all this ahead...?

"Now we sit." When they were both seated on the narrow mattress, Fairchild squeezed some foam into his hand and patted it on Holland's face. "This will pull a little."

Holland sat still as Fairchild shaved him. The operation seemed to require much placing of hands on his head and shoulders. At one point Fairchild eased behind him and wrapped an arm around his neck—to steady him, he said. If Fairchild had been using a straight razor, Holland thought he would have had cause to worry. As it was, he just sat it out.

When he was finished, Fairchild wiped his hands on the towel and said, "There, that's done. Don't you feel better now?"

"Yes, much better."

"Well?"

Holland gritted his teeth. "Thank you."

Fairchild smiled in approval. "You are most welcome. Let's see, bath, shampoo, shave—did I forget anything?"

"Toothbrush. Toothpaste."

Fairchild looked stricken. "I didn't even think of that! I'm so sorry."

Holland sulked.

"I said I was sorry! I'll take care of it the next time I go out."

Holland forced himself to smile. A little.

"Ah, a smile! You have an attractive smile, do you know that? You should smile more often. You look so *disapproving* all the time."

"I do?"

"Indeed you do."

"How odd," Holland said, careful to keep the sarcasm out of his voice.

What on earth do I have to disapprove of?

TWENTY-SIX

PAULA DANCER sat in Captain Murtaugh's office, squinting at the TV screen.

Marian had asked the graphics technician to come take a look at the tape; Murtaugh was dubious but had raised no objection. Marian tapped her fingernail on one tiny spot on the left side of the screen. "Right here," Marian said. "Do you see it?"

Dancer leaned in closer to the screen. "It just looks like part of the shadow to me," she replied.

Murtaugh grunted. "That's what I said."

"The shadowy part starts in a pretty straight line," Marian persisted, drawing her finger along the left edge of the narrow strip of white tile that showed. "All except this one little speck here. It sticks out. Like a bump."

The speck Marian was concerned with was high up on the screen, almost out of the picture. Dancer shook her head. "The lighting is too spotty. It's hard to tell."

"It's just shadow, Marian," Murtaugh cautioned. His tone said: *Don't get your hopes up.* "It's only a speck."

"Maybe so, but can we make sure?" Marian asked. "Can you work some computer-enhancing magic on a VCR tape?"

"Sure," Paula Dancer said. "I'll need to get that frame converted to a graphics file that my viewer program can read. You won't get a sharp picture, but I can give you an enhanced enlargement that'll tell you more than that little speck does."

"Great," Marian said with relief. "And, Paula—this is urgent. We need that enlargement immediately."

"I'm on my way." She ejected the tape from the VCR and left.

"Don't get your hopes up," Murtaugh said.

FAIRCHILD HAD BROUGHT not only toothbrush and toothpaste but mouthwash as well. He'd also brought two steak sandwiches and two cartons of chicken soup. Holland had devoured everything in sight and asked for dessert. Fairchild produced a bag of pears.

Holland sat munching one as his captor applied salve to his back. Fairchild's touch was soft; while one hand smoothed on the antiseptic cream, the other was fondling Holland's shoulder and upper arm.

A lot had been made of the relationship that frequently developed between captor and hostage, Holland mused. A strange form of bonding often took place...frightened women trying to mother equally frightened young gunmen, strong men becoming buddies with their captors instead of attempting to overpower them. Holland wondered if any of the studies done of the psychology of intimidation had ever included a situation quite like the one he was in now.

That Fairchild was attracted to him was obvious; what to do about it, less so. That odd attraction was what was keeping Holland fed and making sure his wounds were tended to. Fairchild had made him as comfortable as he could under the circumstances—circumstances he himself had created. But Fairchild clearly enjoyed pampering him. No question but that it was in Holland's best interests to keep the pampering going as long as he could.

Holland finished his pear and asked, "How did you find this place?"

"Pure accident." Fairchild screwed the top back on the tube of salve and wiped his hands. "I was trying to get a picture of a homeless pair. Two androgynous bundles of rags—I never was able to determine whether they were men or women or one of each. But they had the most extraordinary faces! Unfortunately, they kept ducking away every time I had a good shot lined up. So I followed them. They led me here."

"Into a subway tunnel?"

"Hah!" Fairchild was surprised. "How did you figure that out?"

"The times you were standing behind the lanterns. You never stood behind the one directly in front of me but always off to the sides. And whenever you threw anything away, you tossed it straight ahead. That indicated a drop-off of some sort. The lack of windows suggested we were underground. But there's no sewer smell here, no sound of water. The subway seemed a reasonable guess."

"Very good." Fairchild stood up and went for his flashlight. "I'll show you." He walked into the darkness in the direction opposite to the way he came in. His flashlight played along the wall, and Holland saw the white tiling for the first time. "They tiled the wall for only twenty feet or so," Fairchild's voice said out of the darkness. "And the platform area has been widened some here—they obviously meant this to be a subway stop, originally. But they never finished." He came back into the light. "The tunnel goes quite a distance in the other direction."

"Where are the homeless pair that led you here?"

"I never found them," Fairchild said ruefully. "There are a number of tunnels branching off not far from the hole they crawled through to get inside. I don't know which one they took. But it wasn't this one."

"And the four young thugs you hired to jump me at Coney Island? You just pushed them off onto the tracks?"

"Not here. Farther in. I didn't want to have to *smell* them."

No, of course you didn't, you finicky bastard. Holland wondered if there was something there he could use. "You're very fastidious, aren't you?"

Fairchild sat down beside him on the mattress. "To a degree. Not overly so, I don't think."

"Then how can you bear to come to a place like this? It's filthy, there's no running water, there are rats—"

"Ah, but I won't be coming here much longer."

Ohh...that didn't sound good. Holland repressed a shiver and said, slowly, "Would you care to explain that?"

"I've given your lieutenant an ultimatum. She has until eleven o'clock tonight to close the case. Come eleven o'clock, everything is going to change, one way or another."

"Eleven o'clock tonight. That's when you kill me."

Fairchild shrugged, didn't answer.

"YOU WERE RIGHT, Lieutenant," Paula Dancer said. "It's a number."

Marian and Murtaugh peered over her shoulder at the computer screen. The enhancement showed a fuzzy but legible figure: *—14.* "What's that before the one?" Murtaugh asked. "A minus sign? A hyphen, a dash?"

"Not a minus sign," Marian murmured. "Dash or hyphen. That's only the end of the number."

"Right," said Dancer. "The first part is lost in the shadow. Another number, maybe a letter or two."

"Can't the computer bring it out?"

The graphics tech said no. "The computer needs *some* light to build on, but there just isn't any there. It's pitch-black. This is all I could get."

"Well, that's something," Murtaugh said. "Fourteen. Fourteen what? Or rather, what fourteen? So far as I know, bathhouses and locker rooms don't number their walls. This is looking more and more like an abandoned subway tunnel."

"Of which there are only about a skillion under Manhattan," Marian muttered. "Could we have copies of that? About a dozen."

Paula Dancer printed out twelve copies for them. "You need anything else, Lieutenant?" Marian told her no and thanked her.

"Why a dozen copies?" Murtaugh asked as they moved away from the computer.

"To show to the Transit Authority people," she said. "That's the next step, isn't it?"

The captain frowned. "I'm not sure how far back they have records for. If that's a very old tunnel—which seems likely—there may be no way of tracing it, even with a partial number."

Marian was thinking. "Fairchild was on his way to Astor Place when Campos and O'Toole lost him. We could ask the Transit Authority to look there first, in the Ninth Precinct."

"He could have been going to Astor Place for some unrelated reason."

"He could have, but does it seem likely, Jim? He'd been going about his business for ten hours or so, before the tail lost him. He'd left Holland alone for all that time. It was about time to go check on him again."

Murtaugh thought that over and then nodded agreement. "We'll ask the Transit Authority to check the Astor Place area first. You may have something there."

"Don't get your hopes up," she said dryly.

"You're going to kill me at eleven o'clock tonight."

"That depends on what your ladylove does."

"No, it doesn't. If she won't close the case, you kill me to prove you weren't bluffing. If she does close the case, you kill me to keep me from identifying you." Holland's voice was bitter. "I knew I was dead the minute you let me see your face."

Fairchild let a long silence build. Then, suddenly: "What do you see in her? She's not beautiful. *You're* beautiful. She's very ordinary."

A photographer who cannot see. "Marian Larch is *not* ordinary.*" He looked at the man sitting next to him. "As I recall, you were rather interested in her yourself at one point."

The remark seemed to rattle Fairchild. He tried to bluff. "I just wanted to get close to her to find out what the police knew."

Holland laughed.

Fairchild slapped him. "Don't laugh at me. Don't you *ever* laugh at me."

"I wasn't laughing at you." Holland said with calculated testiness. "I was laughing at myself. Here I sit, with only hours left to live, worrying about a woman."

That mollified him. "You haven't thought far enough ahead." Fairchild massaged his temples. "Did you know I was married once? She left me. She said I was too…kinky."

Holland said nothing to that. Then: "What do you mean, I haven't thought far enough ahead?"

Fairchild was scowling. "Say Marian does go on TV and announce the case is closed. Then what? If you die, she just reopens the case. I'll have gained nothing."

Holland's eyes narrowed. "So you need to keep me alive."

"For a while. I can't turn you loose, now that you know who I am. But I could send her a videotape every week showing you holding a newspaper with the current date. Just until it's safe. The police aren't going to worry about an old case forever."

"I see. And how long would you keep me chained up here? Six months? A year?"

Fairchild turned to face him. He casually put a hand on Holland's knee. "I haven't decided yet."

Holland fixed his eyes on the hand holding his knee. "That wasn't originally part of your plan, was it?" he asked softly. "When you set those young thugs on me, you meant to kill me no matter what Marian did. But now you're having second thoughts. Now you like the idea of my being chained here, you like knowing how dependent on you I am." *Had he gone too far?* "Do you want to keep it that way? Are you changing your plan?"

The other man began slowly fondling Holland's knee. "I like to stay flexible. I can adjust to new situations." Fairchild locked his captive into an eye contact that made his meaning unmistakable. "There's only one test question I ask when I'm deciding what to do. What's in it for me?"

"And?"

"What's in it for me looks tempting."

Time for a diversion. "But what if Marian won't close the case?"

That spoiled Fairchild's mood; he jumped up and began to pace, agitated. "Then I'll have to kill you, don't you see? Goddam stupid woman. I hate letting everything depend on Marian Larch!"

I don't. "Why do you have to kill me? She'll never know."

Fairchild stopped his pacing. "What?"

"If I don't come back, she'll assume I'm dead. That will let you decide how long you want to...keep me alive."

Fairchild looked at him suspiciously. "Why are you so cooperative all of a sudden?"

Holland sighed. "This is my life we're talking about, remember. Of course I'm going to cooperate. Look, you could even send her one last video—if she doesn't close the case. I can play a very convincing dead man."

The suggestion made Fairchild smile. "So then Marian-the-not-so-Magnificent gets to mourn her lover's death twice? The second time when your body turns up? Oh, I rather like that." He bent over so his face was level with Holland's. "What an amusing idea."

It was the first time since childhood that Holland had had to suppress an urge to spit in someone's face.

THE MEN they'd talked to at the Transit Authority all agreed that the —14 on the videotape was from a numbering system so old that there were no records of it…and no way of identifying the tunnel in question. But it was a subway tunnel, no doubt about that. One of the men suggested that the number might mean the tunnel was the fourteenth branch off a main line, but that was no help without knowing what the main line was. The only way to locate the tunnel was to go underground and look for it.

The New York City Transit Authority had faced similar problems before—the homeless taking up residence in abandoned subway tunnels, kids who went exploring and got lost, even killers dumping victims they didn't want found. Most of the abandoned tunnels were no longer used for a reason, the primary one being that they were not safe. A few tunnels still remained that had been dug as aids to the original construction of the subway system, but none of those had been tiled. What they were looking for was a tunnel that once housed an operating line that had since been shut down.

All known accesses to such tunnels had been barricaded, either with cinder-block walls or with hurricane fencing set in cement. But the key word was *known;* there was no systematic way of tracking the old accesses, as the Transit Authority's predecessors either hadn't kept records or did keep records that had vanished over time. And there was another problem: old walls could crumble and fencing could be cut through. Maybe the known accesses were intact, maybe not. The men at the Transit Authority dug up the locations of all such blocked-off accesses they did know about and sent out a team to check for signs that an entryway had been found or forced through one of them.

The team was supplemented with detectives and uniformed officers from Midtown South Precinct.

For such an extensive deployment of manpower, Marian had Jim Murtaugh to thank. Not only had he put more Midtown South personnel on the search than could really be spared, but lord knew how many favors he'd called in to get the Transit Authority to move so quickly. But when she tried to thank him, he wouldn't let her. "If we can't protect our own," he'd said, "we can't protect anybody."

Now he was trying to get her to go home and grab some sleep while she could. "How can I sleep?" she protested. "I want to know the very minute they find something!"

"And you will. I'll call you myself. But it could be a long search. If they find all their known barricades are intact, they're going to have to search for a new way in. That's *miles* of track in the Astor Place area alone."

She shook her head. "I'll wait here."

"No, you will not," he said bluntly. "Marian, how much sleep have you had in the last few days? You look like hell. Your face is pinched and white, you have purple pouches under your eyes. You're no good to me if you're dead on your feet. Go home and sleep. I'm not asking you, I'm telling you. That's an order."

Marian sighed. "You will call me?"

"The minute I hear."

"I'll be only a few blocks away. I'm staying with a friend."

Marian walked through the blistering heat to the brownstone on West Thirty-fifth; it was empty when she got there, but Abby had given her a key. Marian didn't go up to her room with the four-poster bed; instead, she curled up in a comfortable armchair in Abby's living room and put her cell phone on the table next to the chair. She laid her head down on the broad armrest, about two feet away from the phone.

Sleep, dammit, she told herself. She raised her head to check on the phone.

It was still there.

TWENTY-SEVEN

THE TELEPHONE ringing woke Marian out of a light sleep.

It was Murtaugh. "They found a breached access. Where are you? I'll pick you up."

Marian's heart pounded. "I'm right up the street." She gave him the number.

She stood waiting on the sidewalk in the heat; at least the late afternoon sun was behind her and she didn't have to peer into the glare for Murtaugh's car heading west on Thirty-fifth. The captain pulled up to the curb and she climbed in. "Ninth Precinct?" she asked. "Was I right about Astor Place?"

"Ninth Precinct," Murtaugh confirmed. "I've already talked to DiFalco. He's giving us some help." The captain smiled. "So long as it's understood *he* is in charge of the operation."

Marian grunted. "That's DiFalco, all right."

Captain DiFalco of the Ninth Precinct was Marian's old nemesis. During the short time she'd served under his command, she'd hated every minute of it. They'd butted heads more than once, and Marian looked upon her transfer to Midtown South as something of an escape. The less she saw of DiFalco, the better...usually. Today she was grateful for his help.

Murtaugh said, "The access point that was breached isn't outdoors—it's inside an IRT tunnel about a half-mile down from Astor Place Station. It's literally a hole in the wall, where the cement had started crumbling and was helped along by person or persons unknown. The hole opens into an adjacent tunnel, long unused."

"Then that's it," Marian said.

"Not quite. There's a whole slew of other tunnels branching off from there—we'll have to search all of them."

"Hmm. The team that's supposed to be tailing Fairchild—have they picked him up again?"

"No."

"Then he could be in there right now."

"He probably is."

That could be dicey. Fairchild would be able to see the flashlights of approaching searchers and duck away into the darkness. Marian wasn't nearly so concerned with catching Fairchild as she was with finding Holland. But she wanted to find him alive; Fairchild could easily put a bullet into his prisoner before making his escape.

Murtaugh read her mind. "We know the place Holland is being held is lighted—the tapes showed a few lanterns sitting on the ground. We'll instruct the searchers to douse their flashlights as soon as they see another light source down there."

"I'm going to join one of the search teams."

"There are plenty of searchers. You don't need—"

"I'm going to search."

Murtaugh said no more.

Astor Place was crowded with men from the Transit Authority as well as cops. Marian spotted Perlmutter and others from Midtown South as well as detectives from the Ninth Precinct. Captain DiFalco was giving instructions in a loud, self-important voice. Passengers scurrying by threw him curious glances but didn't stop to see what was going on.

Gloria Sanchez detached herself from the crowd around DiFalco and came straight to Marian. She threw her arms around her and gave her a big hug. "God, I'm sorry, Marian," she said. "What you musta been goin' through! But don't you worry—we find him."

"Yes," Marian said, grateful for the hug. "We'll find him."

"I been tryin' to call you—both your place and Holland's. I didn't know about Holland until today."

"Oh...I've been staying with Abby James."

Gloria's eyebrows went up. "I thought she was in California. For that movie."

"She was. But they kicked her out." Marian moved over to hear what DiFalco was saying.

Gloria stared after her. "They kicked her out of *California?*"

"This little gizmo," DiFalco was saying, holding up a black plastic object about half the size of a remote control, "sends out a beacon signal. Everybody carries one. Everybody." DiFalco caught sight of Murtaugh and nodded an abrupt acknowledgment. "To activate it, just push this button here." He demonstrated. There was no audible sound; only the pulsing of a green light the size of a pinhead showed the instrument was working. "We're not using walkie-talkies because we need a silent approach. Walkies don't work too good down there anyway."

A man from the Transit Authority was passing out the beacons and flashlights as well. Marian took one of each; Gloria joined her and did the same.

DiFalco said, "The signal will show up on this tracking device." He looked around. "Sanchez, you got the tracker."

"Gee, thanks, Captain." She took the tracking box and slung the strap over her shoulder.

"If you spot the victim or the perp, start your beacon immediately. Sanchez's team will follow your signal and act as backup. Don't use the beacon if you get lost." He smiled sourly. "Don't *get* lost. Stick with your teams, all of you."

"I'm going with your team," Marian said to Gloria. Gloria nodded.

Murtaugh spoke up. "May I add one thing?" He emphasized the necessity of stealth. "The minute you see a stationary light in there, turn off your flashlights. And move quietly—don't make a sound. We mustn't give this perp any advance warning at all. It could prove fatal to his prisoner."

"And start your beacons the minute you spot them," DiFalco added, needing to have the last word. "All right, people, you all know which tunnel you're taking. Let's move."

The searchers started filing through a service door that led to the walkway along the main tunnel. DiFalco stepped over and placed himself directly in front of Marian, forcing her to stop.

"Captain?"

"How're you holding up, Larch?"

"Well enough, thanks."

"It's been a while since we first worked with Holland, back when he was still FBI. A lot of things have changed since then." He grinned nastily. "Your lover boy has got himself in real deep shit this time, hasn't he?"

Three voices spoke at once.

"That's enough of that, DiFalco," Murtaugh said sharply.

"You're an asshole, DiFalco," Marian said tiredly.

Gloria Sanchez cussed him out in Spanish.

The two women pushed on by, leaving Murtaugh to deal with DiFalco.

The walkway along the tunnel was narrow, forcing the searchers to move in single file. A low guardrail protected against that false step that could send them tumbling to the tracks eight or ten feet below. The tunnel lights marking the approach to the station cast just enough illumination to make the flashlights unnecessary but not enough to do away with shadow. It was hot and close. The line slowed down as they reached the hole in the tunnel wall.

The hole was on the ground level, necessitating that the searchers crawl through one at a time. Marian dropped to her hands and knees and followed Gloria Sanchez in...and found herself in a darkness so heavy it was almost tactile.

The beams of the searchers' flashlights cut through the dark like Darth Vader lightsabres. One light caught the tunnel ceiling. "Keep 'em *down,*" somebody growled.

Marian played her own light across the tracks below and to the opposite wall. No tiling in this tunnel, but that meant nothing; only the areas of the subway stops were tiled. No service walkway on the other side of the tracks. And unlike the walkway in the main tunnel they'd just left, the one they were standing on now had no guardrail.

"Watch your footing," Gloria called out. "And no talkin' from now on."

The search team started moving to the right. The beams cast by other teams' flashlights showed to the left, following to other branching tunnels. Last in line, Marian felt disoriented and kept her eyes fixed on the small pool of light in front of her feet. *I'd probably flunk a sensory-deprivation test,* she thought unhappily. She had to keep her hand touching the wall to her right, a second point of reference in addition to the light at her feet.

When she'd gotten a little more used to walking with so little visibility ahead of her, she raised her head to see the dots of light cast by the other team members' flashlights. She'd fallen a little behind; Marian hastened to pick up her pace.

The service walkway was covered with a fine grit. Among the footprints left by the searchers ahead of her, Marian thought she could make out track marks. Something on wheels had come this way? Something narrow enough to fit on the walkway?

Marian turned her flashlight on her watch and was surprised to find they'd been walking only fifteen minutes. It seemed longer.

The next time she looked up, all the other searchers' lights had disappeared. Marian felt a stab of panic in spite of knowing that the tunnel had probably just curved. She raised her flashlight and shone it along the wall, confirming the curve. Then her heart jumped: there was something else. Inset into the wall a few feet was the unbarricaded entrance to another tunnel.

No, not a tunnel proper, but a set of iron stairs leading down *to* another tunnel. The Transit Authority had provided locations to all the known *barricaded* access points; they might not even be aware this opening was here. As quickly as she could, Marian made her way around the curve in the tunnel they'd been following; ahead of her, the other searchers' lights were small dots in the distance. She started to call out Gloria's name but stopped herself in time; silent approach.

Shit. They'd all been doing what she had done, keeping their lights on where they were walking; they'd missed the other entrance completely. This one must be one of the shorter branching tunnels, but it would be enough to separate Marian from the other searchers. By the time she checked it out, they'd be too far ahead for her to catch up and she'd have to return to the station. But she couldn't just leave this new tunnel unexamined.

Nervously, she stepped onto the iron steps. At the bottom when she'd reached the tunnel proper, Marian realized this was no minor branch that could be checked out quickly. She needed help. Well, Gloria and her team would just have to backtrack.

She reached in her pocket and activated the beacon.

FAIRCHILD WAS ANGRY. "Do you take me for a fool? Do I *look* like a fool?"

"Of course not," Holland replied mildly. He sat on the mattress, watching his captor pacing back and forth. "You asked me what the problem was, and I told you."

"I am *not* unlocking the manacles."

"I don't expect you to. I do expect you to understand."

Fairchild laughed derisively. "Oh, I understand. I understand you're trying to con me into setting you free."

Holland played the sulking child again. "You aren't even trying to understand."

"Oh, don't be like that!"

"It's all right for you—you have the upper hand. But it's different from where I sit. This isn't just a game for me."

"A game? You think I'm playing a game?"

"A bondage game, yes. Normally when two people play at master-and-slave, they both know at the end of the game the cuffs are coming off and everyone goes home happy. But I don't know that. This is more than a game—it's real. These manacles are real. That chain is real. How can you expect me to believe you won't kill me at eleven o'clock?"

"Because I say I won't."

"You could change your mind again."

Fairchild bared his teeth in feral imitation of a smile. "Yes, I can change my mind again. And again. And again. And you can't do a damned thing about it."

Holland tried another tack. "What if our positions were reversed? What if I was the one running this show and you were the one chained to the wall? What if I talked casually about killing you if I didn't hear something on the eleven o'clock news I wanted to hear?"

"It wasn't casual," Fairchild said harshly.

"But can you imagine yourself in my position? Would knowing you might have only a few more hours to live make you believe whatever I told you?"

Fairchild sighed. "No, I suppose not. But if Lieutenant Bitch doesn't come through at eleven o'clock, you get to play dead for the video camera. Maybe that will convince you."

"Unless you change your mind again."

Without warning Fairchild lashed out a kick that caught Holland in the ribs. "I decide when I feel like deciding! And I'm beginning to wonder if you're worth the trouble."

Holland was bent over in pain; he'd overplayed his hand. He'd meant to lead Fairchild into thinking more about what it would be like, having his own pet slave for a while longer. But the man was so volatile, so changeable...what would work now?

The Nixon approach. "If you get rid of me," he gasped, "who will you have to kick around then?"

The silence grew so long that Holland was beginning to think he'd made another mistake. But then Fairchild laughed, softly and indulgently. "There's no end to your arrogance, is there?" he asked rhetorically. "It's one of the things that makes you so intriguing. Here you are, only inches from death—and you're still baiting me. Oh, I've caught myself a wild one here!" He laughed again.

Holland picked up his cue and snarled. "So glad you are amused."

"Oh, you're very entertaining. I wonder what other tricks you know." Fairchild knelt down behind Holland and began massaging his neck. "I've never come across anyone quite like you before. I think it's going to be fun, playing with you."

Holland submitted to the massage, wondering how long he could keep this bizarre charade going.

TWENTY-EIGHT

MARIAN DIDN'T WANT to admit it, but she was scared.

The oppressive blackness around her, being alone this far underground—that in itself was enough to give her the willies. But if she should happen to blunder on to the spot where Fairchild was holding Holland...she could cost Holland his life if she wasn't careful.

For the last ten minutes she'd noticed a new pull on her Achilles tendons; the tunnel was sloping downward to a new level. The gradient was slight but unmistakable. The temperature was dropping as well; it was almost cool.

Marian's heart was pounding because she thought this was surely the tunnel they were looking for. The layer of grit on the service walkway showed footprints and the same wheel tracks she'd noticed in the last tunnel. Both footprints and wheel tracks could have been made by a homeless person pushing a grocery cart, but she didn't think so. As well as she could make out, these tracks were left by four wheels evenly spaced, unlike those on the carts in the supermarkets. But *somebody* had been using this tunnel lately. She passed an empty cardboard carton of the sort fried chicken came in, but it looked as if it had been there a long time.

A rat ran across her foot.

She stopped dead still, swallowing a cry. She shone the light around and behind her, but the rat had disappeared. Marian took a deep breath and started forward again, her already cautious approach now even more so.

Two or three minutes later she came across a whole pack of them, red eyes gleaming in the beam of her flashlight as they swarmed all over the walkway and blocked her path. Marian shuddered. How to get rid of them? She couldn't fire her gun into their midst...or make any noise at all.

What she needed was something to throw. Marian had left her shoulder bag locked in Jim Murtaugh's car; no help there. And she wasn't about to throw her gun away. She went back for the chicken carton she'd passed. Not much weight, but at least it wouldn't make any noise when it hit.

The rats squealed when the carton landed among them and darted off in different directions. Two of them headed straight for Marian.

She kicked them off the walkway onto the tracks below.

The rats quickly regrouped, swarming around the empty carton looking for any remaining bite of food. Breathing shallowly, Marian started tapping one foot. A rat came to investigate. She kicked it off. Aha.

On her next attempt, she got three. Even better.

But when she tried it again, the remaining dozen or so all turned on her. Then Marian was kicking and kicking, pressing her lips together to keep from screaming. One rat started climbing her trouser leg; she knocked it away with her flashlight. She kicked and kicked and *kicked*.

Then suddenly she was kicking at empty air. She steadied herself and flashed the light around. What rats she hadn't managed to knock off the walkway had retreated. She aimed her light ahead and behind; no sign of them that she could see.

Marian slumped against the tunnel wall and momentarily gave in to the shakes. She was sweating and breathing heavily. But almost immediately she pushed away from the wall and started forward again. Moving was better than standing still.

The gradual downward slope of the tunnel ended, and the air had turned decidedly chilly this far underground.

The tunnel started a long curve to the right. At the end of the curve, Marian stopped.

There was a light up ahead.

Quickly she turned off her flashlight. She couldn't make out anything about the light; it was still too far away. Marian flattened against the wall and started inching along the walkway in the pitch-dark, trying not to think about rats.

When she'd gotten a little closer, she could see movement around the light. But who was there, homeless or Holland, she still couldn't tell. She continued her crablike progress.

Then she was able to make out two figures. One of them was naked.

Marian pulled out her beacon signaler to check; the tiny green light was still pulsing regularly. *Gloria, hurry!*

She inched her way forward.

FAIRCHILD HAD started to extend his massage beyond the neck, but Holland complained that his ribs were hurting where his captor had kicked him. Fairchild was still on his knees behind him, contenting himself with fingering Holland's hair.

"You have nice hair. Soft, good body, a nice shine. Do you use a blow-dryer?"

Holland grimaced; it was his one physical vanity, his hair.

A light slap across the back of the head. "Answer me."

"Yes, I use a blow-dryer."

"Thought so. I wonder what you would look like bald? That might be an interesting experiment."

"I'll just grow some more."

Fairchild's fingers trailed lightly down Holland's back. "Most of these lash wounds are healing, but there's one here that still doesn't look quite right. Time for more of the salve." He got up and headed toward the cart of supplies.

Holland quickly pulled himself to his feet and stepped over to stand by the wall. He didn't like Fairchild kneeling behind him.

He came back with the salve. "Lie down. It's easier that way."

"I've been sitting too long. My legs are cramping." Holland gave one leg a little shake by way of demonstration.

The other man shrugged and told him to turn around. "I'll need to get some more. The tube's almost empty."

The salve felt good going on. But when Fairchild's fingers started dancing around Holland's waist, Holland jerked away. "That's fine. Thank you."

Fairchild tossed away the now empty tube. "Ticklish?" he said with a laugh. "Don't you let the lieutenant touch you? Or does she just lie there for you without moving? Tell me what it's like, you and her."

Suddenly, like a switch being turned off, Holland had had enough. He was drained by the effort of concealing his contempt, of keeping the cat-and-mouse game going. And now he was expected to entertain his captor with stories of intimate moments shared with Marian? No. When he turned to face his tormentor, his eyes were like ice. "Marian can touch me anywhere she likes, anytime she likes. She is the *only* one I permit to touch me. Have you got that, Fairchild? The *only* one."

Fairchild's face turned an angry red. "Do you think I need your *permission?* I can do anything to you I want!"

"Yes. You can. But you can't do it with my permission. That, you will *never* have."

Fairchild's voice went up. "I'm in control here! It's what *I* say that counts! I can end your life like *that!*" He snapped his fingers.

"You can do that too. What you can't do is solve your problems without using violence. Don't you know coercive violence is the last resort of the incompetent? You're a loser, Fairchild.''

Too late, Holland saw he had goaded him too far. Fairchild lost it completely. He screamed curses at Holland in a high, constricted voice. "Who do you think you are, talking to me like that! You speak to me with respect, do you understand? By god, you are going to *learn* respect. Before you die, you are going to call me 'master'—and mean it!'' Wildly he looked around for a way to hurt Holland.

It was probably too late for damage control, but Holland tried anyway. "Then prove me wrong! Resolve this one problem—me—without using violence. Just this once. Fairchild! Do you hear?''

If he did, he gave no sign. Fairchild had fetched the matches he used to light the camp stove and was squatting down by the mattress. "Have you ever wondered what it's like to be burned at the stake?" he spat out. "Well, you're going to get a taste of it right now." Holland watched in dismay as Fairchild ripped open one end of the mattress with a pocketknife and held a lighted match to the cotton stuffing. It took him several tries before the material caught fire.

Fairchild grabbed a safe part of the mattress and swung the burning end around toward Holland. "Maybe this will teach you respect, hah? How do you like that?" He pushed the mattress right up against Holland's legs. Holland twisted and turned and kicked frantically at the blazing, smoking mattress while Fairchild laughed at his efforts. The flames licked up around Holland's legs and he screamed.

Then, to his utter amazement, Holland saw Marian Larch come flying through the air to land on Fairchild's back. They both went down with a crash. Marian was on top; before he had time to react, she grabbed Fairchild by the hair and smashed his face against the cement floor hard…three, four times. And then a fifth time. She jerked his hands behind his back and cuffed him. Fairchild gave out a few bubbly moans and went limp.

Marian scrambled over to the burning mattress, which was sending out a stench so foul that it made her gag. She grabbed the only corner that wasn't on fire and dragged the mattress to the edge of the platform, knocking over one of the lanterns on the way. With an effort she pushed the mattress over onto the tracks. Her eyes were watering; the thing was smoking like burned peppers.

Marian hurried back to Holland. He lay slumped on the ground, grimacing with pain; both legs were burned up to the knees. The twisting and kicking he'd done had opened up the cuts on his abdomen; he was bleeding again. Marian was screaming inside, horrified by the condition he was in. She touched him hesitantly, afraid of hurting him more. "Help is coming," she told him gently. "I've already signaled."

Then she went back to Fairchild and started searching through his pockets but stopped at a sound from Holland. He raised his manacled hands to point along the wall. He gasped, but couldn't get any words out.

Marian retrieved her flashlight and went looking where he'd pointed. There it was: a key ring on a nail. She grabbed it and ran back to Holland. Even though she tried to be careful, he winced when she unlocked the manacles. As soon as she had them off, she saw why: his wrists were bloody and raw.

Holland was struggling not to pass out. "So nice…to see you…again." The effort left him gasping for breath.

"Ssh. We'll have plenty of time to talk later. Just be as still as you can."

He grimaced, said no more.

Fairchild began to moan. Marian ignored him.

The moaning grew louder and turned into a scream. "My node! You broke my node!"

"I broke more than your nose," Marian told him. "I broke your whole goddam face."

He called her a bitch.

"You'd better stay still or you'll injure yourself even more," Marian said. "On second thought, why don't you jump up and down for a while? With luck, you might fall off onto the tracks and break every bone in your body."

He started screaming at her—a gurgly, incoherent stream of curses, calling her every filthy name he'd ever heard. Marian just waited him out. But after he'd finished, he gulped in several mouthfuls of air and started in all over again.

Marian sighed and went over to hunker down beside him. "If you don't shut up right now," she said pleasantly, "do you know what I'm going to do? I am going to shoot you." She unholstered her gun.

He shut up.

She replaced the gun and went back to Holland, who was making a gesture with one hand that she interpreted to mean he wanted to sit up. He was still dizzy with pain, but no longer seemed on the verge of passing out. She eased one arm around his shoulders and helped him to a sitting position; he slumped against her, resting his head against her bosom. Carefully she put both arms around him. "Does that hurt?" When he didn't answer, she left them there. Marian wished he could retreat into sleep; that might bring him some relief. She kissed the top of his head.

And sniffed. Some sickly sweet, perfumy smell. "What have you got on your hair? You smell like a Turkish...barbershop."

His lips moved.

"What?"

He tried to say something, but Marian couldn't make it out. She put her ear down close to his mouth.

"Let's screw," he whispered weakly.

When Gloria Sanchez and her team came in, they found Marian both laughing and crying over the naked, battered man she held cradled in her arms.

EPILOGUE

THE NOVA SCOTIA sun was kinder than the one currently broiling New York. Holland sat in a porch chair staring out at the Atlantic Ocean, resting his chin on his two hands clasping the head of his cane. A pleasant breeze blew in off the ocean, tangy with the scent of saltwater. Inside the house, Marian was talking on the phone.

Across the narrow street and down a small rise was one end of a public dock. Holland watched a family arrive and start readying a sailboat for an outing. The family's two small children began playing a game that involved bouncing a ball against the steps that led up to the street.

The house was in Yarmouth, and it belonged to Abby James and Ian Cavanaugh. They hadn't owned it long; they'd stayed there only twice themselves and only briefly both times. Consequently the house still had a somewhat impersonal feel to it…except for the books. Abby couldn't stand an empty bookshelf.

Marian came out of the house and sat down on the top step of the porch.

"Was that Murtaugh?" Holland asked.

"Yes. He says Rita Galloway's trial is scheduled to begin next week."

"Both of the Fairchildren on trial for murder, brother and sister. But separate trials, for different murders." His eyes turned inward. "I owe that man a lot." He meant Murtaugh.

"We both do." Marian had explained how the captain had organized the hunt, drawing upon all the resources available to him and even a few that shouldn't have been. "He wouldn't even let me thank him."

The two children were running up and down the steps from the dock, calling out incomprehensible commands to each other in whatever game they were playing. Holland asked, "What are Rita Galloway's chances?"

"Of getting off? Fairly good, I'd guess. Once it hit the news that it was her own brother who manipulated her into killing her husband, that won her a lot of sympathy. She was Fairchild's weapon. He's the puppet master, she's the puppet."

"You want her to get off, don't you?"

Marian took her time in answering. "No, I don't," she finally said. "She took a life. I don't know what kind of man Hugh Galloway was—I never did get a fix on him. The only times I saw him, he was either ferociously angry or visibly controlling his anger. Maybe he was every bit the bastard Rita said he was. But that didn't give her the right to kill him. And she killed him for something he didn't even do. She had a number of alternatives, and she picked the worst possible course of action open to her. No, Rita Galloway belongs in prison."

"Marian the Moralist."

She shrugged. "It's why we need law. Personal justice can so easily go wrong."

The two kids were playing in the street now, trying to see which of them could bounce their ball the highest. Holland used his cane to lever himself out of his chair. He walked slowly over to stand near Marian. "This is a very handsome cane," he remarked. It was made of carved cherrywood and was a gift from Kelly Ingram. "I'm going to hang on to it. It should come in handy when I reach my crusty old curmudgeon stage."

"Oh? When's that? Next week?"

"Watch your mouth."

The children's ball came bouncing up against the porch steps, barely missing Marian's legs. The two kids came running after it.

Holland raised his cane in the air and shook it. "You get that ball out of here, you young whippersnappers!" The kids giggled and ran back down to the dock with their ball. Holland turned to Marian. "How was that?"

"Not bad. Your voice needs more of a quaver, though."

"I'll work on it." He lowered himself to the front step beside her. "If Rita Galloway does get off, she's going to try to get Bobby back."

"Then she's got a fight on her hands. The court gave Walter Galloway custody and he's not going to give it up just because she beat the rap."

"Which would be better for the boy?"

"To stay with his grandfather, I think. The old man had the sense to hire the nanny that Fairchild found for Bobby. She seems to be doing a good job as a mother substitute."

"And when Walter Galloway dies? Do the courts ever give custody to nannies?"

"It has happened. That probably would be the best thing in Bobby's case. They could stay on in the Sutton Place house and avoid still another relocation. Bobby needs stability more than anything else."

Down below on the dock, the family was ready to leave. Marian and Holland watched as the sailboat drifted away, graceful as a bird in flight as the sails slowly began to bellow outward when they caught the wind.

"When my legs are better," Holland said, "we should rent a sailboat."

Marian cleared her throat. "I don't really care for boats."

"You know, neither do I. It's just that when one is staying in a seaside resort like Yarmouth, it somehow seems a dereliction of duty not to be doing something on, in, or under the water."

The sailboat was smaller now, its wake barely visible. Another sailboat slid into view, heading in the same direction as the first.

"Holland. I'm going to move in with you."

He shook his head. "You've played nursemaid long enough. I can get around all right now."

"No. I mean I'm going to move in with you."

He slowly swiveled his head toward her. "Permanently?"

"Permanently. It turns out I'm one of those stupid people who nearly have to lose a thing before they realize how precious it is. I'm moving in with you. I've made up my mind, so don't argue about it."

Then Holland gradually began to smile, the first genuine smile she'd seen from him since his ordeal. The remnants of pain lingering in his face seemed to ease a little. He was still smiling as he looked back out at the ocean.

"I'll think about it," he said.

In September 1998
watch for

BURIED IN STONE

by ERIC WRIGHT

Retired Toronto detective Mel Pickett is intrigued by the body discovered
near his cabin in the woods. The corpse is that of a local lothario, and
Larch River folks are busy guessing who might be the culprit: a jealous
husband or a jilted lover.

Someone is arrested, but Mel, with instincts honed by years as a big-city
cop, suspects there's more to the case than meets the eye. His probe
reveals secrets buried in stone...and a clever, nearly perfect crime and
a devious killer.

Available at your favorite retail outlet only from

Looking For More Romance?

Visit Romance.net

Look us up on-line at: http://www.romance.net

Check in daily for these and other exciting features:

Hot off the press

View all current titles, and purchase them on-line.

What do the stars have in store for you?

Horoscope

Hot deals

Exclusive offers available only at Romance.net

Plus, don't miss our interactive quizzes, contests and bonus gifts.

PWEB

Lost & Found

All new...and filled with the mystery and romance you love!

SOMEBODY'S BABY
by Amanda Stevens in November 1998

A FATHER FOR HER BABY
by B. J. Daniels in December 1998

A FATHER'S LOVE
by Carla Cassidy in January 1999

It all begins one night when three women go into labor in the same Galveston, Texas, hospital. Shortly after the babies are born, fire erupts, and though each child and mother make it to safety, there's more than just the mystery of birth to solve now....

Don't miss this *all new* LOST & FOUND trilogy!

Available at your favorite retail outlet.

HARLEQUIN®
Makes any time special ™

MURDER & SULLIVAN

by Sara Hoskinson Frommer

A JOAN SPENCER MYSTERY

OPENING NIGHT IS MURDER

The town of Oliver, Indiana, is ready for opening night of Gilbert & Sullivan's *Ruddigore*. Joan Spencer, flexing her bow arm in the orchestra pit, doesn't see a thing. The victim, Judge David Putnam, was awaiting his cue, before he became too dead to hear it.

Who wanted the good judge dead? Local detective Fred Lundquist and his lady love, Joan, discover that the sparse trail has a surprise twist—with a vengeful killer waiting at the end.

Available at your favorite retail outlet
in September 1998.

 WORLDWIDE LIBRARY ®